Kiss Me And Die
Book One of the Kiss Me Series
M.N. Lash

Kiss Me And Die

M.N. LASH

Contents

Content Warnings

B efore you even begin to flip through the pages of this book, read this list. This is a paranormal romance and has several dark elements involved. Those include:

—Graphic death (murder, accidental, in-the-process-of-dying)

—Graphic violence/gore

—Sexual activities (explicit content that includes light BDSM play)

—Kleptomaniac Activities

—Depression

—Rapid and internal monologues (ADHD)

—Impulsive behaviors

—Loss of spouse (Not MC)

—Creepy aging that may make you uncomfy

Chapter 1 — Ruin Me by Sebastian Schub

Chapter 2 — The Night We Met by Lord Huron

Chapter 3 — But I Am A Good Girl by Christina Aguilera

Chapter 4 — Ain't No Rest for the Wicked by Cage The Elephant

Chapter 5 — Ghost by Confetti

Chapter 6 — Are You Gonna Kiss Me or Not by Thompson Square

Chapter 7 — Do I Wanna Know? by Arctic Monkeys

Chapter 8 — PRETTY PLEASE by Dutch Melrose and benny mayne

Animal I Have Become by Three Days Grace

Chapter 9 — Way Down We Go by KALEO

Chapter 10 — Hellfire by Barns Courtney

Chapter 11 — Wicked Game by Chris Isaak

Chapter 12 — I Feel Like I'm Drowning by Two Feet

GHOST CLASSIFICATIONS

FREE-ROAMING AND HARMLESS APPARITIONS

USUALLY NOT HARMFUL AND DO NOT OFTEN ATTACK LIVING SOULS

TYPE ONE – DRIFTING SPIRITS (DRIFTERS)

- NO PARTICULAR PURPOSE
- LONELY
- WANT TO BE AROUND PEOPLE/SEE THE WORLD

TYPE TWO – LINGERING SPIRITS (HAUNTERS)

- STICK TO A PARTICULAR PLACE/PERSON/OBJECT THEY WERE TIED TO IN LIFE BY CHOICE

TYPE THREE – TEASING SPIRITS (JOKESTERS)

- WANT TO FOOL LIVING SOULS
- ENJOY PLAYING PRANKS AND SCARING HUMANS OF THEIR CHOOSING

GHOST CLASSIFICATIONS

Almost always have ill-intents

Type one – Rejcted souls

- Died with broken hearts/rejected aspirations
- Often lash out at living souls they associate with these wrongdoings to make themselves feel better about their deaths

Type two – Wronged souls

- Treated poorly in life or died from poor treatment (i.e. murder, starvation, bullying, etc.)
- Get aggressive with living souls to punish everyone for the way they were treated and due to the unresolved trauma they hold

Type three – Corrupted souls

- Died after being corrupted by someone or something in life (i.e., switching political sides, accepting bribes, turning a blind eye to wrongdoings, etc.)
- Take out their aggression on living souls because they are angry with themselves

GHOST CLASSIFICATIONS

CLASSIFIED INFORMATION

IF YOU ENCOUNTER A CLASS THREE SOUL, DEATH AWAITS YOU

Author's Note

There will be a few paragraphs in this book that may make you think, *What is happening?* and that's okay.

They will look like this and will be in a different POV from the rest of the text. You may think they seem weird or a little out of place, and that's okay. Most minds don't function the way an ADHD mind might, and most minds don't have rapid, chaotic thoughts with a random song placed in between. I didn't include any songs (copyright, duh), but I tried to be as authentic as possible. So if you see these paragraphs, know they aren't random or out of place. They are representations of my mind, and the minds of many others like me. I am—Maybe if—They are—

I hope I have done justice to this topic and that I accurately displayed my mind to you all. Enjoy, and don't forget...

Don't fear the reaping.

For the love I will spend an eternity cherishing.

Chapter 1

The first time Cassiopeia Jaynes killed a man, it was an accident; the second time, it was entirely on purpose.

Cassy knows how that sounds: homicidal, psychotic, a tad bit (or, admittedly, a *lot*) insane. But she isn't any of those things, not in any meaningful way. Everyone has bad days, and hers just so happen to include murder. Personally, she doesn't call them bad days. Truthfully, they're the best ones.

She glances around the busy rodeo-themed bar, casually sipping her beer as she searches the crowd of wannabe stars for her next target. She always conducts extensive research before committing to the act, and her chosen victim is known for not taking no for an answer. She taps her fingers on the bar as she searches, her mind racing in its usual chaotic manner. She thinks about the lights (too bright and headache-inducing), the noises (stereotypical country music and lots of conversations she can individually pick out nearby), her outfit (skin tight and uncomfortable but a beautiful baby blue that she adores), and the itching on her scalp (caused by the auburn wig she's sweating all over).

Flipping some of the auburn curls over, her attention snags on Erron Gates. She can see him pressed against some poor woman across the room who looks extremely uncomfortable with Erron's hand slipping too far down her backside, causing Cassy's racing thoughts to pivot toward various rescue attempts. Her body moves on its own accord as she starts to stand from her bar stool, preparing to intervene on the woman's behalf and get the ball rolling on her plan of attack. But just as she does so, the woman is shoving Erron off and disappearing into the crowd, no doubt to seek out whoever she came with to rant about the disgusting perv who just tried to assault her in the middle of the dance floor.

"That your boyfriend?" The guy next to Cassy has a distinct voice, one she immediately notices because it lacks the usual Southern drawl practically everyone in Nashville owns. And even if they don't own it, they pretend to, at least. This voice has a low timbre, which isn't an oddity in itself, but something about it sends warning signals through her brain. She can't pinpoint what kind of accent the man has, but it's something old, deep, and thrilling.

"And if it is?" Cassy purrs, turning to face him. She sends him a sultry smile, her heart racing as fast as her mind.

How am I supposed to kill Erron Gates now that somebody has seen me stalking him from across the bar? I could wait until tomorrow, but tomorrow is a workday for Erron and he won't be in a random bar where I can disappear into the crowded streets once my work is done. Being caught is not an option. I can't let them catch me. I can't—I won't—Maybe if—

Cassy's heart pounds at the thought of being caught, the motion interrupting the spiraling thoughts she was delving into. Anxiety clutches onto her so tightly that she stops breathing, restricting her blood flow. She would hate to leave a rapist like

Erron on the streets for even one more night, but it's that or risk being caught. In the three years she's been a killer, she's never once been close to being caught. Not only are her methods...unorthodox, but she's also *very* careful. The debilitating anxiety demands nothing less of her.

"Then it's a damn shame." He grins flirtatiously and shows off pearly white teeth, pointing at the beer in front of her. "Do you really like that stuff?"

"Not particularly." She grins back, falling into the familiar role of flirty party girl. This is the worst part of her job—being someone she will never be. It's a good alibi, sure, but it's also fucking *hard*. "It's just cheap and gets the job done." In all actuality, she has been nursing this one drink for over an hour, but the strange man doesn't need to know that. He also doesn't need to know that she actually hates beer, which keeps her from getting drunk since the taste is so abhorrent she can't bear to take more than a single sip every ten minutes.

"Ah, I see. I'm not much of a drinker myself. I have other vices." He flips his long, dark brown hair out of his face, the rest of his hair a disheveled mess that her gaze lingers on. A silver streak races across the front left side, the color similar to that of her own hair. Long strands fall across gorgeous, hooded hazel eyes as his wide lips turn up into a smirk. She blinks up at those lips, at the cupid's bow she's definitely not noticing, and forces herself to move her gaze back up to his.

"Hence the bar," she says, gesturing around them playfully. Each word to the handsome man makes her heart pound so viciously she's sure it's going to come right out of her chest; her fingers tap away on the bar in a poor attempt to control herself.

She can't help but flick her gaze back to that long, copper-toned face, watching his jaw sharpen as he clenches his teeth. He relaxes again, a pleasant smile back on those entrancing lips.

"Just looking for some entertainment," he drawls, long fingers tapping on the bar all too close to hers. She quickly pulls her hand back into her lap, fingering the hem of her dress instead. It calms her mind when she moves, soothes her chaos to have something else to focus on.

"Well, you haven't found it here." Cassy pretends to take another long sip, watching him under her false lashes as she waits for him to take the hint and find someone else in the crowded space to bother.

"I haven't?" The man raises a bushy eyebrow, and she can't help but notice the thin line cut into it. A scar or purposeful, she wonders? Not that it matters. As soon as she can get him to turn his attention elsewhere, he'll never see her again.

Clucking, she says, "Boyfriend, remember?" She glances toward the last place she saw Erron and—*Fuck. He's gone. Where could he have gone off to so quickly? Did he follow the girl from earlier? I need to stop him if he did. I need to find him. Did he—I need—Where is—*

Shaking her head and taking a deep breath banishes the convoluted, overlapping thoughts as the handsome man says, "Your boyfriend is a dick who doesn't deserve you."

She chokes on a laugh, nodding enthusiastically even though she certainly shouldn't be. "Yeah, but he's a *big* dick." Normal, quiet, shy Cassy wouldn't ever say such a crude thing. But that's not who she is right now. Right now, she is badass, super spy, killer-on-the-hunt Cassy, and she can't care less what comes out of her mouth or what others perceive of the words she lets loose.

She winks at the handsome man, trying not to seem frantic as she does another sweep of the room for Erron. Slowly, she scoots off her seat, dusting invisible lint from her dress when she still can't spot him. With a confidence she doesn't actually possess, she states, "I should go find him before he does something more than a little harmless flirting."

"Sure, sure." He waves his hand, that unusual, large nose of his scrunching as he judges her. She doesn't need or care for his judgment, though; Erron Gates will be dead soon, and she can't bring herself to care how hard someone judges her for allegedly dating him.

She struts off, swinging her curvy hips in a precise way that will ensure the man's eyes fall to a particular asset of hers. It's a trick she uses often: distraction via jiggling ass. She chooses to use it now in case the man does remember her by this time tomorrow. She may be anxious about him spotting her watching Erron, but she's also fairly confident the man won't be able to point the real version of her out in a lineup. Besides, she came here to get her fix. She came here to *kill*.

Cassy feels the stranger's eyes burning a hole into her back, or if things are going according to plan, her backside, but it's okay. It's the whole reason for her getup: attracting strangers. The red lipstick, the tight dress, the high heels that have been pinching her feet all night; it's all meant to direct eyes straight to her. No one ever suspects the girl who *wants* people to look at her is doing things in the dark that no one *should* see.

She finds Erron in a hallway that leads to a set of restrooms ten minutes later, exiting from the men's room and rolling down the sleeves of his plaid button-up. It's only half tucked into his tight jeans, his belt buckle large and obnoxious on his waist. "Hi, handsome," she purrs, putting herself in his path and blinking long lashes up at him drunkenly. He is mildly attractive with his short blond hair and sharp jaw, but scum isn't really her type.

Erron pauses his long strides, grinning down at her from at least a half a foot difference. "Hello, darlin'." His thick accent is hardly decipherable underneath the music, but she grew up in the heart of the bible belt: she knows how to pick apart a true Southern accent.

"Want to dance?" She shouts to make sure he hears her. His nod is so enthusiastic it's sickening, but she grabs his hand and pulls him out onto the dance floor anyway. Well, what the bar patrons have turned into the dance floor.

Cassy spends twenty minutes with the disgusting man, hyping him up and whispering sweet nothings into his ear. She tells him that his hands are so strong and wonders what they could do to her body. She tells him she is picturing her body underneath his, picturing him dominating her. All the while, she's thinking of the too-bright lights, of the smell of sweat, of the horrible, slimy feeling in her throat as his hands roam *everywhere*. Her fingers twitch nervously behind his neck as all the things that can go wrong flash in her mind, but she knows none of the insane scenarios are going to happen. And when Erron squeezes her in a spot that makes her want to gag, she's ripped abruptly from those self-doubting thoughts. Unfortunately, she's used to treatment like this from people like Erron. It's part of her job, after all. Well, her kind of job.

No one pays Cassy to kill; she just likes to do it. She likes to rid the world of the trash littering its surface, and she doesn't mind doing it for free. Especially considering it's been a fixation of hers that's lasted longer than anything else ever has before. That being said, she does have bills that need to be paid and a million other hobbies that need funding. So, she takes a little fee from her victims. A...performance fee, as she often refers to it. She has to act like someone she's not for hours at a time, despite the anxiety curling inside her gut the entire time, so she believes she deserves a *little* something for the performance of their lifetime.

She digs in pockets in search of cash, credit cards, gift cards, and anything else she might find valuable. The thicker their wallets, the better, she always says. Besides, lots of her victims are rich, and who's going to notice the chum cash that's missing anyway? Or, if she happens to have access to cars or homes, missing laptops, clothes, makeup...

Erron Gates isn't rich. And, unfortunately, he isn't going to have any cute clothes or makeup for her to relocate to her home. Needless to say...he's worthless. She's performing a mercy killing, really. And it's relieving an itch that's been digging inside her brain for a week now.

It takes Erron a full thirty minutes to beg Cassy to go home with him. Shocking, because he usually doesn't ask. She knows because of the excessive, obsessive research she performed in the days prior. It's basic protocol for her to check every social media account, to look into every family member and their friends, to stalk her little heart out until she's content with the evidence she's captured. She learns her victims' types, their hangouts, and their preferences in companions. She dresses for the occasion, and she acts for it, too.

She isn't delusional about her body; she knows anyone with eyes will look at her in appreciation. And no, that's not her being cocky or overconfident. She understands she's not a size small, but she does have a decent ass and boobs that equate to a handful, which means she attracts attention practically everywhere she goes. She's been told she's beautiful her entire life, been complimented on almost every single physical feature, either back-handedly or outright.

"Wow, Cassy, your eyes are so icy they could hide in a glacier."

"Cassy, your face is so perfectly round; you're so lucky!"

"You know, Cassy, your face isn't completely proportionate, but at least the giant beauty mark on your cheek pulls attention away from it!"

"Between those dick-sucking lips and those wide eyes, you look so innocent, and damn is it a turn on."

"Your hair is so silky and long, and that color is...otherworldly, Cassy. It'll look so beautiful wrapped around my hand."

Unfortunately, men who are attracted to her blubber out the stupidest things, and women who are jealous of her spout off some harsh truths. She knows her lips are stuck in a permanent uptick that gives off the dumb, naive vibes so many salivate over. She knows that her eyes are weirdly glacial, memorable even on the best of days. She knows that her silvery blond hair is unique, and not only because of the many awed whispers of, "Is it real?" She always laughs and nods, but it's the most annoying comment of all. It reminds her of the reason why her hair and eyes turned so light—of how the natural, dirty blond she had adored as a child faded away, along with the almond-colored eyes and tan skin she inherited from her mother—in the days after she received the best gift of her life. She tells herself often that sacrifices have to be made. She'd give up her natural coloring all over again to keep what she received in exchange.

Cassy learned relatively quickly that the blond hair, blue-eyed combo draws the attention of practically every creep in the world. Although it makes her feel uncomfortable, it is helpful in her line of work. Why go searching for targets when they'll come right to her? They take one look at her innocent, young face and her attractive body, and they swoon. The idiots think she's their prey, that she's a blushing fawn waiting for the hissing cobra to strike. Cassiopeia Jaynes is anything but a fawn.

She's more like the devil's worst nightmare hiding in an angel's dream.

"Let me grab one last drink!" she shouts to Erron, squealing in mock delight when he squeezes her ass as she walks away. He thinks he's about to get laid, the poor simpleton.

"Hey!" she calls loudly toward the woman who was sitting on the other side of the handsome hunk from earlier. "Where did the man who was sitting here earlier go?"

"No one has sat here all night." Her eyebrows pinch together. "The seat's broken, so people have avoided it like the plague."

"No, there was definitely a man here earlier." How could she not have noticed *him*? He was attractive and alluring, everything and more that the average bar-goer would be searching for.

"No, honey. No one was here. I saw you, though, drinking beer. Maybe you had too many? Do you need a ride home?" The woman gives her a sad tilt of her head, smiling lightly.

Instead of reacting the way she wants to, she giggles and says with a drunken slur, "Yeah, you're probably right. And, no, I'm good."

The woman gives her a once-over, chewing on her lip. "Be careful, okay? Be safe."

Cassy nods, smiling brightly and fighting her way back over to Erron.

Whoever that guy is, he's long gone now. Even if he does hear about Erron's death, it'll look natural, and he won't suspect the random girl in a bar on a busy Friday night. Actually, he'll probably be glad for me, considering his comment. He will—I don't—Even if—

"Hey, babe, ready to go?" she calls, tugging Erron toward the door impatiently. Even if that man had been more of a problem, she's not sure she can stop herself at this point. She's already set her mind on doing this, and the shouting in her brain won't stop until it's done. She won't be able to focus on normal, everyday things until she kills Erron Gates. It'll nag at her like a bug under her skin, and she can't deal with that any longer. That's the curse of ADHD, especially for someone like her who's unmedicated.

Erron follows her like an obedient dog, trailing after her into the cool early October air. She tugs and pulls on him until they are in a dark alleyway between the bar and the clothes store next door. It's relatively secluded, hidden from sight if you are standing on the sidewalk nearby. She giggles as she stumbles into him, shoving him into the wall a little harsher than necessary.

"Couldn' wait any longer?" he breathes out in a low groan, taking her by the hips. "My apartment is only five minutes away."

"But I want you now," she whispers into his ear. "Here." His shitty little apartment is of no interest to her. She knows he sleeps on a futon and his cat pees on the carpet—she doesn't want to step a single overpriced heel into that place.

"You look so sweet," he whispers into Cassy's neck, lips trailing down sloppily to her shoulder. Her heart pounds as the adrenaline pumps in, the unbearable need inside her nearly sated. Soon enough, the dopamine will seep in, and she can get her fix.

"That's what they all say." She can't help from grinning as he lifts his head, taking the opportunity to lean in and press her lips to his. There is no warmth, no spark, no indication that anything has happened at all. But as soon as her lips break away from his, he is pushing away, moving to clutch onto his chest as he groans and falls to his knees.

"What did you do to me?" He barely gets the words out, another loud groan of pain echoing in the otherwise silent alley. She simply sighs, bending down and tugging her heels off one at a time. She lets out a small noise of relief, stepping toward him with them swinging off her fingers.

"Only what you wanted me to do." She glances down at her watch, the pounding of her heart slowing only marginally. "Should be any second now."

"You b—" He falls onto his side, dead. She chuckles lightly under her breath, crouching down and patting the pockets of his jeans. She finds his wallet in his back pocket, her sticky fingers snagging the forty dollars and Olive Garden gift card inside. If she's lucky, there will still be money on it.

She stands with a satisfied grin, taking two steps back. "Thanks for the great night, babe."

Finally, *finally*, the endless, roaring waves in her brain have calmed. She wonders how long it'll last this time.

Chapter 2

Using all the facts as a guide, Cassy knows one thing...she wasn't born a killer. She was made into one.

Growing up, Cassiopeia was normal. Well, as normal as anyone can be, she supposes. She can't remember most of her childhood, but sometimes she'll get little flashes of random, happy memories and thinks, "How did I become this?" She never had an emo phase, never rebelled against her parents (who were mostly perfect in every way, despite her casual relationship with them), and never even skipped a single class. She was a goody-two-shoes; everyone told her so. But that didn't make her virtuous.

Her first boyfriend came along when she was sixteen, and she let him go as far as second base in the two months they dated. They made out plenty, groped a lot more, and she never let it go any farther. Her second boyfriend came six months later: same story. Only, they made it nearly four months before things came to a crashing halt. Around that time, she began realizing that it wasn't just men she liked, but women too, and everything in between.

Her romantic interests lie with anyone whom she finds attractive, regardless of what is or isn't in their pants. So, she dated *whoever* she wanted *whenever* she wanted. By the time she turned twenty-one, she had had plenty of sex, despite her demure appearance and personality. It often surprised people and made her less attractive in their eyes when they found out she wasn't quite as virginal as expected. It's always made her undeniably angry.

Two months after that twenty-first birthday, Cassy saw someone die for the first time. That day is the day her own deathly capabilities were awakened. She was riding in a taxi, staring out the window glumly as the idiot driver blabbered on about places to see in Nashville, assuming she didn't know everything she needed to about the place. She'd visited the city plenty of times for work and pleasure, as it's only an hour's drive away from Rosehollow, the small town she grew up in. Out of all those times and the many since, she's never seen anything as gruesome and macabre as she did that day. She isn't sure she ever will again, nor does she necessarily want to.

Cassy stared out the tinted window in a haphazard attempt to ignore the driver, her eyes catching on a woman standing by a streetlight. The woman was waiting for the light to change, or so she assumed. The woman stood out because she was wearing odd funeral attire, a vintage black dress accompanied by a mourning veil hanging across her head. Cassy couldn't see her face through that veil to mark any noticeable features, but something about the woman drew her in, and she threw the door open before she could talk herself out of it.

The driver was screaming at her, raving about ratings or something. They were stopped at the same light, so she didn't know why he cared. Despite his angry shouts, she grabbed her purse and left the car to walk toward the hypnotizing woman.

More like run, really. Cassy ran to her, weaving through cars and waving her hand in the woman's direction. Music was playing somewhere in the distance, probably at one of the many bars lining the streets. She remembers the song playing because it seemed to be moving at a slug's pace, each word pronounced in a precise way. "The Night We Met" by Lord Huron, a song that still crawls around in the back of her mind to make occasional appearances in the forefront.

The woman looked at Cassy with a devastating calm. The woman looked her in the eyes, and she realized those eyes were *black.* The pupils were so dilated that they swallowed whatever was there before, and the upper lids were covered in smudged eyeliner that ran down the woman's cheeks and to her neck. Cassy could barely see it through the veil, but she remembers it so vividly now. She reached out and put a hand on the woman's shoulder, opening her mouth to say what, she didn't know. But the moment her hand touched the stranger, the woman leaped away into the road and stopped in the middle of the intersection. When she turned back to look at Cassy, something was glinting in her hand.

Cassy didn't scream when the knife buried itself into the woman's chest. She didn't even cover her mouth in surprise. She knew something was wrong, that something bad was about to happen. She knew, and she wasn't sure how. She listened to other people screaming, and she listened to other people reacting, but she never did so herself. The woman watched Cassy as she fell to her knees, her veil blowing in a gentle breeze as blood dripped onto the asphalt. No one moved to help her, too scared of walking into traffic, but Cassy didn't even register the danger.

She walked to the woman with a calmness she shouldn't have possessed, with a clarity she didn't realize lay within her. Cars honked, some even trying to inch past, but she wasn't worried about them. She fell to her knees before the injured woman so they could be face-to-face, scraping them on the dark asphalt as she did so. Then she lifted the veil, touching her hands to tear-stained cheeks. The woman had a beautiful face, with a sharp nose and almond-shaped eyes. Her lashes were so long, her brows so uniform, her cheeks so plump. Her jaw was soft and so was her tan skin, her blond hair peeking out from underneath the veil. But despite all that beauty, Cassy took one look at her and knew she was ugly inside.

She has always possessed a good intuition, especially when it comes to people and their personalities. She's always known with one look who will be a jerk and who will be worth her while. She's managed to avoid relationships with toxic people, especially men, and she's always chalked it down to luck. Her whole life had been like that up until that moment: lucky. Boring. Uneventful. But staring at that woman—Trisha Underling, she later discovered—she realized she was never *just* lucky. She was different. Because this beautiful woman who just walked out in front of the busiest street in Nashville and stabbed herself in the heart wasn't to be pitied, and Cassy was the only one who knew it.

"What did you do?" Cassy asked her, tilting her head curiously.

Trisha's grim smile was answer enough, and she slumped into Cassy unceremoniously. She felt a warmth on her chest, a wetness that should have grossed her out but mostly made her annoyed. Just like that, Trisha's life was gone. When Cassy first touched her, she was alive, and then suddenly she wasn't. It didn't affect Cassy much. She felt Trisha's death like a cold chill down her spine, and she remembers shivering underneath the humid air of the summer afternoon. She remembers feeling someone's gaze on her—someone who wasn't part of the crowd screaming from the sidewalk—and a sliver of movement against her hand. Maybe it was Death watching her that day, admiring her. Maybe it was an accumulation of all that luck she never truly had. Either way, *something* was there. And that something gave her a gift she'll never be able to repay.

The cops got there quickly enough, and they questioned her thoroughly. After two hours, she was finally allowed to leave the crime scene, a large splotch of blood on her chest the only evidence that it had happened at all. That night, after bathing and changing into something not stained with a stranger's blood, she went out and found a companion. A man at one of those cheesy country bars hosting mediocre singers. He took Cassy back to his apartment, the two so drunk they were stumbling around and laughing loud enough to have someone knock on his door and shout as they passed by. When he kissed her moments later, she realized that whatever had happened to her that day was *monumental*. Extraordinary.

When he kissed Cassiopeia Jaynes, he died.

He collapsed onto the floor of his apartment, his death instantaneous. He just...died. It was later ruled as a heart attack, but the poor man was only twenty-five. She couldn't quite understand at first *why* he died. She blinked down at his body in surprise, her addled mind swimming with confusion. For the second time that day, she had to talk to the cops. "Cassy," they hissed as they showed up, as though her name was a curse. She supposed it was, because her second kill was one of those cops a week later. That was his fault, though. He shouldn't have tried to tell her he would get her out of the entire mess if she sucked him off. He thought he was getting lucky when he kissed her, but the only lucky one that day was whatever victim she was saving from him.

She managed to get out of the messy ordeal on her own.

In the days following, her body had begun leeching itself of color. No more dirty-blond hair, no more almond-colored eyes, no more tan skin. Everything about her felt different and new, and it was exhilarating. She had to lie to her family and friends, convincing them her tan had been a spray tan all along, her blue eyes were contacts, and her hair was dyed. It was hard—it still is, some days—but it was the only thing she could do about the situation.

It's been three years since Cassy saw Trisha die, and those three years have turned her into the world's largest serial killer. And the best part? Not a soul knows. Not a single one. Not even her best friend, Winter Stokes, to whom she tells everything. She thinks Cassy is unfortunate in love, that her dates suck, and her youthfulness sets her back. Winter often attempts to dress her up in sexy garb and send her out to bars, and sometimes Cassy allows the poorly executed scheme to carry out; it always drags the dirt into the house for her to clean up.

Once Cassy realized what she could do, what power she held, she knew what needed to be done. How can anyone prove she is the killer when these people die from heart attacks? How can anyone look at her, the picture of innocence, and say she is a serial killer? Quite simply, they can't. So, after killing that cop, she decided to use her powers for good. Well, as good as killing people can get.

Her friends and family think she works in tech. She never goes into specifics, claiming she works for the government with a top-secret clearance and she couldn't possibly tell them more than that. Of course, no one bats an eye. No one's ever pressed her for more details. Why would they? She's the girl who's never so much as gotten a parking ticket.

She doesn't know what led her to this cold, uncaring job. Like she said, she's *normal.* She doesn't have trauma, nothing sustainable, anyway. Sure, living in Tennessee has its downfalls. Anywhere in the south does when you're like her: different. But she wasn't bullied, her parents are perfect, and no one ever so much as laid a hand on her. She has just always been the nice, smart girl who everyone likes but doesn't love. Does that count as trauma? Knowing that no one loves you but everyone gets along with you? That you are enough of a person for them to acknowledge you, but not enough for them to get to know you?

No matter what led her down this path, she's glad for it. She's glad that she was given a gift to make her stand out, that she was acknowledged for *once* in her fucking life. She's glad that whatever it is that gave her this gift chose her.

The slow clapping behind Cassy startles her into awareness and has her spinning around on her heels, the multitude of thoughts in her head fleeing at what she finds there. "Wow, what a delightful show." The man's wide grin is one of true delight as he pulls a cigarette from his mouth, blowing out smoke slowly.

"Fuck. Fucking *fuck*," she moans under her breath, sizing him up. *I could probably take him, honestly.* He's not a bodybuilder by any means; not that she is, either. But she is pretty good with the element of surprise, even with his near six-foot height. She's at least six inches shorter, but it's not about length but what you do with it, right?

Her pulse jumps as her mind tries to come to a conclusion that doesn't include fighting him.

There's a gun strapped to my thigh. I can always shoot him. If I shoot him, there will be a mess to clean up, though. DNA analysis might not find anything on him, but it would show up on Erron. I've never worried about it before, because no one investigates heart attacks. Especially when the bodies are found outside bars after partying too hard. They would investigate a gunshot wound, though. If I—Should I—Does he—

"Not going to comment?" he questions, throwing what is left of the cigarette onto the ground and stomping on it with one of his fancy, black leather shoes.

"You wouldn't happen to want a kiss, would you?" she questions, swallowing hard. All hints of the flirty party girl from before are gone, replaced with the anxiety-ridden Cassy whose fight-or-flight response is a jumbled mix of both options.

"Oh, no, sweetie. I've seen what those delectable lips can do already." He grins at her, shoving his hands down into his jeans pockets and leaning against the brick wall behind him. Fucking hell, now she's actually going to have to use the gun.

She puts a new mask on now, a confident super spy badass who isn't scared of an inconvenience, and sighs in mock disappointment before sending him a chilling smile that would make a sensible man run. "That's too bad." She pulls the pistol from her thigh in one swift move, unlatching the safety and pointing it at his chest. The suppressor attached to the barrel will reduce the sound, ensuring that no one will hear the shot over the loud music emanating from the bar. "I hope you deserve this."

"I wouldn't—"

This version of Cassy is a shoot and ask questions later kind of girl, so she does what her instincts tell her: she shoots.

The bullet speeds through the air, and she hears it embed inside the wall behind him as it passes through skin. Except...there is no dramatic fall to the ground. No clutching of his chest and mouth gaping like a fish. He just...stares at her. There's no blood, no hole, no evidence whatsoever that he just got *shot*.

He sighs and dusts off the front of his black button-up, looking at her as though she's a disappointment. "I told you not to do that, Shadow Kisser."

"What are you?" she whispers, but not in fear. In all her years as the...Shadow Kisser, as he has so eloquently named her, she's never once considered that there could be someone else who defies Death.

He fades in and out of existence, his smile lingering longer than the rest of him. "A smart girl like you can't figure it out?"

"You're a ghost." She knows it's the right answer before it leaves her lips. Ghosts aren't a topic she's put much thought into, considering she's never seen one. She never didn't believe, but she never had reason to, either. And she's never, *never* considered that she may have needed to.

"Ghost, apparition, poltergeist, spirit...I've been called lots of things."

"And *are* you any of those things?" She trembles as Confident Cassy begins to fail in her one job. To be fair to Confident Cassy, she didn't know that ghosts existed *or* that one had been watching her like a creep from the shadows.

He smiles, clearly pleased. His smile is beautiful and deadly, and it brings a sharp twisting in her stomach that could almost be butterflies. "What a wonderful question. Maybe I am. Maybe I'm not. I don't define myself by any of those terms, but I let others do so."

"Right," she drawls, sighing loudly and shutting her eyes tightly as she tucks the gun back into its holster. "Well, what do you want? You going to haunt me now or something? Wait, you can't do that, can you? Were you haunting this guy?" She kicks Erron, frowning in distaste. "Ghosts are usually stuck to a person or place, right? And it's about circumstance, isn't it? You have a rough death day or something?"

"What do you know about death?" He scoffs, dismissing her entirely.

She *really* doesn't want to be haunted, so she says simply, "How to defy it." She taps her fingers against her thigh to keep herself from imploding into tears. "How to bend its rules to fit my game."

"Interesting." He watches her for a few more seconds before walking forward and crouching down next to Erron. He touches Erron's cheek, holding his hand there and searching for...something. He makes an annoyed sound, face lighting in anger briefly as though the thing he is searching for is no longer there. "And to answer your question, no. I'm not stuck to a place or a person.

I'm not bound by my circumstances. I get to roam where I please."

"Great, just great. So I'm guessing I can't banish you, huh? Fuck, I don't have any salt, either."

He wrinkles his nose, standing and dusting his pants off. "Salt? You watch too much television."

"If you just tell me how to get rid of—"

"I don't want you to get rid of me, Cassiopeia Jaynes. I want to help you."

Chapter 3

"You want to...help me?" Cassy questions, eyebrows raised. This cannot be real. Is insanity a side effect of her power? If it were, she'd be certifiably insane by now, wouldn't she? "I appreciate the offer, strange ghost who knows my name and calls me Shadow Kisser, but I'm good. See you...hopefully never."

She steps around Erron's body, readying to make a beeline for the end of the alley when the ghost says, "You aren't a little curious?"

She pauses, sighing deeply and pinching the bridge of her nose, because *yes*. Of course she is. "Should I be?"

"Of course you should. A strange ghost who knows your name is talking to you, right?" He looks at her as though she should know better. As if she were a naive, gullible child. "Calling you by a nickname you've never heard before, but I've heard many, many times over the years."

"Actually, my mother always told me never to talk to strange ghosts, especially ones who are men. So I'm going to just skedaddle out of here—"

"No, you aren't." He steps closer, body wavering in and out of existence. He reaches out and grabs her wrist, tugging her toward him. She lets out a small noise of displeasure at the cold that ripples up her arm, and moves to push him away, but her hand passes through his body entirely.

She scowls, hating the smug look on his face. "Oh, great. Just fucking great. You can touch me, but I can't touch you? How original." She huffs as he releases her, watching her with an amused smirk. "Just tell me already, then. To hell with all my good sense."

Why am I sassing a ghost? Can ghosts kill? Oh, I hope not, because I've probably pissed it off. I'd be pissed off. I wonder—Maybe if—I would—

"Death is angry," he says simply, shoving his hands back down into his pockets as her spiraling thoughts are brought to an abrupt halt. "You keep taking people who aren't on his list. Lots of ghosts know your name, Cassiopeia, and lots of them will be rewarded for telling him where you are. I'm not the only one who has been watching you, Shadow Kisser."

She can *feel* her face go white, her mouth opening and closing like a fish. "Death? Isn't he the one who..." It doesn't surprise her that Death exists and is a literal figure, because her theory for years has been that he is the one who chose her, that *he* gave her the powers she covets more than anything. She thought...she thought he *wanted* her to use them. Why else would he have given her the kiss of death? Why else make her the...the Shadow Kisser?

"The one who...?" he drawls, looking on the edge of laughing at her dismay.

Cassy lets a careful mask of nonchalance cross her face, shrugging carelessly. "Nothing. Never mind. If he is so worried, why doesn't he come get me himself?" Why send ghosts? And what do ghosts even *get* out of this whole ordeal?

"Do you know how many people die a day? He's a busy man. Besides, why do the dirty work yourself when you have an army at your disposal?" He brushes some of that dark hair out of his face and tucks it behind his ears before plucking another cigarette out of his pocket, a lighter following suit.

"Smoking is a disgusting habit." She wrinkles her nose at him, watching him put the cancer-inducing stick up to his enticing lips. Not that he can even develop said cancer anymore. "Wait—how can you even smoke? You die with those in your pocket or something? Also, what did Death offer the ghosts in exchange for finding me? You guys have ghost currency or something? Ghost crypto?"

"It's not like I can die again," he says with a chuckle as though reading her thoughts, blowing the smoke directly in her face. And, damn it, she can *smell* that disgusting smoke as though it's real. "To answer your question about how I get them: or something. And, to answer your question about the ghosts: or something again."

"Great, that cleared it all up," she says snarkily as her face pinches into what she's certain is an unattractive snarl, crossing her arms across her chest. If she stops and thinks about the way she's talking to this strange ghost who probably wants to turn her in to Death, nothing good will come of it. So, she keeps going. "Listen, I won't run from you, okay? But can we please get away from the dead body? It's making me nervous." She glances around the alleyway, but she doesn't see a single person nearby. Of course, that doesn't mean someone won't show up.

She's narrowly escaped being seen with bodies before, and she doesn't plan on being behind bars anytime soon.

"Let's walk and talk." He glances down at the body with an angry frown before gesturing for Cassy to follow him. She does so reluctantly, ducking her head and turning her back to the security camera by the front entrance of the bar as they pass. Once they are alone and down a street with fewer people around, he informs her, "Ghosts are a nuisance to Death. In his free time, he comes to collect them, but that time is limited. So, most make it many, many years before attracting his attention. But, in the end, all ghosts attract attention. It's an unnatural distortion of what Death represents, so he despises the very existence of ghosts."

"Oooookay," she says slowly, not entirely sure what she has to do with Death's hatred of ghosts. Someone on the street glances at her with confusion, and she jabs a finger at one of her ears and gives them a pointed look. They look embarrassed, having not considered the fact that she may be talking on the phone via earpiece, and move along. Most people don't give her a second glance, though—people talking to themselves isn't an unusual situation in large cities like Nashville.

"He despises your existence, too," the ghost declares solemnly, gravely. His facial expression matches the sentiments. "You were an accident and should have never been allowed to run astray."

"Oh. Well, then." She swallows the lump in her throat, breathing in through her nose, out from her mouth. *I was supposed to be different. Chosen. But I'm not. What am I? Am I—Is he—I don't—*

"What does he want from me?" She counts to five, not trusting herself to make it as far as ten, and keeps forcing her breaths.

"Does it matter? *He wants you.* That, in itself, should be alarming."

"Valid point," she murmurs, picking at the skin on her lips nervously. She bites the inside of her cheek, trying not to let the worry show on her face. "What happens to me if a ghost snitches?"

"That's unclear," he says monotonously, unsympathetic to her plight. "What happens to the ghost is an entirely different matter."

She blinks, mouth opening and closing before she asks, "What happens to the ghost?"

"He's offered to let them stay. To not force them to cross the veil."

"And you're not going to take that offer?" She's assuming he won't, anyway, because he's offered to help her. Although he can be taking her to the damn man himself right now for all she knows.

"Not interested." He takes another puff of the cigarette, releasing it on a loud exhale. "I am interested, however, in striking a bargain with you."

"So you *want* to cross the veil? And what kind of bargain?" Is that who she is now? The girl who strikes bargains with ghosts? This is *not* the dopamine high she wanted.

His lips curl up sadly, a humorless chuckle leaving his lips. "I will never be allowed to cross the veil, no matter how desperately I wish to. As for the bargain, I have a few...pests I want you to take care of. Some people will pay you a lot of money to get rid of ghosts. It's a lucrative business, if you're legit."

Cassy laughs loudly, too surprised by the notion to straight up strike it down. "You want me to become a ghost hunter?"

What does he expect her to do, walk around in old buildings while calling out to ghosts who may or may not exist and beg them to communicate with her? That's what they usually do on TV, anyway. And does he seriously believe people will *pay* her to "hunt ghosts"?

"If that's what you want you to call yourself, sure." He looks down at her with a grin, clearly amused by her.

An annoyed scowl crosses her lips, eyebrows dipping in. "What's in it for you?"

"I no longer have to deal with the pests." He says it as though it should have been clear from the second their conversation started, and it certainly wasn't.

"And what are you offering me in return? Protection from Death?"

"Basically."

He shrugs, flicking his cigarette to the ground and stepping on it as they continue forward. She grumbles and bends down to pick it up, throwing it in the nearest trash can with a huff. Ghosts litter now? They're already dead, do they really need to take the Earth down with them?

"And I won't die if I take this bargain, right?"

"A ghost won't kill you."

Cassy sighs and rubs her nose again, annoyed and frightened. "That's...too specific for my liking."

"Take the deal or leave it, that's not my problem."

"The annoying ghosts are your problem," she points out, rolling her eyes. Confident Cassy isn't here anymore; Original Cassy is too overwhelmed to be anyone else.

"Not for much longer." He grins, and her heart plummets, the sight so hypnotizing that she almost stumbles over a crack in the sidewalk; she knew she shouldn't have worn these heels.

She can't stop staring at the silver streak in his hair; it glints in the dim lights on the streets. Something about it is so...*attractive.* Is this how people feel when they look at her hair? Dumbfounded, amazed, hypnotized? "You haven't even told me your name."

Hazel eyes clash with hers, his tongue slipping out to lick his wide lips in a devious way. "It's Ruin. Ruin Morrigan." The name sounds old and intriguing, like something straight out of the Dark Ages. It fits him so *well.*

"How long have you been dead, Ruin?" she questions stupidly, flinching when his face curls into anger.

He pushes long brown locks out of his long face, the thin line in his eyebrow scrunching up until it is nearly non-existent. "You do *not* ask a ghost how old he is."

"Can I ask how—"

"No! You cannot ask how I died, either. It's entirely impolite." He huffs, and the anger dissipates with the smoke from earlier, his face relaxing back into a pleasant smirk.

She sighs, turning away to hide her disappointment. "Are you going to help me with these ghosts, Ruin? I'm not exactly an expert...or even an entry-level beginner. I don't know anything about ghosts or how to get rid of them. I didn't know ghosts *existed* until about ten minutes ago when you showed up. I hope you don't expect me to just...take care of them without a little guidance."

"I'll help," he confirms, grinning again. "Do we have a deal?"

She swallows hard, closing her eyes and swaying on the spot. Death by...*Death* or getting rid of a few ghosts? Yeah, one of those definitely sounds better than the other. As improbable, unlikely, and outlandish as they both sound, she knows in her heart that the ghost isn't lying to her. "Alright, Ruin Morrigan. I'll vanquish your ghosts if you keep Death off my ass."

"Deal."

He grins triumphantly with those blindingly white teeth as he reaches out and grabs her hand, and though she can't feel it this time, they shake. She *can* feel the icy cold from before stretch even farther up her arm, and with it comes an inked mark on her bicep.

"What the fuck? You didn't mention this part!" She glances down at the new mark, tilting her arm to stare at it better: A bright red lip print.

"What? I thought it was suitable!"

She scowls at him, rubbing at the perfectly shaped lips printed on her arm. It looks as though someone kissed a stencil and used that to tat her up. And...and it is actually kind of cute. She's not telling him that, though.

She frowns, dropping her arm. "I guess I have to live with it now, don't I? It isn't like I have a secret well of paranormal knowledge that will help me get rid of it. So...what do we do now?"

"Now, you go back to your hotel. Avoid killing anyone while you are working for me, yeah? It'll give Death fewer reasons to come sniffing around." He pauses to give her a pointed look, but she only purses her lips tightly in response. "I'll give you one week to find somewhere in the city to stay, then you're stuck with me."

"One week—" Ruin disappears so suddenly that she stumbles, her eyes wide as she looks for even a hint of copper-toned skin. But he is no longer striding along the sidewalk, no longer looking at her with disdain or anger. He's…vanished.

She groans, kicking at the ground with a huff. Her life is no longer what it should have been, and her night is ruined. The only repetitive thought she has now is one she repeats aloud. "What the fuck am I going to do?"

Chapter 4

Finding somewhere to stay in Nashville on such short notice is practically an impossible feat, but Winter, as always, is a godsend who knows somebody who knows somebody. Cassy loves her apartment in Rosehollow; she would have to, considering it's in one of the most expensive neighborhoods, complete with a heated indoor pool *and* a gym. She's not giving it up entirely; she hopes these new jobs will help her pay for both places. If not...she will probably be evicted from the most perfect apartment to ever exist.

Winter said that the new home Cassy is renting is owned by one of her exes' grandmothers. At least that's what Cassy retained from the conversation. Unlike her, Winter's always left on good terms with her exes. She actually tries to make things work, and those relationships almost always last over six months. *Every. Single. Time.* Cassy's partners are lucky if she gives them more than six weeks, if they're even given the chance to make it that far.

She is grateful for Winter's loyalty today, though, because at least now she has a home to rent for the foreseeable future. It's...well, tiny. A one-bed one-bath, the living room blends into the kitchen in a way that makes it hard to see a distinction between the two areas. In its single bathroom, the toilet is pressed between the sink and the shower so tightly she can't even spread her legs out. But it's a place to stay in Nashville and gets her one step closer to not being hunted by *Death*, so...it'll have to do for now.

Unfortunately, she has a lot of things. Like...*a lot* of things. It's an occupational hazard because she often takes things she shouldn't. But if she wants it, she gets it, and that's that. If she doesn't, her mind will obsess for hours, for days, for weeks, until she gets the thing that's been driving her crazy. It's only temporary happiness, temporary content, but at least she gets relief from her own mind. And, *yes*, that mindset does fuel a horrible shopping habit.

Boxes are piled throughout the living room and spill into the kitchen, more hiding in the bedroom that she shoved to the side to give herself the space to walk. She sighs as she pushes the glass coffee table across the room, attempting to convince herself not to complain. She's used to...more. More room, more things, more comfort. At least she has a washer and dryer. There's always an upside to things, as Winter often tells her.

She grabs the remote to her TV and turns on her exercise tutorials, hating herself already. She tries to do these at least three times a week, just in case she needs to hit someone or run away quickly. She hates every second of it, though. Working out just isn't fun for her. She'd rather be curled in her reading chair with a book, escaping into a different world entirely. Reading is another good way to turn down the volume of her mind, so she clings to it just as tightly as she clings to her feather-filled pillow at night. It's something she enjoys greatly, unlike the exercise regimen she forces herself to get through every other day.

Cassy only gets ten minutes into the video when she hears a disgusted, "What are you doing?"

"Holy shit!" She spins around, clutching her hand to her heart and panting hard. Ruin watches her with a raised eyebrow, leaning against the door casually as though he belongs there. She blurts, "You can't just walk in like that! I could've been naked!"

"So what if you were?" His gaze roams over her, trailing down her body in a seductive way that she doesn't like at *all*. Ghosts shouldn't be looking at humans like…like they're snacks!

"That's so pervy," she snaps as a flush rises from her neck to her cheeks. She turns briefly to pause the video before setting her glare on him once more. "Fucking knock, you creep."

"Has anyone ever told you that you have a dirty mouth?" Those wide lips curve into a sensual smirk, and his eyes light up in a way she shouldn't be noticing. Just like she shouldn't notice the golden ring around his pupils or the tiny specks of green hiding inside the hazel.

"Only the ones who want a taste of it," she says with her own flirty smirk, falling into her alternative personality with ease. It's always been easy to flirt, easy to play with people's emotions. Easy and *fun*. It sounds horrible, but it's the truth. She's not a bad person. At least, she doesn't think she is. And, besides, she really only does it to people who deserve it. She's not sure there are many people who do deserve to know how weak and fragile she actually is behind it all. She especially doesn't think a ghost deserves anything more than the surface-level, flirty, confident version of Cassy she's offering up.

"As I said last week, I've already seen exactly what those delectable lips can do. I'm not interested in becoming your next victim." He pushes off the door with his foot, running a hand through his dark hair and tucking it behind his ears before heading over to her. She eyes the silver streak in the front, mouth opening and closing as she takes a moment to process his words. Ruin waits patiently, staring at her with a raised brow.

"You're already dead," she snorts, waving her hand dismissively and purposefully turning her back to him in an attempt at ignoring the palpitations that are happening…*everywhere*. "My lips wouldn't hurt you."

"Oh, I think they would," he says softly, clearing his throat afterward. "Ghosts aren't immune to Death, after all."

She spins back around, mouth open wide again as she tries to comprehend the implications of *that* statement. "I can kill ghosts by kissing them?"

That can't be true. Ghosts are already dead, right? Or is everything I know about ghosts not true? I suppose that is plausible because most humans think ghosts are fictional, therefore marking all "facts" about ghosts as untrue to begin with. So, I suppose I should assume I don't know anything. And if I don't know anything, then I'm fucked. I may—I don't—I suppose—

He shrugs, face neutral. "I have my theories. The most logistical one is that your kiss will send the ghost to Death, who I'm sure will promptly collect them." Her frantic thoughts falter, then reform into new ones.

"So if you get on my nerves…?" she purrs, putting a hand on her hip and watching him stride around the small house, peeking his head inside boxes.

"I'd love to see you try, C.J." He digs around through a box of books, holding up one with his signature raised brow. There's a woman on the front in nothing but some lingerie, a shirtless man behind her with his hands on her hips and his face in her neck.

"No nicknames." She grits her teeth, jabbing her finger at him and hissing, "And get out of my things. I like what I like, and you aren't allowed to shame me for that." She can't remember what that one's about, but it's not hard to guess what the contents inside are. Actually, she doesn't remember what most of the books on her shelf are about. After she reads them, she forgets about them after, at most, a year. At the least they're stored in her memories for six months. Anything that truly sticks with her...well, that gets a longer hard drive. One of the few benefits of ADHD: She can reread and rewatch practically everything and experience it like she's never seen it before.

He grins, showing off his pearly-white teeth. Why does he have to be so annoyingly perfect? Are ghosts even allowed to be pretty? Being haunted shouldn't be a good thing. "No shame here. I've seen, and tried, it all."

She flushes again, tapping her fingers absentmindedly before settling on saying, "Quit snooping, then."

"Why shouldn't I snoop? I'm staying here, too, after all." He struts into the kitchen next, running his hand over dated, yellow-tinged countertops and wrinkling his nose at the very old appliances.

"You absolutely are not," she hisses, nose crinkling angrily as she points her finger at the door. "And you certainly aren't coming and going as you please."

"I disagree." He exits the kitchen to stalk off toward the bedroom, ignoring her entirely as he passes through the living room.

"This is my house. That *I* pay for, you leech. You can't disagree." She stomps after him, frustrated and feeling a little queasy. He can't be serious? He has to be kidding.

"Only one bed?" he jokes with another heart-stopping grin, jabbing a finger at her elegant black bed frame that definitely doesn't belong in the smoke-stained room.

"Do ghosts even sleep?" she exclaims, throwing her hands up in frustration.

Is that another thing I don't know? I should do some research. Is there a way to research ghosts without finding a bunch of B.S., though? If there was, would he tell me what's true? If there—I should—Maybe if—

"Some do." He shrugs and moves to the attached bathroom, scoffing at the small space.

"Then there's a really nice couch right over there for you to do that on." He wrinkles his nose at the tiny shower, seemingly displeased with the new arrangement. "You got a problem?"

"This house is tiny," he says plainly with a harsh frown, as though it should have been obvious.

"Yeah, and? You didn't give me much notice; this was the best I could do in a week. Trust me, I don't want to be here any more than you do."

"You like the nicer things in life, don't you?" He watches her with careful boredom, leaning against the door frame.

I wish he would stop doing that; he looks too real and too handsome. I refuse to be attracted to a ghost. Can ghosts even feel attraction?

Actually, do they feel anything at all? He says he's seen and done it all...was that before he died? Maybe I could ask. I should—I can't—If he—

"I think I deserve to have nice things, don't you?" She sniffs at him impatiently, turning around and striding back into the living room to finish her workout and distract herself from absurd, intrusive thoughts.

"Does being a killer make you more deserving?" he questions. She has this gut feeling that he is being genuinely curious and not judgmental, mostly because of the interested tone he used to ask the question.

"I see it more as...taking out the trash. I just do community work," she snips, hitting play and beginning a series of punches and leg raises that usually leave her out of breath after the full minute is up.

"Interesting that you believe doing bad things will result in receiving good ones, C.J."

"What bad things?" She blinks at him innocently, smiling flirtatiously over her shoulder. "I'm a good girl."

She can feel his eyes on her when she turns back to the video, but she doesn't pay him any mind. She ignores his presence entirely, spitefully, in hopes he feels exactly like the ghost he is.

When she finishes, she heads straight to the shower, slamming the door to the bedroom *and* the bathroom shut behind her. Logically, she knows that he can probably walk straight through the wall to get in. She hasn't seen him do that, but the majority of the knowledge she has about ghosts includes the walking-through-walls aspect of their lives. She wants to prove a point, to be stubborn, to show him she doesn't care if he's there or not; she'll do what she wants when she wants to do it.

Cassy doesn't hear him when she gets in the blazing hot water, and she frequently checks to make sure he doesn't follow her inside the shower. But he never shows up, never appears in front of her to stare her down with those intense hazel eyes. She's grateful that the ghost she brought home turned out not to be a pervert after all.

"Are you going to speak to me now?" Ruin seems annoyed when she finally struts out in her pajamas, a crop top paired with oversized plaid pants. She watches his gaze go directly to the shiny gem in her belly button, and her cheeks flush at the attention. She doesn't know what's happening to her; she never gets nervous around men, or anyone else, for that matter. Flirty, Confident Cassy takes care of Ordinary Cassy, ensuring the nerves never bleed through. Though she *is* usually in control in the situations where Confident Cassy is needed. She doesn't feel close to being in control around Ruin. It's proven by the all-consuming thoughts about him she can't seem to stop when he's near.

"Depends on whether you have anything interesting to say." She moves to the box of books he so graciously opened for her earlier, dragging the heavy thing over to a bookshelf on the wall next to the door with a loud groan.

I hope he doesn't make comments about any of my other books. Ooh, this one is good. I should display it, but it isn't as pretty as the others. And what will he say when he sees the monster with horns on the front? I shouldn't care about his opinion. It's my house. Maybe he won't comment. I shouldn't—Maybe if—He can—

"I was going to tell you about the job I have lined up for you this week, but..." he trails off, shrugging sheepishly. He's made himself comfy on her black leather couch, lying out with his long legs hanging over the armrest.

"Alright, that qualifies as interesting, then." Her mind is reeling again, already resetting and preparing itself for the conversation to come. It fills in blanks she wasn't even provided, running through how and what he might say about the ghost he wants her to find.

I have a ghost hiding in a graveyard two streets away, Cassy. Cassy, I desperately need you to hunt the ghost hiding in my great, great relative's house. Cassy, I—Cassy, I—Cassy, I—

"So glad to have met your standards," he grumbles, sitting up and watching her carefully organize books into piles.

"Go on, then. Don't leave a girl hanging." Cassy forces herself to quit with the make-believe conversations, using the books as a way to focus on his actual words and not the ones she's put into his mouth.

He watches her with that stoic expression she's begun to associate with him, his gaze intense. "There's a man who lives at the edge of town, secluded, old. He's been haunted by this ghost for years now, and he's desperate to get rid of it. Desperate enough to pay someone fifty thousand dollars."

She chokes on air, coughing and banging her chest with wide eyes. "Did you just say fifty thousand dollars?"

"I did." His lips turn up into a small smile, clearly amused by her reaction.

"How did you find this man?"

"Ah, ghosts talk. They think it's funny. Arnold's been hanging around that house for nearly a hundred years, and the current owner, Ben, has only been there for five. Arnold waited until he was nice and settled before starting up, causing a little chaos here and there until he had the poor old man petrified. You'll be doing Ben a big favor. He's made several attempts to get rid of Arnold already, but no one has been legit. You know, because the only legit way to get rid of a ghost is to send them to Death, and there aren't many people who know how to do that."

"Oh, I'll be very legit for Ben." She grins, thinking of the money already. That amount of money can go a long way if she plays her cards right...

I could pay the rent at my other place for a year and still have twenty thousand left over. I could buy a car, even though I don't really care to. I could buy matching wedding gowns for Winter and me, even though neither of us is in a relationship. I could—I could—I could—

"I know you will. All you have to do is show up, find Arnold, and kiss him."

"I've never seen a ghost before you," she says with a weary pause, turning over her shoulder to watch him with a raised brow. "And you said the kissing thing is a theory."

He nods, seeming to contemplate her words for a few seconds. "Most choose to hide. And what better way to test said theory than with a harmless ghost?"

"Okay, then how do I get him to choose not to?"

His lips tilt up into something soft and comforting. "You're a beautiful woman; I'm sure you'll figure something out." She flushes again, nodding her head. Why can't she stop this insistent redness from invading her skin?

She forces her lips into a snarl. "Yeah, that makes perfect sense, Ruin. I'll just seduce the *ghost*."

"That's the spirit!" He grins brightly, and the treacherous organ in her chest flutters *again*.

"Is there anything I should know about this ghost? Like…is he dangerous? Is he a trickster? Is he ugly?"

Ruin lets out an abrupt laugh, choking and silencing it just as quickly. "He's just a low-level ghost, C.J. He can only hurt you if you let him. As far as ugly goes…Well, I guess that's in the eye of the beholder, isn't it?"

She scrunches her nose in disbelief. "There are levels?" She starts placing the books on the shelves in order of color and genre, carefully placing each one into the space they will stay for as long as she's here.

How are the levels divided? Is it by strength, age, or something else? Do ghosts have powers? Can they all touch me? Can they—Do they—Are they—

"Sure, sure."

Cassy blinks. "Are you going to explain the levels?" She raises an eyebrow, huffing. Does she have to pry *everything* out of him?

"Not today. I want to see how you handle things before I decide to keep you around."

"Oh, great. So this is a test, then? And if I fail, you'll send me to Death's doorstep?" Her heart drops into her stomach, the attraction from before gone entirely now. He's such an *asshole*.

"It is, and I will. I told Ben you'd be there in three days, by the way, so that's how long you have to prepare."

She stands and spins around fully now, scowling. "How did you…?"

"You need to change your email password," he says simply, moving to lie back down on her couch and closing his eyes with a barely contained smile.

"No way!" She plucks her phone out of her back pocket and checks her email; sure enough, there it is.

To: benishaunted@email.com

Hello,

My name is Cassiopeia Jaynes, and I am a professional ghost hunter. I saw your post on helpmebanishmyghost.com and am very interested in the job. If you send me the address, I will be there in three days to check things out and let you know my professional opinion on the matter.

Thanks,

Cassy J.

From: CJKisses@email.com

In disbelief, she says somberly, "I can't believe you did that. I don't even know *how* you did that."

What other kind of information can he get? Can ghosts hack bank accounts? Should I worry about my Social Security number now? Does he have access to my birth certificate? Can he take my money and reroute it? Does he—Can he—I need—

An infuriating smirk graces his features. "I may be old, but I do know how emails work, C.J."

"I told you to quit calling me that!" She's always just been Cassy. Never Cassiopeia, never C.J. *Always Cassy.*

"I'm not as limited as you might think I am," he says after a brief silence, chuckling to himself. "I guess you'll find that out in your own time since I'm living here now."

"You are *not*—"

Ruin tilts his head up as though listening to something, popping out of existence so suddenly that she doesn't even get the chance to blink. One second he's there, and the next he's just...not.

"Ruin?" she calls, wondering if he's still in the house somewhere. When she doesn't get an answer, she assumes he's left. They were in the middle of a conversation, for goodness' sake! Making up her mind about his species' personalities, she declares to the empty room, "Ghosts are assholes."

Chapter 5

B en Craigmore's house isn't *just* a house: it's a mansion. Cassy has to be buzzed in at the front gate, and the taxi driver is just as impressed as she is with the large white palace in the middle of nowhere. The front door could fit a Trojan Horse through it, the giant fountain in the driveway circling to greet her before she ever set foot in front of said door.

This isn't the kind of haunted house I was expecting. I wonder what kind of job this guy has? How does he have fifty thousand dollars lying around to pay me? What if he stiffs me? What if this isn't a ghost and it's just a creepy old guy trying to lure unsuspecting strangers in to murder them? What if I fall for it? What if—What if—What if—

"You live here?" the driver questions in awe, her jaw slack.

Cassy clears her throat and shoves the paranoia from her mind, moving to get out of the car. "Just know somebody who does."

"Oh, I see." The driver smirks as she looks at the entryway, coughing as she tries to hide a laugh. Cassy glances in the direction the driver is staring, groaning when she realizes why the woman is trying to hide a laugh. Ben Craigmore is exactly as Ruin described him: old. He hobbles out on a cane, the handle shaped like a rabbit's foot. A lucky omen, if she had to guess. He's mostly bald, his thin white hair sticking up around the tops of his ears and disappearing around the back. The man is wrinkly all over, his small, hunched frame making him seem weak and insignificant in front of such a commanding entryway.

"It's…never mind. I don't care, anyway." She sighs, not bothering to correct the driver's thoughts. She'd think the same things if she saw herself coming to an old man's house dressed the way she is. She'll never see the driver again, though, so it doesn't matter.

She exits the vehicle, smoothing out her skin-tight dress and straightening to her full height. She strides forward in her tall heels, glancing around at the beautifully towering hedges and vibrant red flowers decorating the front of the place in appreciation.

"You must be Cassy Jaynes," the old man says, his voice scratchy and rough. He coughs into a handkerchief as he watches her, beady gray eyes roaming over her form. She had tried to keep the dress business-like, but also ensured it ended above the knees and showed off cleavage. If Ruin thinks she needs to seduce the ghost, then she'll seduce the ghost. Not that she would know if he approves of her attire: he hasn't been around for days.

I wonder where he went? He said he was going to stay with me and just disappeared. What if Death found him? What if I'm no longer safe? What if he actually sent me into a trap? How did I fall for this? I'm so stupid. What if—How did—What if—

"I am," she says, smiling brightly to banish the anxiety. She doesn't usually go by Jaynes or Cassiopeia when meeting her victims, and she certainly hadn't planned on changing that tactic. She doesn't want anyone finding her outside of business, certainly not people who attract ghosts. She already has one of those herself, and she doesn't want another, thank you very much. Too bad Ruin had to...well, *ruin* her cover.

"You aren't what I expected," he murmurs, his gaze lingering on her hair. Today, she decided to wear a brown wig, the curls ending at her waist. The contacts are brown to match, a perfect disguise that she often uses. She probably didn't need to bother with the disguise, since he already has her real name, but it's a safety net she isn't prepared to rid herself of yet.

"Am I too beautiful to be a ghost hunter?" she asks with a tight-lipped smile, following him inside. The door shuts behind them, and the quiet in the house is discernible. Immediately, she gets the shivers, goosebumps traveling up her arms and down her legs.

"Most definitely," Ruin purrs beside her. She jumps so hard she almost falls over, clutching onto her heart as it attempts to pound right out of her chest.

"What the—" she starts hissing, stopping to smile as Ben turns around with a raised eyebrow.

"Were you saying something, Cassy? I have old ears; you'll need to speak up." He taps one of his ears and smiles weakly, glancing around his home wearily.

The room they are in is large and open, with two sets of stairs curving around and leading up to a hallway on the next level. The floor is a beautiful white marble, the walls a light gray. There is a singular table between the stairs, a vase with sunflowers sitting on top of it. Otherwise, the space seems empty. It's large and cold, the air still and full of warning. And the white...ugh, it's all so blinding and *boring*.

Does he live in this giant house alone? Did he decorate himself, too, or did it come this way? Why hasn't he just moved? Surely, he has the money to. If I were him, I would paint these walls a color to represent the dark and broody atmosphere. Why did—How would—Did he—

"No, I didn't say anything, Mr. Craigmore," she tells him loudly, forcing herself not to shoot daggers at Ruin, who seems to be hiding his presence from Ben

"Ah, well. You saw my post, correct?"

"I did," she agrees, because she *had* briefly read over it. The post claimed he was in search of someone to get rid of the ghost in his house because he's sure it is trying to kill him. Though from the sounds of things, the ghost is mostly having fun. Arnold, Ruin said, is his name. Ben posted that he has been knocking things over, flickering lights, and throwing things across the room. His final straw was when the cane was ripped from his hand and thrown down the stairs. She has to admit that *that* particular action sounds less like a funny prank and more like a cruel joke.

"Great. Then you know what you're up against." He is so serious, so fearful, that she almost laughs. It probably wouldn't be nice to laugh at the man willing to pay her fifty thousand dollars, though, so she refrains.

"I have an idea." She glances around again, not seeing any hints of a ghost yet. "Where should I start first?"

"It likes the kitchen," he snarls, jabbing his rabbit foot cane toward a doorway on the right. "Probably died in there doing something idiotic."

She snorts, unable to help herself. "I'll start there, then."

He stops her, wrinkled brows drawing in. "You didn't bring anything with you. How are you going to get rid of it?"

She tucks a strand of hair behind her ear, smiling cautiously. "Ah, I, uh, have a special method. A chant."

"A chant?" He seems skeptical now, and rightfully so. Cassy is a fraud, after all.

"It's hard to explain." She clears her throat with a barely hidden wince, heels clicking as she starts making her way to the kitchen. "But it's a secret not easily taught. Don't worry, Mr. Craigmore. I'll take care of your little problem."

"And if you don't?"

"Then you don't have to pay me." She shrugs, not bothering to glance back. "But you will."

"I'm glad one of us is confident," he murmurs, but she doesn't respond. Telling him the truth—that Confident Cassy isn't real—isn't in her best interest. Fake it 'til you make it and all that rubbish, right? "I'm going to the library to sit for a while by the fire. Let me know when you kill it."

She doesn't bother correcting him: she can't kill what's already dead. She only continues into the kitchen, the large space beautiful and a little intimidating. The cabinets are blood red, the counters deep black. The floor is the same marble, though, and all the accents are gold. It's dark and gloomy, the exact kind of space she could picture a ghost hiding out in, and the kind of moodiness she thought would fit in the entryway. It seems a little out of place now, though, compared to everything else she's seen.

Ben mentioned in his post that his cook would blame him for moving things around, for slinging pots and pans on the floor overnight for the cook to clean. He almost quit several times, apparently, because he is convinced Ben is a bitter old man trying to make his life miserable. She's sure Arnold thinks that's hilarious.

What kind of things does a private cook make? How much money would you earn as a private cook? Has the cook ever been attacked by a runaway, flying pan? Has this—What happens—How does—

"What do I do now?" she murmurs, glancing over at Ruin, who followed her into the kitchen. His hands are shoved down into his pockets as usual, his brows furrowed. He pulls out a cigarette, starts to light it, then abruptly changes his mind and shoves it back within the depths of his denim jeans.

"I don't feel his presence here."

The atmosphere *is* rather peaceful. She, herself, doesn't feel any chills down her spine, nor does she feel as though someone is watching her. But she doesn't really know how being around a ghost who is purposely hiding feels, so she scowls at Ruin in discontent. "How helpful. How do I get him to come out and play?"

"You walk by him." He looks over at her fully, eyes roaming down her body slowly and purposefully. "He'll like what he sees, and he'll feel the urge to come out. Lots of ghosts have fun with the living by making them think they are alive, too. Then, later, when no one has heard of the person they were talking to, they write it off as a strange encounter and never think of it again. Arnold's known for his...feminine attraction."

She groans, covering her eyes. "He's a pervert, isn't he? Is he going to grope me?"

"If he tries, I'll send him to Death myself," Ruin says firmly, head tilting to the side. He looks as though he's listening to something, a familiar move she's noticed more than once now. "I have to go."

"You cannot be ser—" Ruin is gone, disappearing as quickly as he had appeared. "—ious," she finishes, cursing his name under her breath.

Where does he go whenever he disappears like this? Who is he listening to? Do ghosts get calls? If ghosts get calls, is it like a ringing phone? Do they have some kind of calling to make them appear at a whim? Maybe he's not a ghost at all, but a demon. Maybe he's being summoned by witches. Do they—Where do—How come—

Cassy glances around the empty room, sighing as she pushes thoughts of Ruin and his whereabouts into the deep abyss that is her mind. Her racing thoughts only increase when she's nervous, and right now she needs to be in control of the nerves.

She makes her way out of the kitchen, heading toward the set of stairs. She might as well start on the upper floors and work her way down. She doesn't know where, exactly, the library is to find Ben and question him some more about where Arnold likes to hang out. So, she'll have to figure it out on her own.

The upstairs of the home is just as empty and dazzling as the downstairs, the walls lined with beautiful artwork that she's sure cost an arm and a leg to purchase. To the right is a series of closed doors, and to the left is basically the same. After absolutely no deliberation, she decides to head right on instinct and pokes her head in the first door. She can feel the same peaceful atmosphere as she felt downstairs, no random cold raking over her spine or still air to give her the heebie jeebies.

It's a guest bedroom from the looks of things, decorated in a tacky yellow and purple theme. She wrinkles her nose and steps in, glancing around for a ghost despite her feelings of normalcy. Unfortunately, she is right about the room...ghost hunting isn't as easy as she had hoped.

She walks out of the bedroom, heading toward the second, but abruptly changes direction when she notices a door with a pretty floral wreath on the outside. She touches the real sunflowers on the wreath, breathing in their scent.

I wonder why he has so many sunflowers. Were they a dead lover's favorite? Did they belong to a dead relative? Did they—Were they—Why does—

She shakes her head with a frown, taking a step back and turning to the second door again. No, she can't lose track of where she has and hasn't checked. She can't let herself be distracted like a dog seeing a squirrel: an experience she, unfortunately, relates all too much to. Taking a deep breath, she opens the door and sticks her head inside.

The second floor is, ultimately, a bust. Cassy doesn't find any ghosts but does find lots of unused rooms that seem wasteful to have for a man who lives on his own.

She pouts as she descends the stairs, beginning to doubt her ability to do this without Ruin's help. "Mr. Craigmore," she calls as she hits the bottom step, swallowing hard.

"Kill it yet?" he questions as he comes around the corner, coughing and sputtering by the end.

"I can't seem to locate it." She glances around, sighing softly when the damn thing doesn't magically show its face. "Does it like another space in the house?"

"Prefers the kitchen," he says solemnly, face pinched as he jerks his head toward the right. "But sometimes it likes the library."

"Alrighty, then, I'll check the library next."

Ben only nods, stumbling off to who knows where with his rabbit foot cane.

She goes through the doorway Ben gestured to, making a few wrong turns before finally finding the large library he had indicated the ghost likes. She takes in the floor-to-ceiling shelves she finds there, most filled entirely with books, before turning to the fireplace located on the far-right wall. There are two reading chairs cozied up next to that fireplace with windows sitting on either side, the view of the pretty garden in the backyard they offer breathtaking. Cassy takes a step forward to examine the yard from the window, not realizing anyone is in the room until she hears a raspy voice greeting her. "You're too pretty to be a guest of Ben's."

Chapter 6

Cassy jumps at the sound of the voice, her eyes falling to the man lying in one of the large chairs. His curly red hair is short, falling just past his ears, but his eyes are what capture her attention. They're a deep shade of gray, alluring and dangerous all at once. She feels drawn in immediately, her body stepping forward of its own accord.

She smiles, her pulse skipping. Arnold smiles back, dimples popping in his high cheeks. "Just here to keep the man company."

This is the ghost. What do I do now? How do I convince him to kiss me? Am I his type? Will this even work? What do I do if it doesn't work? I can't just make out with a ghost for funsies. Will he grope me? I hope he doesn't. If he does, I may go postal. What is—How do—If he—

He gestures toward the seat next to him. "Want to keep me company instead?"

"Sure. Ben disappeared on me, anyway." She swings her hips softly, seductively, as she approaches, sitting in the chair opposite him and watching the small man with a sultry smile. It's her signature move, and it always works. Humans are simple creatures, after all.

"What's your name?"

She watches him under her lashes, wishing she could laugh about the ridiculous situation. Maybe she can once she's at her new home, fifty thousand dollars richer. "Cassy. What's yours?"

"Arnold." He watches her with such fascination that it's pathetic.

"You're much more handsome than Ben," she says on a giggle, matching his level of patheticness. Damn, she should be better at this, but she feels a little off her game knowing this is a *ghost*.

What do ghosts like? Do they still feel lust in the same way as they did when they were alive? If I flashed my tits, would he get hard? That's inappropriate, but what if? Can he—Would he—Does he—

"Anyone younger than sixty is." He grins again, leaning forward. "Want to find a better way to pass your time?"

"Depends on what you have in mind." She leans forward too, their faces so close now she could easily kiss him. Is it really going to be this easy? *Ghost hunting isn't that hard when the ghost is desperate*, she thinks.

"Find him yet, C.J.?" Arnold lets out a girly yelp, eyes flickering to the dark and imposing man behind her before disappearing. Cassy barely catches a glimpse of the fear on his face, of the impossible paleness hiding there.

"Seriously, Ruin?" she groans, leaning back into her chair and slumping over. "I almost had him!"

"I'd offer you a kiss as an apology, but I don't think I would like the outcome." He struts into her line of vision, crouching down in front of her. His chest is level with her knees, his body a mere foot away. His dark hair falls across his face, and he brushes it and that infuriatingly attractive silver streak to the side, tucking it behind his ears with a sigh. A cigarette hides there, tucked neatly away and waiting for his nimble fingers to grasp it.

"Yeah? Want to get the sneaky little pesk you scared away to come back, then?" She scowls at him, raising her heeled foot and pushing it against his chest angrily.

His hand slips around her ankle, a matching scowl on his face as he pushes up and forward, forcing her leg to rise and her knee to bend. "You were supposed to have this taken care of already."

"You didn't tell me how!" she defends, not liking the position they are in. She's positive he can see her underwear with the way he has her leg pressed up, which is *not* the kind of compromising position she wants to be in with a ghost.

What would it feel like to have his hands roaming other parts of my body? Would the chill he always leaves behind feel good in other places? Would he want to kiss me if my lips weren't so deadly? I haven't truly kissed anyone in so long and I miss it. Would he even want to kiss me, consequences aside? Would he—Would I—Could we—

"Here." He hands her a small bundle wrapped in a stained cloth, dirt crumbling off it.

"What is this, and *how* did you carry it?" She wrinkles her nose when the decaying smell hits her nose. She gags. All thoughts of kisses and foreign touches are certainly gone now.

"Quit acting like you know what ghosts can and can't do. Watching a few shows about ghost hunting doesn't make you a professional, you know? Those guys only think they know things because jokesters like Arnold like to play with them. And don't worry about what is in it; it's just a little alchemy at work. All you need to know is that it'll call Arnold to you. Just go somewhere alone, whisper his full name, and he'll be forced to make an appearance for a full minute before he's allowed to disappear again."

"I don't *know* his full name," she hisses, frozen in an awkward position. She can't kick him with her other foot—he'll only press that one up, too. And then she'll really feel bared to him.

What would it feel like to be truly bared to him, though? He's all dark and mysterious, surely that makes for a good run in the bed. He seems like the kind of guy who would take a woman's needs seriously, the kind who pays attention to what you want and what you need. The kind who would talk you through it. He seems—I wonder—What if—

She shoves away the embarrassing thoughts, trying to ignore the wetness below and fighting a blush as she tries to concentrate on his next words. "It's Arnold Goldletter."

"That name screams rich," she says after a pause, just as Ruin disappears again. "Seriously? What are you so busy doing that you don't have time to help me with the mission *you* sent me on?" Of course, she receives no reply.

She grumbles curses under her breath, heading toward one of the guest bedrooms up the stairs. She'll shut and lock the door behind her, caging Arnold in. Surely, she can leap across the room and plant one on him before he realizes what's happening? Maybe if she catches him off guard enough, she can grab him in the first ten seconds and be done with it.

Before she can make it up the stairs, her phone rings so loudly that she lets out a little shriek. Her heart races as she pulls it from her bra, glancing down at the caller ID: It's Winter trying to do a video chat. Because why wouldn't she want to do that while Cassy is in the middle of a ghost hunt?

"Hi, babe!" Winter greets, her beautiful black and blue hair pulled up into the messiest of buns. The electric blue is hidden whenever her hair is down, located on the underside of her thick, wavy hair.

"Hi, Chilly," she responds, the familiar nickname—gifted to Winter by Cassy in preschool when she told Winter that her heart was chilly after a fight over a doll—rolling off her tongue. She tiptoes up the stairs, clutching onto the bag of dirt in her hand like it's her lifeline. "What's going on?"

"I just miss you. I stopped by your apartment and noticed a lot of your stuff was gone. Did you move out without tellin' anyone? I thought that place I helped you find was for one of your work buddies."

She flinches, chewing on her bottom lip. "Why did you think that?"

Winter makes an annoyed huffing noise, the camera flopping up and down as though moving with her hands. "Because that's what *you* told me!"

"I'm just staying in Nashville with a...friend for a while." Cassy makes it to the top of the stairs, slipping inside the hideous purple and yellow room with a wrinkle of her nose.

She can practically see her best friends' ears perk up, a mischievous grin on Winter's plump lips. "A friend, you say?"

"Yes, *friend.*" She scowls at Winter, flipping her a bird.

Winter's brown eyes narrow as she takes in the room barely visible behind Cassy. "Is that where you are now? That room is certainly...*interestin'.*"

"Ugly, you mean?" She laughs, shaking her head. "No, that's not where I'm at now. Just at one of his friends' places, that's all." It's a gross minimization of where she is, but she's not great at lying. She's usually honest to a fault, whether she wants to be or not. Things just come out of her mouth, and she has to work really hard to keep them in. It's not a great trait for a serial killer.

"His?" Winter quirks a pierced brow, no less interested. "What's *his* name?"

"Ruin," Cassy chirps before she can stop herself.

"Ooh, that sounds dangerous. He a biker boy? That sounds like a biker boy's name. *Ruin.*" It sounds funny coming from her Southern Belle accent, thick and syrupy instead of dark and gloomy. Although...that's Winter herself. She's all dark and gloomy on the outside, butterflies and rainbows and everything sweet within. She often shocks people when she starts talking: no one expects the Southern Belle from a girl who is covered in tattoos and piercings.

"Nah, just an unfortunate name choice from a misguided mother."

"Is he hot?" Winter is wiggling her eyebrows at Cassy, as though that will make her more likely to admit the truth.

"Very." She's glad Ruin isn't here to hear this.

Would he like knowing I'm attracted to him? I shouldn't be attracted to a ghost. I kind of want the ghost to be attracted to me. Is that wrong? I shouldn't care this much, right? Wanting a ghost is wrong. It's not—I shouldn't—I won't—

"Ha!" Winter giggles, wagging a finger at Cassy partially off-screen as her brown eyes dance. "I'm hurt, Cassy darlin'. Why didn't you tell me you'd been seeing someone? You didn't have to lie about moving in with him. I'm your best friend, honey. I may judge your decisions, but I'm always going to support them."

"I haven't been lying! I just want to hang out in Nashville for a while and he offered. It isn't anything serious. Just a roommate situation." Cassy can't stop the blush from rising to her cheeks.

"*And history will say they were just roommates,*" Winter mocks, giggling again. "Alright, whatever. I'll let you go play with your boy toy. Don't get murdered!"

"He's not—" She hangs up before Cassy can clarify, *again*, that she and Ruin aren't together.

She huffs in annoyance, shoving her phone back down into her bra before twisting around and locking the door. She doesn't have time to deal with Winter right now; she has a ghost to kill. Or not kill. Or—whatever.

She glances over her shoulder, eyeing the bed pressed against the right wall and the nightstands on either side. The only other furniture is a dresser directly across from the bed, and it looks much too heavy for her to move. So, she heads toward the closest nightstand and shoves it against the door. Then she repeats the process with the closet, ensuring she buys herself enough time to jump on Arnold if he tries to exit either way. That leaves the window as the only exit, which she triple-checks is latched before feeling confident enough to summon the ghost.

Her heart races with the uncertainty of it all, the fear of this altercation becoming violent rising in her mind. *Will he attack me, or will he just run? How much damage can a ghost do? Ruin can touch me all he wants, and I can't always touch him...does that mean I can't defend myself? What happens if I can't kiss this ghost? Will this even work? What if Ruin is wrong and I'm about to get hurt for no reason? Will I be slung into the wall? Will Ruin save me? I don't need a man to save me, but it would be kind of hot. Will I—Can he—What happens—*

No, no. This is what's going to happen: Arnold is going to be so surprised that he won't fight her, she'll plant her kissers on him, and then she'll collect her money from the frightened old man. Easy peasy lemon squeezy. Right? Right.

She holds out the gross dirt bag, swallowing hard as she calls, "Arnold Goldletter, I summon you." She adds on the last bit just so he knows her intentions, not that he will care. Not that it *matters* what her intentions are.

Arnold pops up so violently that he falls to the floor, a scream locked in his throat. A girly one, if she's being honest. She jumps the moment he hits the ground, landing on top of him and shoving his face down into the hardwood floor. He squirms underneath her weight, screaming, "No, no, no!" He makes a horrible, choked wheezing noise that has her entire body flooding with guilt.

"Just let me kiss you," she begs, a little whine to her tone. Arnold moans as though in pain, throwing her off his back and sending her tumbling down. She groans as she lands on her back, her breath leaving her violently. She forces herself to choke down air, forces herself to spin and grab him by the ankle as he tries to crawl up to his feet. She's not very strong, but Arnold isn't very large.

She drags him, somehow feeling his full weight, pulling him toward her body as harshly as she can. But Arnold kicks out with his free foot, shaking her off him when that foot lands a hit to her jaw. He leaps up to his feet so fast that she can't leap up with him, forcing her to stumble into a standing position as she rubs her aching jaw. His eyes are wide as he darts over to one side of the bed, his entire body shaking. She slowly inches toward him, pinning him between her, the bed, and the walls.

"*Please*," he pleads, eyes flickering toward the blocked door as though looking for someone there. His eyes widen when he turns back to her, as though a realization has hit him. "Don't make me go with him, Shadow Kisser. If I had known…well, it doesn't matter now, does it? Listen, I know he's still nearby. He has to be. *Please, don't make me go.* I don't want to die!"

Is he talking about Ruin? It seems he has a reputation among the ghosts. Has Ruin been hunting others of his kind? Is that why Arnold is so scared? Why would Ruin do that? Maybe he—Does he—Arnold is—

"You're already dead." She cracks her neck, screaming in frustration when he jumps onto the bed. She's quick to follow, the two of them landing in a pile of tangled limbs. He screams and thrashes underneath her, pleading for her to stop, but she doesn't. She grabs his head and forces him to turn it, bending over at an awkward angle and planting her lips on his so fiercely that he sags.

"I'll haunt you," he growls out the parting words as angry and terrified as a caged animal.

"I'll be looking forward to it," she whispers sweetly as he disappears from underneath her. She sighs in relief, jumping when she hears a knock at the door.

"Cassy? Cassy, what's going on in there? What did you do?" Ben is shouting as loudly as he can manage, falling into a coughing fit as a result.

Cassy grins, laughing as she collapses onto the bed. "I just killed a ghost."

Chapter 7

By the time Cassy makes it back to her new home, Ruin is already there to greet her. Ruin and a…guest.

Her mouth opens wide in an unattractive gape, stammering noises coming out of it until she finally manages, "You did not bring a fucking ghost dog into my house."

"You don't like dogs?" He grins and pets the giant thing's head, its very short, black hair unruffled by the touch. She can't be certain as to what kind of dog it is, but it doesn't look like one she's ever seen. Its teeth are *huge*, its body is *huge*, and its paws are *huge*. If it can be as physically present as Ruin is…this is going to be a problem.

She swallows, looking the thing over wearily. "Dogs are fine. Giant ghost dogs who can destroy my already very tiny rental home are *not* fine."

He waves his hand dismissively, squatting to love on the dog some more. She hates the little voice in her head that admits it's endearing to see his eyes light up as he coos into its ear.

Ruin glances up at her, eyes dancing with humor and lips twisted up into a snide smirk. "You have fifty thousand dollars, don't you? I think that's enough to repair anything that gets damaged."

"Twenty-five," she corrects him, glaring. "Remember?" Ben had been hesitant to give Cassy any money at all after finding her locked inside one of the guest rooms with his furniture moved around and had been even more reluctant to proclaim the ghost dead. Or undead. Or, whatever it is you call a ghost who is sent to Death to cross the veil. She had to sweet-talk him into giving her half now and half in two weeks after he verified Arnold was actually gone, and she only managed to do that after blithely telling him that she can bring back ghosts just as easily as she can get rid of them. She's not entirely sure that it was a truthful statement, but she feels certain that she can convince Ruin to nag the man for a while until the money is in her hands.

"Eh, it'll be fifty soon enough. Don't worry, C.J., Cerci wouldn't harm a fly. She's a little sweetheart, aren't you darling?" He coos at her again, rubbing her short ears and allowing her to lick him across the cheek. He outright laughs in amusement, the sound so unusual that her chest clenches. Who knew this was hiding underneath the hard exterior he shows the world?

What else makes him this happy? How do you take care of ghost dogs? Does she have to eat or is she just happily existing? Are all animals ghosts? Does Death have to reap animal souls, too, or is this different? How can I make him laugh like that again? Cerci is actually cute. I like pets. Maybe if—I like—Ruin is—

"Cerci is certainly not welcome here," Cassy hisses, hands on her hips as she watches the dog with a forced frown. Cerci tilts her head, dark black eyes watching Cassy with such earnest enthusiasm that she begins to physically wilt. "Well, I don't know, maybe I can get her a bed…"

A startled cry leaves her lips when Cerci leaps forward and tackles her, the dog's body practically the size of Cassy's own. She falls to the floor holding the dog, Cerci's giant tongue sweeping across her face frantically as the long tail wags. It bangs against the back of the couch and makes a noise loud enough to leave her wincing, her head already aching from the fall. Well, it probably also hurts because of the giant, throbbing bruise on her jaw, but that's neither here nor there. She tilts her head to the side and lets out her own joyful laugh, rubbing Cerci's face and sides lovingly.

"For a ghost dog, you sure feel real," she attempts at another hiss, but it comes out more like a bored statement than anything else.

"You don't know everything about the dead, C.J.," Ruin annoyingly points out again, coming to relieve her of Cerci's weight. He picks the dog up easily, and she can't stop her core from fluttering. If he can pick up a dog that huge, what could he do to her? Her preference would include being slammed against the wall, his lips all over her, his body—no. No, she can't allow herself to think about Ruin sexually. It is entirely inappropriate, and the two will never work out, as she has often reminded herself since meeting the blasted ghost.

"So you've said."

She wipes her face with her sleeve, accepting the hand Ruin holds out for her. It feels sturdy and calloused, and she blinks down at where they are joined for a moment in disbelief. But then she's being pulled to her feet and their hands drop, the hint of warmth she felt gone with it. Are...are ghosts supposed to be *warm?* The last time they touched it was so cold she could have been touching ice.

"Cerci goes where I go," he says casually, clicking his tongue at the dog. She goes and curls by the front door, tail still wagging as she watches them intently. "She obeys every order. She protects me. And most importantly of all, she's my best friend." The tail slams down harder, and Cassy swears she can feel the floor shake.

She raises an eyebrow, moving to grab an ice pack from the freezer before proceeding to plop down on the couch. Ruin's turned away, staring at Cerci with an intensity so deep it's as though he's trying to mentally convey something. She allows herself to take him in for a moment, entranced by the love he's showing the ghost dog. It's not a side of him she's seen yet: a doting, caring friend. With a hard sigh, she asks, "You need protecting?"

"Not everyone wants to meet Death," he whispers softly, smiling knowingly at Cerci. "Most ghosts know who I am and what I do."

"So you send ghosts to Death often, then? You two have some kind of arrangement?" Her eyebrows fall in, her mind chewing on this new information. He's basically an informant, like she suspected after Arnold's strange reaction to Ruin. He finds ghosts, tells Death about them, and gets...what? Is this why he isn't interested in Death's bargain when it comes to finding her: He already has his own deal with the devil?

What if Ruin is lying to me? I don't know him that well. He's handsome and endearing around dogs, but that doesn't make someone good. What makes someone good, though? I consider myself good.

What if what he does makes him consider himself good, too? At what point does it become not good? How do I tell when it crosses that point? What if—I am—Is he—

"Something like that." He clears his throat, coming to lie next to her. He stretches his feet into her lap, casual and lazy like usual. She ignores the burst of explosives in her stomach, ignores the awareness his touch brings. She likes this casual chatter, the banter that the two share. The only other person she can speak to as freely is Winter. She has to put on a show for everyone else. Everyone except Ruin, now. She doesn't want to mess up a potential friendship with the imaginary hard-on she gets every time she looks at him.

"Alright, great. So, theoretically, does that mean you get hunted down a lot?" If a ghost mob shows up at her house with actual torches...

"Never hunted, always preyed upon." His eyes are directed to the ceiling, watching the fan move in lazy circles. She watches with him, trying and failing to decipher his words.

After taking too long to decipher, she finally grinds out, "What does that even *mean*?"

"Don't worry your pretty little head over it, C.J. My business matters little to you. All you need to know is that Cerci will take care of any...outliers. She'll keep you safe. *Us* safe."

"I'm more of a cat person, you know?" she lies, glancing back over to the dog again. She's had lots of pets in her life, but dogs were always her favorite. She had a Great Dane named Lucy when she was eight, and Lucy was her best friend in the whole world. She was sixteen when she passed, the eight years Lucy lived considered a long life for that particular breed, and she hasn't dared to own another pet since.

"She'll grow on you," he says knowingly, a little twinkle in his eyes as he turns his gaze onto Cassy.

"Like you will, I suppose?" Her fingers tap against the side of the couch; she's always moving, never still.

"I've already grown on you, silly thing." He mocks her with a devilish grin, the grin falling as he spots the bruise she's sporting as she adjusts her ice pack. "Did Arnold do that to you?"

"Like you care?" She scoffs, tilting her head back against the cushion and letting out a small noise of displeasure as she presses the ice pack deeper. She's had worse, of course, but knowing a ghost gave her a physical injury…well, it makes this bruise a little more terrifying than the previous ones.

"Of course I care." He looks almost confused, as though it should be obvious that the ghost haunting her gives a fuck about her well-being.

"You didn't say anything at Mr. Craigmore's house," she points out, adding on bitterly, "Or was Cerci's presence supposed to be an apology?"

He looks positively offended. "Why would I apologize? I didn't hurt you!"

She laughs bitterly, unable to stop herself from biting out, "No, but you sent me to kill the ghost who did."

"You can't kill—"

"Semantics." She waves her hand around, closing her eyes and trying to ignore the throbbing in her face.

How long does it take for a bruise this large to heal? I've never been kicked or punched in the face before. All my victims are dead before they get the chance to fight back. They barely get the chance to understand what's happening before keeling over. I like that, though. The realization in their eyes. It's a little addicting. Lots of things are addictive for me, though. I get so focused that I can't let things go. Killing bad people gives me dopamine, and I crave it like a drunk craves alcohol. Is that wrong? Should I see a therapist? A therapist would turn me in, though. Should I—I like—This is—

"I *am* sorry you got hurt." Ruin's voice is in the distance, loud enough to penetrate through the random thoughts spinning inside her mind.

"Huh?"

She opens her eyes just in time to see his brows crinkle, his mouth parting automatically as he starts to repeat himself. "I said that I was—"

"Oh, yeah. Well, I suppose it's the thought that counts, isn't it?"

His frown is deep and annoyingly attractive, and his legs swing off her lap in a move so fast she doesn't have time to track it. "What's wrong with you?" He moves so that he's sitting directly next to her, his eyes worried and his body stiff. He reaches out to touch her head, pulling off her wig and examining it thoughtfully. "Do you have a concussion? Is this thing on too tightly?"

"What? No. Nothing's wrong with me, other than the fact that I have the sudden urge to murder the nearest person. Oh, wait...that's you." She pouts at him sadly, as though it's a travesty. She leans forward, popping her lips playfully. "Pucker up, buttercup."

"As tempting as that offer is…" It's like he can't stop himself from leaning forward, from tempting fate, as he lets his lips hover so close that she's sure they'll meet if he speaks. He leans back only slightly before he does speak, as though thinking the same thing. "I'm quite certain you've had enough kissing for one day."

She jerks back and barks out a laugh, her cheeks so hot she's sure they're blazing red. Her fingers dance across her lips absentmindedly, a repetitive motion she makes throughout each day. "It's quite the contrary, actually. I *haven't* had enough. It's something I always crave."

If she kissed Ruin, it wouldn't be because she wanted to kill him. Or to send him to Death. It would be because she wanted to, because she *needed* to. And that…that would be a mistake. She can't want Ruin. She can't need him. Ghosts and humans can't mix for a reason, and that reason is beyond explanation. She can flirt and tease and play with him all she wants, but it can never be more than that in her mind. She won't allow it to be.

"You definitely have a concussion," he concurs, lips twitching up into a smile as his fingers begin to part sections of fake hair.

"Quit that." She smacks his hand away, huffing as she yanks the wig back into her hand. She tries not to touch her head, tries not to smooth down the ruffled, wild hair she's certain is present there. "You won't find evidence of a wound. I just have delayed processing, that's all. You'll get used to it if you hang around me long enough."

"Delayed processing?" He says it slowly, the words haughty on his tongue.

"Yes, and it seems I may not be the only one in this room with it." She scowls, offering no other explanation. He doesn't need to know personal stuff about her. He doesn't need to know about the inner workings of her brain, or its very unfortunate malfunctions.

"Is that a result—"

He's so close, so real, and I am on fire. I am on fire for a funny, genuinely nice ghost, and I shouldn't be. Would he mind if he knew? Would he want to do something about the ache building in my core? I bet Ruin knows exactly how to take care of that. Would I want him to? Yes. I shouldn't. This is ridiculous. I've known him for two weeks. Sure, I think we talk as though we've known each other for years. Sure, I think we have some kind of weird magnetism. But that doesn't mean I'm allowed to want him this deeply so quickly. I've always craved sex, but I don't know if I've ever had such a visceral reaction to someone before. I haven't gotten laid in months, though, so maybe that's the problem. It's definitely not because I like his personality and how he coos to the giant dog he calls his best friend. I'll call Winter. I'll go—We can—Would he—

"What are you staring at?" Ruin is snapping his fingers in front of her, concern written all over his features. He reaches out to touch her face, his thumb running over the edges of the bruise gently.

"I'm staring into space because this whole nice guy act of yours is boring me. I know to wait for the other shoe to drop," she says monotonously, shoving herself off the couch and forcing herself into a standing position to get away from that contradictingly warm touch. "I'm going to get a shower and I'm going to bed. Cerci is welcome to stay with me; you aren't."

"It's not an act, and there is no other shoe," he says softly, but she pretends not to hear. And when Cerci comes trotting in her room after her, she pretends not to notice that he ordered his companion to follow.

Chapter 8

The next day, in a desperate haze, Cassy calls Winter to invite her on a girls' night out. The sexual tension between her and Ruin is too overwhelming, too new, and she needs to find an outlet for the strange feeling wriggling around inside her gut like a bundle of worms.

"I'm so sorry, Cassy, but it's going to be two weeks before I can go," Winter is telling her, her voice fading in and out as though she is moving away from the microphone and drawing back in. "You know how work is."

Winter is an E.R. nurse, meaning free time can be nonexistent at times. Winter enjoys her job, though, and is constantly taking shifts for others and volunteering for overtime. Weekends off for Winter are as rare as patients who don't flirt with her. Cassy has always applauded her best friend for the work she does, for the time and effort it took Winter to make it into the profession. On the flip side, she hates Winter's guts for finding something she's so passionate about that she'll blow Cassy off for it. Winter is practically her sister, but lately it seems that their chosen career paths are steering them in opposite directions. It fucking *sucks*.

After spending two days alone moping about the long wait, Ruin shows up to direct her toward another ghost. It's a welcome reprieve from her impatient mind, and it helps her to have something new to obsess over. His visit is brief but satisfying, and she finds herself laughing hard and relaxing deeply for the first time in...well, a while.

"Why don't you stay longer?" she asks when he tilts his ear toward the sky, his signature move before he departs. She and Ruin were in the middle of a conversation about books, a topic she'd never bonded over with anyone else before. Winter doesn't read, and she isn't artistic in any way, so she and Cassy never discuss shared hobbies. Ruin, on the other hand, has revealed to her that he reads, draws, and paints; it's an endearing discovery, and she eagerly awaits more details.

"I want to," he says softly, watching her with those beautiful, entrancing eyes. "But there are things I have to do. Things I can't put off any longer."

She frowns, tucking a strand of silver hair behind her ear. "You're a ghost. What could you possibly have to do? Do you have a job or something?"

He smiles widely, winking playfully. "Or something." Disappointment flutters in her heart when he disappears, so she pulls out her phone and searches the hotel Ruin had told her about in an attempt to redirect herself. Fortunately for her, the distraction works. Researching is an area of expertise for her, after all.

When Cassy arrives at the old hotel a week later, the owner greets her in the lobby. The woman is the only person there, the space eerily quiet and still. The woman admits to her business failings, most of which are from the loss of customers due to the strange occurrences in the rooms. She listens as the owner details her life as a single mom of three, the heavy bags under her eyes an indication of her struggles. The owner offers Cassy five grand for the hunt, which she readily accepts. She feels too bad to ask for more, and not every job can pay her on such a grand scale as rich Mr. Craigmore's could, anyway. She also has a feeling Ruin will ruthlessly pick at her for having such a soft heart, but she can't bring herself to care. She may be a killer, but that doesn't make her heartless.

"Room one-seventeen," the owner tells her with a hearty, relieved sigh. "That's where it usually stays. And take—" A tightly wrapped bundle of green is pressed into Cassy's hand, along with a small matchbox. "—this. The ghost hates this sage stuff."

She slowly curls her hand around the bundle, nodding lightly and trying not to laugh. "Of course. Thank you, ma'am."

Cassy makes her way to the room swiftly after, knocking on the door to room one-seventeen politely before entering. There, sitting on the bed, is an aged lady. She can tell the woman is a ghost because of the slight iridescent hue to her severely wrinkled skin, her frame bent over as she weeps. Cassy merely sits next to the woman, resting a hand over her cold, shaking one and asking softly, "What's wrong?"

The woman's head snaps up, a snarl on her lips despite the sad tears dripping down her cheeks. "Get out!" She balls up her hands, raising them as though about to hit something. A clothes hanger falls to the ground, clattering loudly in the otherwise silent room. "Get out!"

"What's wrong?" Cassy repeats herself, understanding that this woman needs an ear to listen to her. Forcefully, she adds with a stoic expression, "And start behaving before I stop asking so nicely. You're an adult, for goodness's sake. Act like one. Don't make me light this sage."

She can see the woman deflate, her lips opening and closing as she tries to form an explanation. The old lady is likely used to people running away at this point. An angry "get out" and throwing objects would certainly do the trick on the majority of people. Unfortunately for her, Cassy isn't most people.

"My life was horrible," the woman admits, beginning her sad, sad story while staring at the sage wearily. She tells Cassy how her husband was abusive, but she still had ten kids with the man. Only five of the children survived. Her husband blamed her and dipped into the bottle a bit too often over the situation. But the bottle only led to more abuse for her and the surviving kids. She worked as a maid in the hotel from her teenage years up until the moment she died because she had to help fund his drinking problem. She had a heart attack when a guest scared her by accident, and she died in room one-seventeen. Her anger led her to stay, and she's been taking that anger out on anyone and everyone she can.

Cassy takes pity on her and poses her options as a choice, even though it isn't one. "You can either stay here, angry and hostile, or go find peace."

The woman leans into Cassy's shoulder and weeps, translucent tears slipping through her into a ghostly puddle on the floor. Cassy rubs the woman's back to her best ability, but the woman is so hysterical that she fades in and out of existence sporadically. Quietly, Cassy says, "Death isn't a bad person. He won't punish you for staying around when you weren't supposed to. That was his mistake, not yours. Crossing the veil is something that happens to everyone, and it isn't as scary as you might think. Most enjoy it, I think. And maybe in the afterlife you can find the peace you couldn't find here." She isn't sure if any of it is true, but it's believable enough because the woman nods eagerly. She can't help but feel as though the job was all too easy as she leans forward and kisses the elderly woman, her bottom lip wavering when she sees the serene expression on the woman's face. Their lips meld only briefly, the kiss tender and friendly. Then the woman is gone, off to join Death and find her afterlife.

Later, as Cassy crawls into bed, she curls into a ball and weeps. Ruin somehow senses her distress, appearing for the first time since delivering her instructions just to pound on her bedroom door. *Cops would be jealous,* she thinks as he bangs away. "C.J., please," he begs outside her door, unwilling to walk through even though he can. She likes his willingness to give her space, his willingness not to use his abilities to his advantage. He's a good guy, as much as it pains her to admit. "Are you hurt? Did something happen? Come on, C.J. I'm worried about you."

She wants to call out and tell him it's fine, that *she's* fine, but the words don't come. Instead, after five minutes or so have passed, he sends Cerci in to replace her pillow. She doesn't offer any explanation to Ruin, who she's certain is still lingering nearby. It's a notion emphasized when a bag filled with her favorite fast-food fries and a cookie and cream chocolate bar is brought in by Cerci later in the night. She cries more at the thoughtfulness, wishing she could explain herself. But she doesn't want him to know she is stuck on these looping thoughts about the old woman; that her story was so sad that all she wants to do is go back and change things for that family. She doesn't want him to know she feels guilty for lying to the ghost about Death and the afterlife she knows nothing about. Most importantly, she doesn't want to admit out loud that her lies hurt her more than they will ever hurt the ghost.

What was her name? Are her kids still alive? Did they know she was that sad? How many people had seen what was happening and left well enough alone? I want to comfort her. I want to stop that

from happening to anyone else. I want to kiss anyone who makes their significant other that miserable. I want—I want—I want—

Cassy shakes her head, turning her attention back to the navy-blue dress clinging to her body and away from the sad elderly woman. The dress is one she hasn't worn before, stolen from one of her victims months ago. It was beautiful, with the dark lace plastered to its exterior and the sweetheart neckline that had practically called her name. It is shorter than she anticipated, stopping just above mid-thigh, but it is more than flattering. Its sleeveless top shows off her new tattoo, the pair of pink lips perfectly stamped onto the contours of her outer right arm. It's a little much for a night out, even for her, but she can't bring herself to care. *She needs this.*

She holds up a pair of black heels in her right hand, leather boots in her left. The boots will make her look more like a badass, but the heels...

She tosses the boots to the side and sits on the edge of her bed, slipping her foot inside and wrapping the attached strings around her ankles and slightly up her calf. Once finished, she tosses a handful of silver curls over her shoulder before slipping matching silver hoops in her ears. Chewing her lip as she stares at the necklaces she laid out, she decides on one coated in diamonds and slips it around her neck before tucking a taser in her bra. With the amount of cleavage the dress shows, and the glittery jewels dangling right above it, not a soul will suspect it's there. Great for her, painful for any would-be attacker.

Grabbing a tiny clutch, she shoves her wallet, house keys, and phone inside. By the time she's done, there's already a knock at the door. She rushes to leave the room before Ruin can answer it, but she's not nearly as fast as a ghost who cheats by strutting through the couch. He swings it open with a rakish grin, welcoming Winter inside and boldly looking her up and down. Cassy can't tell from her position at the bedroom door if it's merely theatrical or if it's flirtatious, but either way, it has this uncomfortable storm of emotions brewing in her gut.

"*This* is Ruin?" Winter gapes, stepping in and allowing Ruin to shut the door behind her.

"The one and only." He grins, adding, "Did C.J. not tell you how handsome I am?"

"No, but I told her how arrogant you are," Cassy states blandly, strutting forward to put herself between them. She isn't sure if it's brought on by the need to protect Winter from him or hide her best friend's presence out of jealousy, but it's a reaction she can't stop.

Winter puts a hand on her hip, her plum purple dress bunching up lightly on her thighs with the movement. "She won't tell me anythin' about you, actually."

That's fair, Cassy admits to herself. Winter has asked about him a few times now, but she quickly changes the topic and avoids saying anything more than, "He's just a friend I'm staying with, Chilly." She repeats the sentiment now.

Ruin's eyes finally fall to Cassy, pupils blowing wide as he takes her in. She shivers in delight, unable to stop herself from taking pleasure in the clear attraction dancing in his eyes. In a low growl, he grinds out, "What are you wearing?"

"Oh, please. Don't act like you're my father." She makes it seem as though she's annoyed, but really, she's thrilled. This is more emotion than she usually gets from Ruin, more attention than she should seek.

"I'm certainly not that," he confirms, Adam's apple bobbing as he swallows hard. His gaze flicks down to her cleavage before shooting back to her eyes, that gaze inevitably falling again.

"I'll be back later," she says firmly, smiling smugly. "Don't wait up."

She shoves Winter out into the crisp November air, bending down slightly and pretending to adjust the ties around her calves to show off a view of her ass to Ruin before the door shuts. Winter is giggling by the time they step into her car, a giggle that turns into full-blown laughter before Cassy can buckle up.

"What?" she hisses, an embarrassed flush already on her cheeks.

"Oh, nothin', *C.J.*," her best friend purrs, grinning. "It's only that, well, you conveniently failed to mention that Ruin is *hot*."

"How attractive he is isn't relevant." Cassy leans far back into her seat as Winter takes off, giggling all the while.

"Sure, sure. Next, you're going to say that how big your tits are isn't relevant to the way he was starin' at 'em."

"Winter!" More laughter, followed by the honking of a horn nearby. "He probably saw my taser," she mutters under her breath, hating the way her best friend cackles like a maniac afterward.

"Yeah, he probably saw a little more than that when you bent over. You better hope he's a tits guy, honey, because you don't have anythin' to call home about in the ass department."

"Winter!" Cassy groans into her hands, embarrassed, before turning to stare out the window contemplatively.

The truth is, it doesn't matter how much he looks at her tits *or* her ass. He's a ghost, and she doesn't plan on joining him in the afterlife anytime soon.

The bar Winter chooses is some old, busy place near the hospital where she works, a place the two often visit. It isn't as busy as the main bars on Broadway are, and more locals loiter around inside the building than tourists do. *Winter chose well today*, Cassy thinks gratefully, because within five minutes of being on the premises, they've been offered drinks. Drinks they watched being poured before accepting, of course. Within the hour, she is happily buzzed, her bank account not a drop lower, and she's feeling hornier than ever.

She came out tonight to forget about Ruin, to try and end her little dry spell so she can stop lusting over the hot, thoughtful, funny ghost at home. The alcohol seems to have the opposite effect, though, and the more drunk she gets, the more she thinks about him. She sees him in the stranger she's grinding on, his brown hair shorter but still full of waves similar to Ruin's. His face isn't nearly as striking as the ghost's, but it's pleasant to look at. He's shorter, too, but she doesn't care about that.

She *does* care about the hardness pressed into her ass, about the aching throb inside her that she needs him to satisfy. She knows, deep down inside, that it won't completely heal her from whatever parasite is inside her making her crave Ruin. But she knows it will at least alleviate the symptoms for a short while, and that's all the reassurance she needs.

Before the end of the night, she convinces the stranger to come back to her place. It may be a mistake, considering Ruin was actually gifting the place with his presence earlier, but part of her wants him to be there. She *wants* him to see her with another man, as devious as it may sound.

Winter stays with the couple until their taxi finally pulls up, and she immediately pops her head into the silver car to instruct the driver where to take them. Of course, Winter finds the time to take a picture of the license plate before doing so. Cassy tries to assure Winter that she's not *that* drunk but, well, it's a bold-faced lie.

Whether scared of Winter or just an honest driver, the taxi makes it back to her rental house in record time. Though they may have just been completely annoyed by the tiny moans and bold touches shared in their backseat. The Ruin look-alike tried to kiss her several times, but after the third attempt, she full-on face-palmed his face and told him she doesn't kiss hookups. He dropped it after that, but only barely.

Her hands are shaky when she unlocks the door, her body brimming with desire as hands roam down her sides and back up. He's whispering something unintelligible in her ear as the door swings open, something about satisfying her, she thinks. But satisfying isn't the goal she has in mind: distracting is. She wants to be distracted from her inappropriate thoughts about Ruin, of course, but she also wants to be distracted from herself. She wants to go into a space where she doesn't think, where her mind is blissfully at peace and she can enjoy herself in more than one way. It doesn't happen often in sex, but when she finds the right partners, it's electrifying.

She giggles as she pulls the guy through, Blake, she thinks? The door slams shut behind them, and she finds herself pressed against it in the blink of an eye. Blake, or maybe Blare, has his lips on her neck, teeth skimming the sensitive area beneath her ear. She lets out a low moan, closing her eyes as he begins to suck.

What would this feel like if it were Ruin's lips, instead? Would he care that I'm bringing someone else into my bed? I barely know him; of course he wouldn't. Just because I have a crush doesn't mean he does too. And he's a ghost. I always forget. He seems so real, sometimes. But isn't he? He's always touching me, always present. He lives with me now, doesn't he? I've never lived with a man. I always thought that, if I lived with anyone besides Winter, it would be a romantic partner. Does he want to be romantic? I do. Sometimes. No, never. Always. I want—Does he—I can't—

She forces herself to focus, forces herself into the moment as she latches her legs around the man who could be Ruin but isn't. "Straight back," she says breathlessly, burying herself into his chest. He's obedient, she'll give him that. He walks straight to her room and deposits her onto the bed, not even stumbling despite the alcohol running through his circulatory system, before crawling over her and tugging at the front of her dress. It slips down, exposing her bare breasts and the taser hidden between them. She tosses it to the side, grinning mischievously.

"Were you going to use that on me?" His eyes are playful, but his words are a low growl.

"If I had to." She bats her eyelashes at him, enjoying the jerk of his cock against her.

"That's way hotter than it should be." The words barely escape before his lips are planted on her breasts, sucking, kissing, pulling.

"I want—" she starts, a gasp wretched from her mouth mid-sentence as his body flies across the room in one brutal moment. She lets out a cry of surprise, jerking up and flicking her head around. Had a ghost followed her here? Where is Cerci when she needs her?

"What's happening?" Maybe Blake groans against the dingy yellow wall, suspended just high enough to make his feet dangle. His words come out choked, as though someone has a grip on his neck. Maybe someone does.

"Ruin," Cassy whispers, blinking rapidly and quickly pulling her dress back up. "Ruin, no!" She isn't sure how she knows it's him, but she does. She can feel it in the air, can taste the dark energy he always brings into a room.

"You're drunk." His words are simple and clipped, his form blinking into existence. His hand is wrapped around Maybe Blake's throat, holding him up effortlessly. The man is choking and sputtering, eyes wide as he tries to pry Ruin's hand off him.

"Yeah, that's a thing living people do," she hisses, leaping up and grabbing his arm. She tugs on it as hard as she can, but it doesn't make a difference. He's too strong, too sure, too angry.

"He's taking advantage of that." Ruin glares at the man who's slowly turning purple, the hatred so intense it could burn a hole through the wall.

"No, he isn't!" she insists, pulling harder. "The only reason I went out tonight was to find someone to hook up with. That was before I ever drank a *sip* of alcohol, Ruin. Some people like sex. Crave it, even."

His grip loosens only lightly enough to allow Maybe Blake to inhale loudly, his angry gaze falling to her. And what she finds in those hooded eyes, for just a moment, is a heat so intense her core clenches. "Do you crave it?"

She can't stop the word that leaves her inebriated lips, but she can regret it immediately after. "Immensely."

He scoffs at Maybe Blake, releasing the man and allowing him to slide down the wall and to his feet. "You chose *him*?"

"He looks—" She almost lets the words slip out, almost admits to something she shouldn't. *He looks like you.* She isn't sure how he would take the sentiment, even if he did look at her like he was going to take over where Maybe Blake left off for a second there.

I couldn't have you, so I got as close as I could. I wanted to get you out of my system. It isn't going well. I'm so horny. I only want you. Why can't you be alive? Why won't my brain just realize you are dead? Why do I have to desire something I'll never have? Why do—I would—I want—

"I don't care why you chose him," Ruin says softly as he takes a step away from the coughing and wheezing Maybe Blake. "I only care that he isn't taking advantage of you."

"Well, it doesn't matter now, does it? You've completely spoiled the mood." She moves to Maybe Blake, getting down on her knees next to him and taking his face in her hands as she examines the red area around his neck before dropping them.

"I'm sorry, man. I didn't know she was taken, I swear. She didn't tell me—"

She sighs, kissing Maybe Blake on the cheek softly. Followed by a gentle pat. "He's not my boyfriend. I'm sorry you got caught up in this." She can practically feel Ruin's rage behind her at the gesture, his breath like dragon fire behind her.

"I—" the man begins, eyes suddenly wide and hands flying to his heart.

"What's wrong?" Her own heart skips a beat as she stares at him, her own hands following his in an instant. "Ruin, what are you doing to him?"

"I'm not doing anything, C.J." His words are soft, his voice cracking. "You are."

"I didn't kiss him," she says vehemently, shaking her head so hard it hurts. She chokes on a sob as realization hits, her heart hammering a thunderous, painful beat in her chest. Insistent, she says, "Not on the lips."

Maybe Blake falls back, hitting his head on the wall and not moving from the awkward angle. Ruin squats beside her, reaching out to brush his hand across her tattoo with a sad, regretful sigh. "It seems that it didn't matter this time."

Cassy covers her lips, her entire body shaking. This can't be real. There has to be another explanation, because this couldn't have been her. Her breaths come out in uneven pants, her eyes wide as nausea creeps up into her throat. "No. No, no, no, *no*.

That's not how this works. It's only on the lips. It's only *ever* been on the lips. I can do whatever else I want with my lips. I can—"

Ruin has his arms around her, gently pulling her away from the body and into the living room. He slips back into her room after depositing her on the couch, and she's not entirely sure she wants to know what he's doing as she tries to squelch her growing panic.

Is he making sure Death doesn't come? How quickly does he come, anyway? I've never run into him before, so surely there's a delay in the response. Or maybe he sends others to collect for him? He won't kill me, right? This one was an actual accident. I didn't mean—I didn't mean—I didn't mean—

"You've never done that before?" Ruin asks quietly as he returns, a glass of water in his hand. He passes it to Cassy, sitting next to her and drawing her into his arms. It's a small gesture, but mighty. Ruin doesn't usually touch her like this, and it has every nerve ending on fire, despite the situation.

"Never," she whispers after taking a tiny sip of the water, still shaking.

"You're getting stronger," he says simply, chin tucked onto the top of her head as he strokes her hair soothingly.

"I don't want to be stronger. I want things to stay the same. I want to have hookups and not have to worry about oral giving my partners heart attacks." Her mouth speaks too fast for her brain to catch the horribly embarrassing words, and a blush spreads across her cheeks. She can't even blame it on the alcohol; it's a problem she's had her entire life.

"You may have to put a pause on that until we can figure out what's going on." Ruin is gentle with the words, but firm.

"I don't want to. I just…I want—" She bites her bottom lip, blurting out, "I just want a little relief. I just want one, single moment where I don't *think*." It hurts to think about so much sometimes. Hurts in a way that isn't physical but is so draining that she doesn't know how else to describe it. And *this*…this guilt is tormenting her mind, her breath still fast and her chest still clenching. Killing has never bothered her before, has never made her feel so…so *evil*. Yes, torment is exactly what this feeling gnawing on her from the inside out is.

"And sex is the only way to do that?" She can feel his brows furrowing, his arms stiffening around her at the intrusive question.

"No, but it's the funnest." She smiles softly, burrowing farther into him to try and escape her thoughts. She tries to focus on him, on his heaving chest and his smoky smell. "And at least I usually get an orgasm out of it."

"Usually?" The amusement is evident.

Blandly, she says, "Not everyone is gifted with knowing how a woman's body works. Which sucks for me, because the orgasm is really the only moment that truly matters. The only moment where the one thing floating around inside my brain is a pleasurable buzz and not a million rapid thoughts that jumble together to form a few coherent ones."

"You're picking the wrong partners," he says just as blandly, but the rapid racing of his heart gives him away. How does he even have a heartbeat when he's dead, anyway? Is it a mimicry of the movement from the organ he had in life? "You should be having several of those moments, not just one fleeting orgasm that briefly satisfies you."

"Yeah, well, it's slim pickings out here, okay? I do what I can. The women are usually better, but tonight..." She forces her mouth to clamp shut, accidentally biting her tongue and earning herself the taste of irony blood. She will *not* tell him that she was searching for his replacement, even if the alcohol and her mouth are working against her in the endeavor. She winces, knowing that the reason the man in her bedroom died wasn't good. It wasn't heroic, or brave, or even plain dumb. It was meaningless. *It was her fault.* In her eagerness to get over Ruin, to move on, she didn't consider any consequences. Not that she knew there were consequences *to* consider.

"You need better partners." It's another gentle but firm statement, one that has anger blossoming in her chest.

"Shut up, Ruin, unless you're offering. I've been fine without you up until now, and I'll be fine after you're gone." Anger is a good replacement for guilt. Anger is something better to focus on.

Ruin doesn't seem to understand that she wants an argument, that she needs a fight, as he asks, "Do you want me to offer?"

She can hear the way his breath catches, the ghostly organ housed inside his chest pounding uncontrollably as he clears his throat. *It's all an illusion*, she reminds herself, clenching her teeth. *He isn't breathing, and his heart isn't racing. None of it is real.*

"You're a ghost," she says simply, refusing to tilt her head back and meet his gaze. The anger deflates, replaced by something much sadder and much less forgettable.

The silence is awkward and too long, but he recovers the moment when he says, "What is it? The thing that so thoroughly fills your mind?"

"ADHD," she murmurs, rubbing her forehead softly and sipping more of her water. "You'll get used to the little nuances of my actions if you stick around long enough."

"You've shared that sentiment before." A pause, then, "That's why you want quiet. Why you crave stillness in moments with strangers."

"Of course it is. I'm not after cheap orgasms; those are just a bonus." She can't meet his gaze, can't let him see the red that coats her entire face and is possibly creeping down her neck. At this point, she'd rather talk about what just happened instead of...whatever this is. "Speaking of, what are we going to do with the body?"

"What do you usually do with bodies?" His voice is humorless, merely curious.

"Leave 'em in dark alleys." She's unemotional about this fact, unattached. She tries to stay that way in the beat of silence that follows, her chest clenching so painfully she's sure she will double over from the sensation.

"Alright, I'll do that, then." Ruin blinks out of existence, causing her to topple over with a yelp. She doesn't want to know how he gets the body out, how he can just evaporate with something so heavy so easily. But he does it. He does it and doesn't make a fuss, only popping back in front of her when the task is over.

His voice is gentle and coercing as he whispers, "Come on, let's get you into bed."

She lets him drag her back into her bed, lets him pull her heels off and force more water down her throat before tucking her in. Another painfully thoughtful gesture from the ghost who shouldn't think about her at all.

"It's so cold in here," she pants, wiggling underneath the covers and whimpering.

"I'll send in Cerci," he murmurs before clearing his throat, avoiding her gaze. "She's comforted me on many cold, disappointing nights."

Ruin turns to leave, but she grabs him by the wrist and lets out a weak, wobbling, "My mind…it won't stop. Can you…Will you stay with me?" She isn't sure how she manages to get it out, how she doesn't erupt into hives from the nerves and the guilt wracking her body. Alcohol *is* known for making people brave, though.

Ruin sighs, rubbing the back of his head. "I don't think that's a good idea."

"Please." The choked beg makes him cave, and he crawls into the bed to curl behind her. The instant relief should be terrifying, but she's too far gone to register anything but that relief. She needs it right now. Needs his comfort to satisfy her ebbing shame. A warm arm wraps around her waist as she whispers contentedly, "Goodnight, Ruin."

She can feel the dip of the bed as Cerci stretches out at their feet, a loud groan leaving her giant body. And after the silence has gone on too long, after her eyes are long shut and her brain has nearly faded into darkness, she hears a faint, "Goodnight, Cassiopeia."

Chapter 9

Waking up the next morning feels like a dream...until Cassy realizes it isn't. She wakes up warm and content, cocooned in Ruin's arms. She stays there for a moment as her memories come crashing in, reality hitting her so hard she jumps. She isn't a caterpillar about to earn its wings: She can't stay cocooned in a ball of lies to make her dreams grow into reality. So, she pushes herself out of the cage formed by his arms and bolts into the bathroom. She can hear him rustling under the sheets afterward, mostly because she had pressed her back against the door and slid to the floor.

She sits there, hating herself and her damned lips, as he murmurs tiredly, "I haven't slept in..." She doesn't hear how long it has been since he slept because she crawls forward and begins to vomit, the sickness hitting her hard and heavy.

"C.J.?" Ruin is next to her, his large form taking up most of the space in the tiny bathroom. He crouches down behind her to hold her hair, rubbing her back gently, soothingly. It is the kind of thing a romantic partner would do, and the thought makes her want to weep.

I'll never have a relationship. I'll never kiss anyone I love. I'll never get to give oral again. I'll never find anyone to love me. I'll never—I'll never—I'll never—

"Do you remember last night?"

Oh, how she wished she didn't. She can't answer verbally, so she gives him an imperceptible nod instead, followed by another bout of vomiting. Softly, he says, "It isn't your fault. It's *his*." She knows who he's referring to: *Death*. She likes that he isn't upset with her; he blames the person they suspect gifted her the powers. It is the logical person to blame, after all, but she still hates herself for what she did.

She crawls out of the bathroom fifteen minutes later, but only after Ruin helped her brush her hair and teeth. He loops a strong arm around her waist, hand staying firmly on her stomach as he helps her stand and begin the achingly slow walk to the bed. He gently lays her back down once they reach their destination, leaving abruptly before she can ask him to stay again. Not that she had planned on doing so; she had made enough mistakes the night before and didn't need to repeat them into the morning. Cerci is quick to replace him, though, and she falls asleep before she can allow herself to miss him.

Neither Ruin nor Cassy bring up the night in her bed again, nor any of the kind gestures that followed into the morning. Not the rest of that first day, the first week, or even the first month. It's a secret they share now, one that doesn't need to be spoken aloud. Yes, Ruin overreacted. Yes, Cassy killed someone by accident for the first time in over three years. Yes, she asked him to stay with her. Practically begged, actually. And despite it all, even though he's a ghost and she's...her, it doesn't change the truth. It doesn't change the way she feels, certainly, even though it should.

She couldn't stop herself from doing some research on Maybe Blake in those first days, who turned out to actually be Blade. She found a missing person's report that was filed mere hours before his body was found in an alley near a strip club, followed by the obituary labeling him as a loving son and a loyal friend. Then, just to make herself feel worse, she looked at all of his social media accounts. He seemed like a good guy, a great one, even.

And she feels so fucking horrible for killing him.

This isn't what she is meant to do. She is meant to kill those who deserve to die, not those who happen to be near her. Ruin isn't very good at consoling, or at least pretends not to be; he shrugs and says accidents happen like he's talking to a toddler who spilled their milk. The kind, assuring man who made an appearance the morning after Blade's death has not come back out. She suspects it's because he is doing the thing she can't bring herself to do: Maintain distance.

She hasn't been able to make the tears stop, hasn't been able to make her puffy face look even remotely normal. She went so far as to cut her hair to shoulder length in the bathroom, dyed strands a rosy pink that didn't last past one wash, then proceeded to go out and get a new ear piercing. None of it helped, but she had convinced herself it would; she had convinced herself those little changes would lead to one big one.

Cassy lied to herself.

Winter thinks she's in a depressed state because the guy she hooked up with died after he left her place. She thinks Cassy wrongly feels a sense of responsibility for his death because she was the last person to see him. "Even you can't make hearts start after they stop, Cassy." But Winter doesn't know. She can *never* know. And that makes all of it so much *worse*. Worse because it means Cassy isn't only lying to herself...she's lying to everyone else, too. She's lying to her parents, to her best friend, and even to ghosts. At what point do the lies become too much? At what point will they catch up with her and bury her underneath their heaviness?

"You're going to have to leave this house, C.J."

She ignores the scowling ghost in her doorway, flopping over so her face is firmly planted in her mattress. The bed is soft and comforting, a great place to wallow in self-pity. It gains bonus points for keeping her protected from the cold December air (the heat in her rental house is minimal at best).

Will I ever get to have sex again? Can I ever have a relationship? I've never wanted one, never wanted to fall in love, but...is it even possible now if I happened to change my mind? Can anyone ever love me when I'm a horrid monster who can't control her lips? Love is stupid. Overrated. I don't want it. I want more than life can offer me. I want to be someone else. I've never wanted that. I need—I see—I want—

"Why? I can order all my meals to be delivered. All my groceries. At least here I can't accidentally kill anyone who isn't already dead." She ventured out of the house a few times the first week, but she hasn't managed to do so since. It became too hard, the world too suffocating. She found herself mid-panic attack in a grocery store, worrying about her lips brushing against a child who had bumped into her while she was crouched down gathering some cans on the lower shelves. It sent her spiraling, and guilt is truly a girl's worst enemy.

"That's no way to live."

"Maybe I don't want to live." She doesn't mean the words, but they're ripped from her mouth, pulled from somewhere deep in her chest even she didn't know existed. The idea of dying has never bothered her, and she loves to kill as long as it's deserved. But this entire situation with Blade? It's different. His death was irresponsible, irreproachable. *It was wrong.*

"Maybe I should let you die, then. What's the point in putting in so much effort when you don't care about living? Why protect you from Death when you crave everything he has to offer?" His words are bitter and touched with a hint of pain.

"You're never here," she says, frowning. He can't deny it; he's always popping off somewhere to conduct some unknown business he refuses to tell her about. Something changed between them that day, something she can't take back. She's not sure if he is scared of her or if he is just plain disappointed in her. The disappointment is worse, she thinks. It may be neither, though. He may just find her disgustingly weak and no longer wants to be friends with someone who can't control themselves.

"And you always are. It makes you an easy target."

She stiffens, turning to look over her shoulder at him. His expression is hard, his lips pinched tightly. "You think he will come here?" *Death.*

I don't want to die. I don't want to live like this, though. I want to keep killing. But I want to kill the right people. What if I keep killing the wrong ones? Is Death angry at me like Ruin says? What will he do to me if he finds me? I'm scared. I'm terrified. I'm—Maybe—What if—

"I'm certain he will."

"Why me?" she whispers, turning away again and shutting her eyes as though that will banish the painful thoughts. They've gotten worse, being trapped at home. More prominent, less obedient. "Why was I given this amazing, wonderful, deadly power?" Not that she's sure she can describe it as such anymore.

She and Ruin have never outright discussed the fact that she has always believed Death himself made her the Shadow Kisser, that for three years she was certain she was doing what Death *wanted* her to do. But Ruin is observant and clever, and he practically told her that he blamed Death, too. It is a relief and a perturbation, and at first, it offered her solace. It no longer does.

"It was an accident." That's all he will say on the subject when she brings it up, *if* she brings it up, and she's sure he will say it again.

"Hmm," Cassy huffs, laughing bitterly as she pushes herself into a sitting position. She keeps her back to him, not wanting to see if there is a hardness in his eyes. "I'm an accident. I'm *his* accident. And he's going to kill me over his own mistakes? He's going to kill me because he can't control his own impulses?"

"Maybe. Maybe not. I think…" Ruin pauses, and she hears his hair moving, as though he ran a hand through it roughly. She hears the click of a lighter but doesn't smell the smoke from a cigarette. "I think he's scared of you. Terrified, even."

"Can I tell you something?" She pauses, waiting for a verbal response.

His breath hitches, his voice rough as he whispers, "*Anything.*"

It almost breaks her, that honest intensity. But she forces herself to be vulnerable for him, for herself, in an attempt to fix whatever has broken between them. "I'm just as scared of Death as Death is scared of me."

She can feel him crawling onto the bed behind her, wrapping his arms around her with a defeated sigh. She takes comfort in the rare touch, in the rare moment they can just *be*. He hasn't touched her since Blade died, and...well, that's just a depressing thought altogether. "That just means you two have common ground."

She lets out a bitter laugh, shutting her eyes tightly and flinching. "Oh, we have lots in common. That's what terrifies me."

"Do you think Death is some villain you should fear?" The words are bitter and angry, as though he's taking it personally. Maybe he is. For all she knows, ghosts can be sensitive about the subject. Death may be their version of a god whom they all worship.

"What, you like the guy?" She shakes her head, huffing lightly under her breath.

Is Ruin friends with him? Is that why he's taking offense? I should quit while I'm ahead. If I keep bashing his friend, he'll turn me in. I don't want to be turned in. Ruin may like me, but he's probably old and has known the guy for a while. He won't choose me over Death. He's kind of doing that right now, though, isn't he? Maybe so, but he's getting something out of the ordeal. I don't think he's told me the complete truth about why. I'm scared. I don't—Why does—How do—

"Not really, no. But I know him personally, and he isn't a villain. He and I...we've bonded over the years. I won't defend his actions, but...I can't lie to you, either. He's not all bad. He's just doing what he's duty-bound to do." His chest rumbles with each word, the warmth of his body comforting. Can he choose whether he's warm or cold? He's been both, and it's confusing to her twisted little brain. How is she supposed to see him as a ghost and not a man when he feels so alive?

"Yeah, and who gave him that duty? Is he just blindly following orders?"

He's grown quiet and thoughtful, as though considering how much to tell her. "He says that he doesn't know. He doesn't remember the early days, the first ones in which he came to be. He doesn't know who told him how to reap souls; he only knew it was natural. So he keeps doing it because it's the only thing he knows how to do. His only purpose."

She frowns, chewing on her bottom lip contemptuously. "Why doesn't he just stop? No one's making him work all the time."

"Who else will do it if he doesn't?"

Sighing, she releases her bottom lip and grumbles mournfully, "Ghosts would rule the world if he didn't collect souls."

His long hair rubs against her head as he nods in agreement. "Yes, they would. And not all of them would be nice. The mass murderer who was sentenced to death? Yeah, he's coming back to keep killing. The mafia guy who started so many turf wars that over five thousand people died as a result of his work? Yeah, he's coming back to continue the legacy. The woman who sexually abused her son and all his friends? She's going to come back and find them again. Do you understand now, Cassiopeia? Do you understand the enormity of it all?"

"Yeah." She swallows hard, feeling strangely...sad. Sad for Death, sad for all the years he will never remember and all the ones to come. "I do."

"Then you understand why you are such a big deal? Why he's so invested in you?"

"I get it. *I do.* But why hasn't he come to find me before? Why didn't he just end this as soon as it began three years ago?" Her chin drops to her chest, the weight of her questions too great to keep it up.

"Three years is nothing to him, my beloved." She sucks in a harsh breath at the nickname, heart pounding impossibly fast.

My beloved. Did he mean that in a romantic way? Did it just slip out? He's not attracted to me. He can't be. We barely know each other, anyway. Not that it matters, but still. He can't be attracted to me. I can't be attracted to him. What would happen if we did try to take things further? I can never kiss him. Never be intimate. It would be a relationship in name only. Why would he want that? Why would—What if—I could—

"And the job he has, Cassiopeia...it's brutal. He's so busy that he hardly has time to think, much less track down the human he accidentally infused with some of his powers during a reaping trip. That's why he sent others to do the job for him."

She leans off his chest to gape up at him, blinking so fast it could start a strong wind. "I...I have some of his powers?" *He knew?* He knew for certain how she was created, *who* created her, and he didn't tell her about it?

His thumb trails across her bottom lip, a dangerous game for someone like him to play. "Yep, and it's all here."

She takes a shuddering breath, forcing herself to calm down as she turns away once more. She can't be angry with him right now; she simply doesn't have the energy for it. "You said you don't like him, but you must be good friends if you know so much about him. If he confides in you."

"Oh, yes. The two of us are as thick as thieves." The words are slimy and bitter, and they leave an aftertaste in her own mouth.

"Then why risk that for me? Why risk his wrath when you were perfectly safe before?" She will never understand why he sought her out, why he decided to help her. Was he like Arnold, unable to resist a beautiful woman? Or was it something more, something deeper, that drew him to her?

"Because there are some things worth risking everything for." His thumb brushes over her bottom lip again, pausing there before dragging it down to her chin. He grips her chin, forcing her to look into those enchanting hazel eyes with the golden ring. "Because you may be the solution to a problem I've long thought unsolvable."

Chapter 10

Cassy frowns up at the grimy storage units before her, huffing her disappointment. She'd traveled ninety minutes out of Nashville to a small town that was reluctant to show up on her navigation app because Ruin had convinced her this would be fun. Ruin had been with her in the car she had borrowed from Winter for most of the drive, his perpetual grumpiness doing nothing to improve her own sour mood. She thought he would be happy to finally get her out of the house, considering he had been begging her to get out and go on a hunt for the past three nights.

After their initial talk about Death, he came sneaking back into her room the following nights, holding her and comforting her in a way only he knew she needed. So this morning, when she announced they were heading to one of the haunting sites he had suggested, she thought he would be thrilled. Or, at the very least, that he would be proud of her. She had even imagined him picking her up and swinging her around, laughing merrily because she was finally becoming more like herself again.

Ruin only seemed annoyed. Though she's not entirely sure he's annoyed with her, because with only ten minutes left in their drive, he disappeared and hasn't returned. It left her no chance to pluck up the courage to demand what his problem was. Not that she has much courage left when it comes to him. He'd wrecked her life in an impossibly brutal way—through the harboring revelation of ghosts and the damning, uncontrollable new emotions he'd plucked out of her—but he'd also pulled it together so it all made *sense*. They've only known each other for three months, but it feels as though he's been by her side for years. Maybe he had been; he could have been watching and waiting for the right time to come along and ruin her. He hadn't admitted to any such thing, but sometimes she wondered if it were true, if only because of the strangely passionate way he speaks of her. *"Because you may be the solution to a problem I've long thought unsolvable."*

Cassy stares at the pale blue storage room doors, most of which are chipped and peeling to reveal white underneath. The rest of the building is white, too, only...it's a gross white. Dirty, dingy, and in desperate need of a pressure wash. The grass is overgrown, some patches giant and nearly as tall as her. Weeds invade the gravel paths, winding through in uneven and random trails. It's nearly sundown, and the place looks...abandoned.

"You can do this, Cassy," she whispers to herself, clinging tightly to the tiny purse hanging around her shoulder. She takes a deep breath and pulls her phone out, glancing over the details of the job one last time as she tries to channel Confident Cassy once more.

An anonymous client contacted her this time, one who claims to own the buildings. She'd already been paid half of the total upfront, so there is no backing out now. Ben Craigmore had actually recommended her to this client, someone whom he'd met online, according to the email she was sent. She glances over that initial email now, despite having committed it to memory.

To: CJKisses@email.com

Subject: Ghost On My Property

Hi Cassy,

You do not know me, but I am an acquaintance of Ben Craigmore. We know each other via the internet, but I trust him implicitly. He recommended your services to take care of a problem I have on one of my properties.

It's haunted.

I've lost customers over the years, and I can't stand it anymore. I'll pay you two grand now and two when the job is done if you can just get rid of the damn thing. It's very loud and abrasive, and it spooks every single paying customer away. I've had three lawsuits on my hands because it hurts clients on my property. My business is suffering, and I need that ghost gone.

I don't have any information on the ghost. I don't know its past. I don't know who it is or how long it's been there. I just know I want it gone. If you agree to the terms, I'll send you the address ASAP.

Please let me know soon,

A Friend

From: Anonymoususer338769@email.com

Your business is suffering from more than a haunting, Cassy thinks bitterly as she glances around, unsure if this can truly be called a business at all. It doesn't look like anybody uses the place besides squatters, and she has no clue how this person could even be pulling in any revenue from such a rundown area.

When she responded to the email, the anonymous sender sent back the address and nothing else. No details on where the ghost likes to linger, no area to specifically search. It's frustrating, especially considering all the research she did on the place beforehand, to know absolutely nothing useful. Nothing other than the fact that this place is listed on one of those *Most Haunted Places in...* websites.

She glances around again with a sigh, taking a few cautious steps forward.

What will I do if I can't find this ghost? What happens if Ruin doesn't come back? Can I do this by myself? Ghosts can be violent, I think. Some people online claim this one is. The email said lawsuits due to hurt clients, so what happened to the people who were injured? What am I supposed to do if it attacks me? What if—How do—I think—

She ignores the terrifying thoughts as best as she can, swallowing hard and straightening her spine as she begins to examine the first building she comes upon. There's nothing out of the ordinary, no chills in the air or ominous feelings crawling up her spine. She wore something casual to this haunt, ignoring Ruin when he tried to suggest she dress sexy again. She also ignored the eager look that danced in his eyes when he suggested it, a clear desire painted there she wished she hadn't noticed because it left a damp spot in her underwear. Cassy had simply said, "I've had enough of dressing sexy for lousy ghosts, thank you very much." She hopes yoga pants and sweatshirts do it for this one, because she couldn't be bothered to wear anything less comfortable than that. If she were lucky, they'd find the messy bun and smeared mascara sexy, too.

"Hmm," she says aloud, moving toward the next building a few feet over. "This place doesn't seem haunted to me." Baiting a ghost is stupid: She knows that. Especially considering she's alone in some seemingly abandoned storage units. But what else is she supposed to do here? Ruin doesn't know anything about this ghost. She grilled him all morning, but even after disappearing and coming back hours later to hop in the car with her, he never admitted to finding anything useful. She assumes none of his ghost buddies, if he has any, know anything useful about this place.

A shrill bang sounds amid the steady blowing wind and the creaking of the old buildings, echoing from inside a storage unit located somewhere in the middle of the rows. Cassy winces, groaning and turning toward the heart of the large area. "That wasn't inconspicuous at all." Of course it's drawing her toward the middle of the buildings, a place where she won't be able to easily escape. A place where there will be too many rows for her to understand her rights from her lefts; not that she gets those correct even on her best days, anyway.

She takes slow, contemplative steps, but it doesn't matter. She's in the middle of the labyrinth sooner than she imagined, the buildings more vast than she realized from the parking lot. There are at least ten rows in the middle, and not all of them are straight. It's almost like it was designed to be maze-like, with dead ends and exit ways that she could only see if she were at a bird's-eye view. She can see some faded signs pointing in different directions with letters underneath, though. Code, she assumes, for which unit the customers would be searching for. The design would be cool, if not annoying, except for the fact that she's hunting a ghost who may or may not be violent inside said maze.

The innocuous bang sounds again, far too close, and she spins around so quickly she almost tips over. Behind her, one of the doors to a unit starts to lift. "Hello? Anyone there?" she calls stupidly, doing the exact wrong thing everyone screams at their screen during horror movies for.

"Hello? Anyone there?" Her own voice is echoed back to her, warped and manipulated in a way that leaves a chill running down her spine.

"Funny trick," she says light-heartedly, clinging to her purse harder. She's Confident Cassy today, not Scared-of-a-Little-Ghost Cassy. She can do this. She has to.

I wish Ruin was here. I feel so alone. If I die, no one but a ghost will ever know. I like to pretend to be fearless, but I'm not. Fearless Cassy is fake. Confident Cassy is fake, too. What will happen to my body out here? Will anyone ever know? Will Ruin tell someone? I have to do this, though. I need to prove to myself that my lips are not bad, that my gift is useful. I need to prove that I am worthy of this gift. Will I—Can he—I miss—

Another bang sounds, lower in pitch and much more terrifying, inside the unit. Cassy groans, shaking off her fear and forcing herself to keep going and step inside the unit. But the moment she crosses the threshold, the door slams shut behind her, and she can't stop herself from screaming in surprise as she's enveloped in darkness.

"Seriously?" she cries, not bothering to spin around and attempt to open the door. "That's so cliche. Surely you can do better than that?"

She shouldn't have antagonized the ghost. It was a stupid, reckless thing to do, and she realizes it the second she feels herself flying backwards. It's as though she is weightless, picked up and tossed as easily as a ball. The pain in her back is the first thing she registers, the tingling along her spine making her head dizzy and numb. She stays numb for a few more precious seconds, that pain suddenly tripling. She wheezes, realizing she hasn't been breathing, dry heaving onto the concrete below her and reaching for her phone. Only…her purse isn't there. It slipped from her arm during those precious airborne seconds, but she can vaguely feel it lying against her feet.

Barking sounds somewhere nearby, a viscous, guttural growl following. It's familiar, but she doesn't have time to think about it as her head is jerked up. Her hair is being pulled, a fist wrapped around her bun, bright white eyes hovering in front of her face in the dark. "Hi," she croaks out, trying to plaster on one of her award-winning smiles. "My name's Cassy. You must be the resident ghost."

Her body slides, slamming into one of the hard, cinder-block-lined walls across from her. Her head smashes into the wall, a warmth sliding down her ear and onto her cheek. She groans, ribs throbbing from the impact. "Leave," it says, the deadly calm infuriating and terrifying all at once.

Cassy doesn't say anything, her shaking hands reaching for the purse that had caught on her foot and been dragged along with her. She reaches for her phone, knowing she needs light. If she can't see the damn thing, she can't expect herself to land a kiss on it. Her hands feel slick as she snaps on the flashlight, whipping it around the small space in search of the ghost. She finds it hovering in the far-right corner, arms crossed over its chest. Her vision is blurry, so she can't tell who or what is waiting for her in that corner. She can only see the large, burly body and feel the anger radiating in the air. She can practically taste it, a mixture of oil and metal, but that could be the blood, too. Her mouth is full of it, which probably doesn't bode well for her. She can only hope her hands are slick with nervous sweat and not with the crimson liquid.

The barking outside has become more intense, the noise loud and rattling around inside her throbbing mind. Is that...is that Cerci? It can't be. She's supposed to be with Ruin, and he isn't here.

Did Ruin hear my thoughts somehow? Does he know I need him? If I pray to him like an angel, will he appear? Did he send Cerci to check on me? Did she come on her own? What if something happens to him without her there? Will she get hurt? I can't get out of this. Winter is going to worry about me. Ruin can explain it to her. She won't understand, but she'll at least know. I should have—I could—Why don't—

Cerci pops through the large door just as the ghost is approaching again, its blurry figure pausing in surprise. It holds up its arms, turning to flee, but Cerci leaps before it can escape. She tackles the ghost and snarls into its face, biting and snapping and clawing. The thing screams, howling in pain, swiping and hitting Cerci over and over and over again. Deep cuts appear on Cerci's sides and face, blood impossibly seeping from the wounds.

Cassy finds the inner strength to push herself up, crying out, "Cerci!" just as the dog's giant body flies back toward the metal door. The dog disappears for a few precarious seconds as she flies through the barrier, and the ghost flickers in and out of existence angrily. Its body is…red. Red and fiery and *dangerous*.

"Hellhound," it spits as though it's an insult, violent gaze turning back to Cassy. "I'll kill you for this, Shadow Kisser. I'll kill you and demand the prize I am owed from its owner."

"Ruin!" she calls pitifully, praying he's out there somewhere. But he doesn't come. And Cerci…she doesn't know where Cerci was flung to. She doesn't know if the ghost dog is too injured to come back.

I didn't know ghosts could injure other ghosts like that. How long does it take a ghost to heal? I'll hit Ruin a few times when I get back and find out. He deserves it for leaving me to die like this. I might actually die, now that I think about it. I should leave a dying voicemail to Winter telling her to hit Ruin when he comes to explain my death. Is that enough justice? Is it—I will—He deserves—

Cerci comes bounding through the door just as the ghost leans over Cassy, slamming it to the ground and growling so viciously it scares Cassy herself. The dog—or maybe hellhound—pins the ghost down, mouth opening to expose dagger-sharp teeth Cassy didn't realize she possessed, and bites down on its neck. It screams and thrashes, but it doesn't manage to push her off this time.

Through her spinning mind, she realizes what Cerci is doing. She's keeping the thing down, holding it until Cassy can kiss it. *Fuck, okay. I can do that.* She tries to stand, using the wall for support, but she falls hard onto her knees. Mind pivoting to a new solution, she bends forward, places her hands on the ground, and begins to crawl. She crawls the mere feet to the two slowly, each move sending jolts of pain through her body and lungs. It's hard to breathe, hard to think, hard to exist. But she pushes through it, reminding herself that it's not just her life, but it could be Cerci's, too.

"Get away, ghost hunter!" it howls, thrashing so violently now that she is sure it'll slip free. Its features are still blurry, but it kind of looks like a woman this close. Its facial characteristics are delicate, the hair long, the body thin and frail. The ghost flashes different shades of red as its anger and desperation increase; something loud crashes in the background. In the back of her mind, Cassy recognizes the ghost is somehow commanding objects to throw themselves against the door outside in an attempt to distract her. She can't be bothered to worry about it, though.

"Fuck you," she hisses, leaning down so her breath brushes against its cheek. "I hope your afterlife is hell." Cassy presses her lips against its burning hot skin, relief flooding her nervous system when the ghost disappears before she's fully pulled away. Cerci stops her vicious growling abruptly, teeth clamping together as she turns to Cassy with a whimper.

"It's okay, doll," Cassy says softly, weakly, as she reaches out a hand to pet her snout. Her lips burn faintly, as though touched by fire. It's a sensation she ignores as she stares into the dog's black eyes fondly. "You did good. Such a good girl."

Cassy sways when Cerci nuzzles up against her, and whines pathetically as Cerci touches the cut on the side of her head. Cassy tips over, wheezing, staring into the area lit by her phone's light. She stares and she stares and she stares, the pain so intense that she wishes she'd just blackout already. But she doesn't. And time is so slow as she tries to convince herself to move, to reach her phone, to call someone, but...she can't. She can't move, and Cerci seems to understand that. She lies down next to Cassy, head on her side, still whimpering and oozing fresh, ghostly blood.

"Good girl," Cassy manages out again, shutting her eyes tightly. "Go...go find Ruin. Ruin. *Ruin. Ruin. Ruin.*" His name on her lips is an invocation, a prayer, a plea, a last request. And finally, *finally*, the blackout greets her.

Chapter 11

"C.J? Please, wake up, C.J. Cassy? Come on, Cassiopeia. This isn't how you die. It isn't your time yet, my beloved; trust me, I know."

Cassy can tell it's Ruin so clearly, despite the words sounding as though they are coming from a mile away. She strains to hear him, to get one more word from his lips to her ears. It's all she wants: to be near, to listen. But she must have moved or twitched when she strained, and as a reward, she's granted his touch.

"Cassiopeia, this isn't funny," he says, words warbled as she's pulled into a cold chest. She feels herself shivering, listening to him curse vapidly as she does so.

"N-N—" she manages out, her lips sticking together painfully. Her jaw strains to open, prying her mouth open with it. "N-No-Not..." *Not trying to be funny,* she tries to say.

"It's okay, my beloved," he reassures her, cold hand moving to feel her forehead. "Take your time. You've got some pretty major injuries." She assumed so, if the pain radiating down her spine and in her ribs is any indication.

"I-I-I—" She still can't get a full sentence out, her throat dry and clammy. How long has she been out? How long has he been attempting to wake her?

"Don't talk, okay?" He runs a hand over her ribs, and she lets out a hiss, involuntarily jerking at the pain that follows. Those strong hands push her into a sitting position, and she lets out a low moan, the throbbing in her spine increasing in intensity and pressure. And her ribs…it hurts to breathe, her lungs aching with each intake and exhale of precious air. "I think you've cracked a rib, and your back…" He pauses to lift her shirt, clucking with a sigh. "There's a lot of bruising. You're running a fever, too. I was hoping my body chill would help you, but…"

"Ce-Cer—" She wants to ask if Cerci is okay, if she made it, if she's somewhere safe. Had she succumbed to her injuries, had that impossible blood leak led to something horrific?

How did she find him? Is there a connection between them that allows her to know where he is? Why did that ghost call her a hellhound and say her owner would owe it a prize after killing me? Is Ruin not Cerci's owner? Ruin is touching me. I forgot. How could I forget? Why am I so cold if I'm running a fever? He said his body chill is supposed to help, but maybe it's just my bones that are icy. I like this closeness. I like having him near. I wonder what Winter is doing, if she knows I'm hurt. Did Ruin come straight here? Did I—Is he—Where's Cerci—

"Cerci is here. Can you see her?" A hint of worry now, and…darkness. She's still in darkness. She can't see. Why can't she see? Panic now, fast and heavy, floods her mind. She finds herself shaking her head, the motion burdensome and difficult.

"No," she manages to get out on the first try, whimpering. "No. No. No." This can't be happening. She can't be blind, can she? She didn't hit her head that hard, so why can't she see?

"It's okay, C.J. It's okay." Not Cassiopeia anymore. She likes it when he calls her Cassiopeia. The way he says it always leaves a wonderful shudder running through her bones, like her body acknowledges it's a sacred word being invoked upon his lips. "It'll go away in a minute. You're not blind, I swear.'"

"H-How do—"

"How do I know?" he guesses when she can't finish, and she can practically see the smug smile when she confirms with a nod. "This isn't the first time I've seen someone attacked by a Class Two Soul. Being around some of them too long can cause temporary speech delays, vision impairment, and other sensory issues. It doesn't happen every time, but the stronger ones tend to cause problems like that."

"A cla-a-class…" The question is so close to coming out, so near, but it is trapped behind her dangerous, deadly lips.

"Ah, yeah. I guess you don't know about that, do you?"

She makes a noise under her breath, wishing she had the strength to slap him. She had tried to get him to explain once, but he only brushed her off and said it wasn't important. *Seems important now, Ruin, doesn't it?* she thinks bitterly.

"Didn't tell me." She smiles softly after saying it, relieved and proud of her strength.

"I'm only doing so now because I thought you were dying," he says with what she imagines is a frown, pausing before adding, "But first I need to heal you. I have this…herbal mixture. It smells like shit, but it will fix your injuries. I need to take your shirt off to rub it in, though. Is that okay?"

Cassy nods, glad she's not able to see him. She doesn't have the energy to blush or the capability of feeling embarrassed right now. Because the pain? The pain is so horrible that Ruin could strip her down naked and she wouldn't bat an eye, so long as it went away.

Ruin doesn't bother being gentle as he lifts the shirt's hem and pulls harshly. The sound of the rip greets her before the chilly air; the realization of what happened follows soon after. "You ripped—" she starts, struggling to breathe through the embarrassment of the moment. She can already feel her nipples hardening, and she can only hope he can't see them through her thin bra. When she had imagined him taking her clothes off before, this certainly hadn't been the circumstances she foresaw. Not that she would ever admit to him she had imagined such a scenario. Or that in other circumstances, she would really enjoy him ripping her clothes off in primal passion.

"Mmm," he lets out a low, distracted noise, and she conjures images of him assessing her body.

What does he think about me? Does he like what he sees? Is he struggling to keep his hands to himself? Does he care? I would care if I were him. If I were a guy, I wouldn't be able to focus with a half-naked girl in front of me. Not one that looks like me, anyway. If I were a guy, though, I would be super embarrassed to have a hard-on in a moment this serious. Does he have one? Should I want him to? I wish I could look. I would—Does he—I'm not—

"You're covered in bruises," he says softly, fingers trailing up her stomach and toward her ribs. Goosebumps follow in his wake, and she hisses when that cold touch hits the bones he thinks may be cracked.

"I'm a ghost hunter," she breathes out, struggling with her words, struggling not to arch into the innocent touch. "Bruises come with the job." She's been a ghost hunter for a very short amount of time, so she can only assume her bland statement is true. So far, two out of the three hunts have ended in physical altercations. This is just the worst of the two.

"If I had known it was a Class Two, I wouldn't have ever sent you here. I should have looked into it more. I never meant to let you see this side of things. I never wanted you to get hurt. You've gotten closer to death today than you should ever be. And I *promised*...I promised you a ghost wouldn't harm you on my watch. I've broken my end of the deal, and I'm—" He's rambling, sad and pained noises leaving between frantic sentences. She can sense his panic, his heartache, his strife. It sends a wave of gratefulness and something more foreign through her, something soft and warm that she decidedly ignores.

"Shhh," she murmurs in an attempt at comforting the ghost, feeling herself blink as a fuzzy white dot enters her vision. "I'm not mad at you."

"You should be," he says darkly, fingers pausing over her ribs.

"Don't tell me how I should and shouldn't feel," she grinds out, blinking rapidly as things slowly start to come into focus. The first thing she sees is his eyes, those entrapping hazel ones that leave her breathless and feeling a bit like melted snow on a warm winter's day.

"I see the ghost attack didn't dim your personality." A thin smile is visible now, dark hair tickling his cheeks. She turns her head to the left, sighing audibly in relief when she finds Cerci curled up into a ball in the corner, watching them intently. She doesn't seem injured, and Cassy can't spot any blood pooled beneath the large body. Maybe the blood had never been there at all; perhaps the head wound was worse than she thought and it made her hallucinate.

"Not even Death can dim my spark," she whispers, turning back to him. "I can see you now."

He nods, brief and curt. "It's already working, then."

The smell hits her abruptly, and she gags loudly, to her utter embarrassment and horror. It's rotten and putrid, the kind of smell that she imagines zombies use as perfume. Ruin outright laughs at her, the seriousness of the moment dulled by the brightness radiating from him. He's so beautiful it hurts, his copper skin radiant in the light of the afternoon sun. He looks like an angel fallen to the earth, and it's so hard for Cassy to look away and remind herself he doesn't even *belong* on earth.

She glances down at her chest, suddenly grateful she wore one of her cute, lacy bras and not the sports bra with holes in it she had debated on wearing this morning. "You ripped my shirt."

"I did." No justifications, no excuses. He doesn't even seem snide about it, and his gaze is firmly glued onto her ribs. He won't look her in the eyes, or at her breasts, and she swears there's a hint of color in his cheeks. That makes her feel a little smug, and maybe a bit too brave.

"I didn't know you were so ill-mannered. You're so feral, like an animal raised in a barn." *That* brings his eyes to hers, his lips pinching as he tries not to grin.

"I'll show you feral when the time is right, Cassiopeia." It's not dripping with humor like it should be, but something more. Something promising, something deep, something *intimate*.

Quickly, she clears her throat and changes the subject. "What's a Class Two Soul?"

I feel so vulnerable right now. Has he noticed? Does he want me the same way I want him? This is an inappropriate time to be thinking about this. I'm injured. Cerci is here, watching. That's his child, basically. It's wrong. It's weird. She saved me, too. What a way to repay her, by jumping her master in front of her after she sacrificed herself for me. Would I—Cerci is—Does he—

"Flip over." She watches his throat bob, the action drawing her eyes to the veins throbbing there. He's...he's angry?

She does as told, flipping onto her stomach and wincing all the while. "That hurt, but damn is it better already." It doesn't hurt to simply exist anymore. Whatever the rancid ointment is, she's grateful for it. Even if he stole it off a zombie, or from a mummy's grave, or wherever he got the stuff from.

"I'm unclipping this." His voice is strained, and she sees his hand clench and unclench out of the corner of her eye. She almost laughs but decides it will only anger him further. Maybe if she makes him angry, he will use it as an excuse to touch her the way she wants him to, and—no. No, she can't bait him into doing all the inappropriate things she's been imagining. *He's a ghost, he's a ghost, he's a ghost,* she chants to herself.

"Yeah, alright." Cassy tries not to let it show that it bothers her, tries to hide the fact that her face is entirely too hot and her body is entirely too eager.

He takes a deep breath and unclips the little clasps with one hand, quickly pushing them to the side and covering her in ointment. He's quiet as he spreads it over her aching back, gentle and focused. It takes a full five minutes before he speaks; a full five minutes of tentative touches and an aching core.

"Class Two Souls are Aggressive Souls. Souls who *can* and *will* hurt you. There are a few different types, actually. Rejected Souls, Wronged Souls, and Corrupted Souls. It's hard to know the difference without a little bit of research, but I suspect this one was a Wronged Soul. Cerci mentioned it turned red? That's usually a sign of a Wronged Soul."

"Cerci *mentioned*? You know what—no. Let's move past that right now. What's the difference between the types? And if there's a Class Two, there must be a Class One. Are there more Classes?"

I thought a ghost was a ghost. If this one was a Class Two, are there worse classes? Ruin should have told me. I should be mad. I can't be mad, though, because I don't really want to know about this. I don't like knowing about the things that exist underneath our noses. Is this an official ranking? Do all ghosts know? Is Ruin a Class One? Is Ruin—Am I—Do ghosts—

"Shush, C.J. Let me explain, then ask questions, okay?" She nods softly in acceptance of the request, his hands continuing to rub her back deliciously as he starts to massage the aching muscles. "Rejected Souls die with broken hearts or broken aspirations. They lash out at people they associate with those wrongdoings to make themselves feel better about their deaths. They have specific targets, typically.

"Wronged Souls were treated poorly in life or died from poor treatment. Stuff like murder, starvation, and bullying; you know the deal. They get aggressive with humans because they want to punish everyone for the way they were treated. It's their way of dealing with the unresolved trauma that traversed through their lives and into their deaths.

"Corrupted Souls are people who died after being corrupted by someone or something in life. You know, stuff like accepting bribes or turning a blind eye to wrongdoings. They take out their aggression on humans because they are angry with themselves."

"Yeah, okay. That makes sense, I suppose." She chews on her bottom lip, refusing to let out the moan threatening to escape when he kneads an especially sore spot below her right shoulder. "A Wronged Soul would definitely fit the bill, with this ghost. What about other Classes, then? What are you? A Class One?"

"I am what I am." An evasive answer if she'd ever heard one. But he's not like the spirit who attacked her, not angry and vicious and hell-bent on harming anyone he comes across. "But, yes, there are other Classes. Class One included."

"Well? Go on, then. Tell me about them. You've opened the can of worms now, Ruin. I won't let you close it."

"Class One is Malevolent Spirits. They aren't usually harmful and don't attack or cause harm to humans. Spirits like Arnold."

"Or you," she points out, but he ignores that.

"Three types of those, too. Type One is a Drifting Spirit, or Drifters. They have no particular purpose for being anywhere and are usually lonely and want to be around people or to explore the world. Lingering Spirits, or Haunters, cling to a particular person, place, or object: something or someone they were tied to in life that they chose to stay by in death. Teasing Spirits, or Jokesters, want to mess with living souls. They like to play pranks and scare humans as they please."

"You're a Drifter," she determines, chewing on the inside of her cheek as she thinks back to the other ghosts she has hunted. "Arnold was a Jokester. That old lady I kissed was a Haunter."

His hands are abruptly jerking off her, the clips on her bra coming back together swiftly. "Not harmful, like I said."

She rolls onto her back, watching him purse his lips as he pointedly stares toward Cerci. His face is close to hers, but not so near that she can lean up and brush against him. His hands clench and unclench at his sides, as though looking for something to hold. "And the others?" she questions lightly.

"There's Class Zero. Wraiths. They are free-roaming apparitions. Harmless, and most of the time not fully corporeal. Little balls of light, usually. Pretty easy for Death to reclaim most of the time."

"And that's it?"

Ruin still seems hesitant, his eyes flashing darkly for the briefest of seconds.

What is he not telling me? Why is he hiding things? I can't expect him not to hide things. We hardly know each other, even if we are technically roommates. Do I hide secrets from him? Probably not, I'm too honest. I always blab things I shouldn't to people. One time—I don't—Is he—

"No."

He doesn't elaborate further, so she pushes herself to her elbows and levels him with a glare. He leans back, eyes wide from the sudden movement that placed her lips too close to his. "There's a Class Three, I presume?"

"That is..." He struggles for a moment with his next words, mouth moving as though he has to chew them up before spitting them out. "Yes, that is something you can presume."

"Is it a secret or something? Something ghosts aren't supposed to, or don't want to, talk about?" Cerci whines from her curled-up position, as though trying to answer Cassy's questions. Has she been around a Class Three Soul before? Not an improbability for a ghost dog.

"Or something." He leans forward, nose brushing against hers in a delicate, soft way that doesn't align with the ghost she knows. He presses their foreheads together, cupping her cheeks gently. "Don't worry about it right now, C.J. You won't ever have to deal with a Class Three. Are you feeling better? Does anything still hurt? Do you need anything?"

"A bath," she breathes, her heart pounding so hard she's sure he can hear it. Why does he do things like this, tempt fate so openly? If she leans forward the tiniest bit, or juts her lips out slightly...

"You do stink," he confirms, leaning back again and dropping his hands with a chuckle before his face hardens once more. "But you aren't hurt, right?"

"Actually...no." She can breathe without it hurting and can move without crying out in pain. "I need whatever that is in my first aid kit, prompto."

"I'll leave some with you."

"Are you going to explain about Cerci mentioning the red ghost, or..."

"I—" He stops and tilts his head, listening to something, or someone, whispering in the wind. "I have to go."

"Ruin, you can't—"

"I've stayed too long already." His hand moves to cup her cheek once more, but he jerks it back abruptly, shaking his head with a sigh. "I should never have come."

"I would have been here alone, suffering, if you hadn't." Why does he always do this? Why does he leave when things get too serious, too involved? Where does he *go*?

"I didn't say I regret coming, my beloved. I just…I shouldn't have abandoned my duties."

"What duties? Are you doing another job for Death right now?" She stares up at him with wild eyes, even wilder thoughts running through her mind.

Will Death follow him here? Will he have sensed how close to meeting him I was? Will he care that I've been helping him with the ghost problem? Will he care that I haven't killed anyone on purpose since meeting Ruin all those months ago? Death must be coming. He must be hunting me down at this very moment. I need to hide. I need to get out of here. I need to—He is—Death will—

"I can't tell you about my duties, Cassiopeia. I won't place that burden over your head, too." She can see the regret looming on his features, emphasized by the wince barely present in his shoulders and neck. She swears he is mouthing, "I'm sorry," but the words don't make an appearance.

"You can trust—" she starts, but he's already gone, his form disappearing in the breeze. "—me." She slams her hand down into the gravel, screaming loudly in frustration. "Fuck you!" she shouts to the wind, a tear sliding down her face. "Fuck you, fuck you, fuck you!" The words escape her in horrible, twisted screeches until her throat aches and her breath comes out in deep pants. She swipes at the excess tears that slip free, disappointment and rage fluttering around inside her like an angry hive of bees.

Cerci lumbers toward her, whining and moving to nuzzle her. Cassy pushes away the ghost dog gently, turning away sourly. "I'm sorry, doll, but I don't even want to think the word ghost right now, much less see one. Just...just leave, okay? Go find Ruin."

When Cerci doesn't move, Cassy turns and snaps harshly, "Go find Ruin, you stupid mutt!"

The guilt invades her like a foreign parasite, slinking through every blood vessel and each nerve. The feeling is intense and harrowing, emphasized when Cerci stands up and bounds off without so much as another whine. Dropping her hands into her hands, Cassy cries. She cries over a *man*, something she can't ever remember doing before.

With a choked laugh, she asks the wind, "What are you doing to me, Ruin Morrigan? And *why* am I letting you do it?"

Chapter 12

Cassy almost ignores her mother's phone call, the weekly one that happens on Wednesdays at six p.m. on the dot. It has been a week since the Class Two Soul incident, and she still doesn't feel fully recovered. Not physically, just…emotionally. Her heart aches, her soul burns, and her mind is never-resting. But she knows she will forget to call back if she doesn't answer the call now, and she also knows her mother will be upset if she ignores it. So, she clicks the little green button on her phone and forces a cheeriness into her tone. "Hey, Mom."

"How are you, little doll?" Her mom has always called her "little doll", a nickname bestowed upon her from the moment she was born and which she likes to bestow upon others out of love. Her parents claim they gave her the nickname because she looked like a baby doll when she came out of the womb, a fake-looking child whom many people did not think was real until she moved. Cassy would have been inclined not to believe them if she hadn't seen the photos as proof. Nonetheless, she loves the endearing name. It feels special, like something that belongs only to her and that only she may pass on to others. She may not be super close to her parents, but she still enjoys feeling loved.

"I've been better," Cassy admits, unable to stop the words from leaving her lips. Quickly recovering from her slip-up, she adds, "Just a long week at work." A long week hunting ghosts, she meant but could not say.

"This have anything to do with that roommate of yours?" her mom questions slyly, her mother's familiar southern accent a comfort to her ears despite the prying question.

"No," Cassy lies, clearing her throat. "Not at all."

"Winter disagrees."

"Winter needs to mind her own damn business." Cassy is scowling at her phone screen, thumbs already typing a heated message to her best friend. Winter has a weekly call with Cassy's parents, too, as hers are out of the picture. Cassy's mom, Lyanne, adopted Winter as her own child the moment she set eyes upon her. She knew, like only a parent could, that Winter needed a mother—a family. And the Jayneses were all in agreement when it came to Winter Stokes: The blood inside you doesn't equate to the love you deserve.

"She says you really like this guy," her mother continues, oblivious to her discomfort. Or maybe her mother just doesn't care. "She says that it could get serious." Winter must have decided that on her own, because Cassy had never said such a thing. Sure, she texts and talks about Ruin often. It's hard not to when he is such a prevalent part of her life. But she's never admitted to Winter that she wanted more. No, her best friend gained that insight all on her own.

"Oh for heaven's sakes, Mother!" she gripes, whispering harshly, "Ruin and I are *friends*."

The accused man pops into her room unexpectedly, an unfortunate consequence of living with a ghost. She throws him a scalding glare, pointing at her door and mouthing, "Get out!"

The two haven't been on the best of terms this week, despite his constant appearances and attempts to get back into her good graces. She and Cerci had made up the next day, the large dog looking all too smug when Cassy cooed at it and begged for forgiveness for fifteen straight minutes. Ruin, on the other hand, has tried every tactic *but* begging. She received a bouquet of her favorite flowers (azaleas, which he somehow knew), a random delivery of books she did not yet own from her favorite author (two entire series she had never mentioned to him), and many deliveries from her favorite restaurants accompanied by varying desserts she adored (some of which she knows he's never seen her eat). He has been trying, and succeeding, to win back her forgiveness, but...he still won't open up to her fully. Still won't trust her with the things she knows he is hiding. And that...that is the perfect way to draw a line between them. It's the tiny crack in their foundation that will bring everything crumbling down. And it *hurts*, oh how it hurts, but this is what they need: a crack, a break, a reckoning. It's the only way to prevent the intense magnetism that continues to draw them in from forcing them into a collision.

"You should invite him over for the family dinner this weekend," her mom says, ignoring Cassy's protests entirely. "Your father and I would like to meet the man."

"I'm not inviting him over for dinner." Cassy grinds her teeth together, watching Ruin's lips tilt up into a smirk. "It's not like that between us."

Sensibly, her mother points out, "You moved out of your *really* nice apartment to a little shack on the outskirts of Nashville to live with this guy, little doll. I think it *is* like that."

"I didn't move to be with him, Mother. I moved because I had a job here and didn't have much of a choice. I still have my apartment, you know. This is temporary."

Ruin leans against her doorway, hands shoved into his pockets while looking all too amused; all too devastating.

"You two are being careful, right? I love you, Cassy, but I don't think you can handle a baby right now."

Cassy chokes a little, eyes wide. Her mother has never really had a sex talk with her before, and it is completely out of character. Though if Cassy stops to think about it, having a possible serious relationship is completely out of character for her, too. "We are *not* sleeping together, Mother."

Ruin chuckles darkly from the doorway, pinning her with a heated gaze. Those intense eyes roam from her feet to her face, slow and purposeful. It is a look that seems to say, "No, but we could be," and she doesn't know how to feel about the bold move.

What has Winter been telling my mom? Why does she think I'm one step away from being pregnant? Why do they want to meet him? I think he would like my family. I don't want to bring him there. They won't understand what we are. I don't even understand what we are. How would that work, anyway? What if—How does—They will—

"Well, Winter thinks you should be."

"As stated previously: Winter should mind her own damn business."

"Don't talk about your sister like that," her mom scolds. She often refers to Winter as Cassy's sister because they practically are. They've been inseparable since they met, and they fight just as heartily as any sibling.

"Tell her to stop lying to you about my love life."

"What love life?"

Cassy's mouth pops open, and Ruin laughs again. She's certain he can hear every word coming from her mother's mouth. "That's kind of rude, you know?" she snaps, glaring at Ruin again.

Unperturbed by her daughter's attitude, Lyanne continues calmly, "Not if it's true. You've never had a serious relationship, little doll. You've never brought anyone home to meet us. If Winter is bringing him up, this is more than just one of your flings. She says you two suck all the energy out of the room, like the moment before a tornado hits. She says the two of you are inevitable."

Cassy winces, not realizing her mother *knew* about her many flings. Like a child, she gripes, "I don't want to invite Ruin for dinner. We aren't together, Mom." What else can she say? Winter has only met Ruin once, and she read them for filth.

Cassy's eyes widen in panic as Ruin strides over, strong hand reaching out and plucking the phone from her ear before she can stop him. "Hi, Lyanne? This is Ruin. I heard Cassy mention something about dinner. I would love to come."

The smirk he sends her way curls her toes in the worst of ways, anger overcoming her good senses as she leaps toward him. Ruin holds her back with his free hand, snarling at her silently. She continues to jump and push back, yelping when

Ruin pushes her to the ground and straddles her. She hastily tries to shove against his chest, but he pins her wrists with ease.

Ruin's on top of me. Ruin's on top of me. Ruin's on top of me. Ruin's on—Ruin's on—Ruin's on—

She can't hear her mother's response, but she *can* practically hear the woman beaming. "Oh, yes. Cassy is a wonderful woman. You did a great job raising her, darling. No, no. Don't worry about me. She won't be upset with me; you aren't getting me into any trouble. None I can't work myself out of, anyway." He laughs, clearly charming her mother despite Cassy's resistance to the situation.

Another quick response from her mother, then Ruin says, "Six o'clock on Saturday evening. Got it. I wouldn't miss it for the world, Lyanne. Oh, no. Don't worry about me. I'm on a restrictive diet, can't really eat much. No, no health problems. Just trying to get in shape. Of course, darling. Can't wait."

Ruin hangs up, tossing her phone to the ground beside them and smiling mischievously. Cassy bites out, "Get off of me, *darling.*"

Ruin glances down at their precarious situation, leaning forward slightly. A knuckle brushes across her cheek, a small *tsk* noise leaving his lips. "I like this position, Cassy. Don't you?"

I like it a lot. I shouldn't like it. I shouldn't want it. I crave it. We can't do this. He's a ghost and I'm not. I can tell he's hard, though. I shouldn't be able to feel a ghost getting hard. A ghost shouldn't be allowed to get hard. I wonder what his dick looks like, what it would feel like. Should I—We can't—I won't—

She jerks underneath his weight, earning another amused chuckle from him. Then he's gone, disappearing to do whatever menial task he was in the process of doing before he'd come snooping. He's been doing that lately, performing small tasks that he knows take a lot of willpower for her to get done: mopping the floors, cleaning the dishes, dusting shelves. She's been appreciative of it all, but now she is too angry to care about all the ways he's been helping her without having been asked. Angry that now he's using her attraction for him against her, wielding it like a weapon so she'll actually acknowledge his existence. She was wrong earlier when she said he had tried everything but begging, and this…this is going to be much harder to resist than watching him bow before her on his knees.

Cassy leaps up and runs to open her door, shouting, "Fuck you, Ruin!"

Panting, she shuts it again, ignoring his laughter. Great. Now she *has* to bring Ruin to meet her parents. She can only hope he doesn't make things worse for her. She is already fighting this thing they have; the undeniable attraction she holds for the formidable ghost. And she…well, she would be a liar if she told herself meeting her parents doesn't matter; if she convinces herself that Ruin being the first, and only, potential partner she's ever brought home means nothing.

A situation like this can only be devastating for her.

Cassy digs around inside the top drawer of her dresser, huffing and cursing at Ruin under her breath. The anger revolving around inside her needs a way to escape, needs a catalyst to ignite the explosion. It's why she's searching for the clump of dried green she hid after the hotel ghost hunt, why she's determined to find a way to make him as angry with her as she is with him.

What if he can't come back after I cleanse the space? What if I never see him again? Will this hurt him? Maybe he will be forced to stay outside the house. Will this affect Cerci? I hope not; I don't want to punish her for Ruin's wrongdoings. I don't—Will he—I am—

She banishes the very logical thoughts away, not prepared to stop until—ah. There it is, hidden underneath a pile of underwear. She grins as she pulls out the sage and the matchstick, clicking her tongue happily. Slamming the drawer shut, she spins and swings her bedroom door open. "Ruin," she calls, grinning like a maniac.

Ruin's head pops up from the kitchen, surprise lit upon his features. She would be surprised, too, if she were him. After she shouted, "Fuck you, Ruin," she doubts he expected her to be out and speaking to him again so quickly.

"Come to beg for forgiveness, my beloved?" His smug smile is large and quick to form, but it visibly droops when he sets his eyes upon the bundle of sage in her grasp. "Cassy…"

"Something wrong?" With a flick of her opposite hand, she's lit a match, the flame dancing above her fingers.

"You don't want to do that, Cassiopeia," he warns, taking a cautious step forward and holding up a hand placatingly. "Why don't you set that down and then we can talk about this?"

His eyes are wide and fearful, as though she's holding a gun to him. Though…she *has* actually shot at him before, and he didn't react nearly as viscerally. Before she can talk herself out of this stupid idea based on his reaction alone, she says plainly, "Talking never works with you, Ruin. Mostly because you tend to run away from conversations you don't like, and even the ones you do. I think this is a much better idea."

She lights the sage.

Ruin curses, leaping at her. Cassy jumps back and waves the smoke forming in his face, squealing when he makes another move to grab her. "I thought this was supposed to banish you," she cries, moving to hide behind the couch.

Ruin's face turns hard, all playfulness gone. He takes two careful steps forward, nearly stepping through the couch. His voice is cold as he says, "What was your plan, Cassiopeia? Cleanse your house to rid yourself of me? Did you think it would be that simple? Did you think at all past your anger with me?"

"Uh…no?" She watches as Ruin's face pinches, as he takes a deep inhale and runs a hand over his face with a groan.

"I haven't smoked sage in a very long time," he says quietly, hand dropping down to his side. His eyes pin her in place as he takes a step into the couch, clicking his tongue afterward. "Sage only gets me high, C.J. It certainly doesn't banish me."

She frowns, glancing down at the sage in question. "Oh. Then why did the hotel ghost lady hate it...?"

"Older spirits are more closed-minded." Another careful step forward, his hand twitching by his side. "And, for some, with their inhibitions lowered, they are more likely to seek out Death to cross the veil."

She screeches and sprints away when his hand snaps out, attempting to grab the bundle from her hand. She laughs as she spins out of his reach, too amused by the new development to be angry. She dodges another of Ruin's attempts to grab her, hair flying behind her as she tumbles into the kitchen. His annoyed grumbling follows her joyous laughter, smoke from the sage trailing all around the living room now.

"Feeling high yet?" she questions with a boisterous laugh, nearly keening over and peeing herself when she sees his eyes already reddened. "No way!" she gasps, clutching her stomach.

"Come on, C.J.," Ruin snips, his steps stumbling. "This stuff works quickly, and I really don't like using a lot."

"I think this is great," she says defiantly, waving it above her head. "Maybe now you'll be a little more truthful with me."

"You want truthful?" He disappears, and Cassy twirls around in anticipation of him surprising her. She only manages to land herself pinned against the counter when he reappears, his face lowered toward hers and his hand clamped around her wrist. The sage is ripped from her grasp and thrown into the sink full of soaking dishes, the flame doused immediately. Ruin leans forward, lips pressed against her ear. Cassy's hands stay stiff, too alarmed to reach out and touch him. "I'll tell you the truth. Being here, with you, in this house…it's exactly what I needed. It's what I have craved for many, many years. But I am a liar for a reason, my beloved. I am not *good*. So if that's what you want from me…you will not get it."

When Ruin disappears this time, it's for good. Likely to go sit out his high somewhere not near Cassy. And she…she only slides to the floor, her entire body shaking. The moment of fun and delight has been ruined, and the anger is slowly making a reappearance. She doesn't want him to be *good*. She just wants…she wants him to want her enough to be honest. She wants, for once, for someone to care so much about her that they will do anything to be with her. Even if that someone is a ghost.

This dose of reality was good. This is what she *needed*. Anger is much easier to feel than love is, after all.

Chapter 13

"I'm not going to fake date you," Cassy tells Ruin for the third time, both hands on the steering wheel of Winter's car as she stares at her childhood home. It's a simple red brick home that appears small from the outside but is actually larger within, especially considering the basement, which could be a small house of its own. The immaculate (for the winter season) front lawn stares back at her, its sharp, dead blades of grass trimmed down to the perfect size. Dying flowers and dead bushes greet her from the front, empty branches waving at her on the gentle breeze.

This house is a haunted place of her past and a cursed place of her future.

"Sure," Ruin says, his answer just as smug and amused as it was before. "Let me know how heartbroken your mother is, won't you?"

"Stop that!" She presses her forehead against the steering wheel, groaning. It's not that she cares about disappointing her parents, or even that she generally cares what they think about any relationship she may or may not be involved in. She only cares that her parents are happy, and upsetting their careful balance is out of the question. Cassy likes being distant from her parents, but she also likes holding them close in her heart.

It is an odd relationship, a healthy one, sure, but...odd compared to those of her classmates and acquaintances while growing up. Her parents love her and she loves them, but they are all happy to only speak to each other once a week and visit once a month. It works for everyone. No overbearingness, no clinginess, no expectations.

Ruin turns his head to stare at her, sending her one of those charming smiles that leave her heart aching. "I'm not sure I understand why you care what she thinks, but I find it amusing."

"It's not that I care what she thinks," she says, lifting her head to try and voice the thoughts she was just processing. "It's just that...I care how she feels. I love her. I love them both."

Ruin nods, reaching out to grip her hand. He lays it over the one closest to him on the wheel, intermingling their fingers and squeezing lightly. "And they love you. That's why they want you in a relationship, you know? They have a deep, unending love, and they want their daughter to have one, too."

She scoffs but doesn't pull her hand out from under his. "And how do you know they have a deep, unending love? You've never met them."

Ruin smiles sadly, dropping his hand of his own accord. "No, but they created you. You, who won't accept relationships because you've never met anyone you think will last. No one measures up for you because you know what it really means to be loved."

Cassy blinks, turning away hastily and beginning to open the door. Ruin quickly leans over, holding it shut and waiting for her to respond. With a sigh and a shudder, she throws out, "Maybe that's true." She has never really thought about it before, actually. Has never considered that she wanted something that exceeded expectations, and *that's* why she never dates. Because, really, how can she find someone like that in Tennessee?

Ruin slowly releases the door handle, clearing his throat before saying, "Let me do it." He exits the car first, jogging around to hold her door open. She knows the action is more to impress her parents than to please her, but she still feels charmed by the notion.

Ruin holds out a hand, and she hesitantly takes it, allowing him to pull her to her feet. She stumbles into his chest for a brief moment, all bodily functions stopping. No breaths, no heartbeats, no thoughts. Not until he places his hands on her waist to steady her before quickly shoving them down into his pockets and muttering, "I need a smoke."

"No smoking on the premises," she remarks breathlessly, head snapping toward the pale blue front door when it swings open. Her mom steps out onto the doormat adorned with a cheerful Santa face, smiling brightly.

"Little doll!" her mom cries, gesturing for them to come in. She has tied her dark brown hair into a messy ponytail, fluffy waves barely contained at the back of her head. Her cunning brown eyes snap to Ruin, assessing him.

I wonder what she thinks about him. Is she impressed? Does she think he's hot? Does he look kind? Will she scare him off? Will he scare them? Can they tell he's not human? Will they—Does she—If he—

Hand on one of her wide hips, Lyanne sends Ruin a crooked smile. "You must be Ruin. It's lovely to meet you!"

Ruin and Cassy begin the walk up the sidewalk to the front door. Her heart nearly explodes as he casts her mother a gracious, awkward smile and responds, "It's lovely to meet you in person, Mrs. Jaynes. Cassy talks about you two all the time."

Cassy is shocked when her mother pulls Ruin in for a hug and his arms wrap around her with ease, no awkward patting of the back or anything. Lyanne releases Ruin, holding him at arm's length and sighing contentedly. "Oh, he's handsome, Cass. And strong."

Cassy's entire face flushes when her mom sends her a wink before turning her back to the fake couple. "He's something, alright," Cassy says bitterly, glaring up at the ghost. The anger and resentment from yesterday have still not faded, despite Ruin's attempts at brushing the incident off with his casual banter in the car.

"And you look so handsome in that outfit, Ruin! It was meant for you," Lyanne remarks as she struts away, assuming they are following.

Cassy takes in the dark jeans that fit his toned legs perfectly, telling herself she hadn't noticed how good his ass looked in them, either. The deep red button-up he paired with it is smooth and soft, the color almost that of blood. She hates to agree with her mom, but he *does* look good. With a bite of annoyance, she mutters under her breath, "Where do ghosts even get new clothes, anyway?"

Ruin chuckles, taking her by the elbow and pulling her to his side. Bending down to her ear, he whispers, "The same place you do, my beloved. From the dead."

Defensively, she says, "Only the ones with good taste!" Ruin laughs boisterously, pulling her into her childhood home for a dinner straight from hell.

Cassy sits next to Ruin at the worn dinner table in her parents' dining room, the wood rough and stained in areas. She focuses on one particular stain, a paint splotch from when she and Winter had decided to paint t-shirts at twelve and used wall paint they found in the garage instead of craft paint. Needless to say, cleaning the green splotch did more damage than the splotch itself.

"Where's Winter?" she asks after a lull in conversation, shoveling a forkful of chicken salad into her mouth angrily. Winter is *always* here for the monthly dinners; she hasn't missed one in three years. As a matter of fact, when Cassy asked if she wanted to ride with them, Winter told her to take her car because she would be taking a taxi straight from work.

"She had to pick up an extra shift at work. She called to tell me this morning; apparently, they were short on nurses. She didn't tell you?" Lyanne swirls her wineglass with an olive-toned hand, watching her daughter above the lip of the glass innocently as she takes a sip.

"No. How convenient of her," Cassy grinds out, stabbing a little too harshly into her food. It seems Winter had planned to feed her to the wolves, despite the many texts Cassy sent her last night ranting about Ruin being an asshole.

Winter is so dead. I'll kill her myself. I wasn't sure I would ever tell her about my deadly kisses, but she'll find out when I plant one on her. She'll probably haunt my ass for it, but I don't care. I'll do it anyway. I will—She is—I can—

Cassy's father, a bald man with a sharp nose and gray-blue eyes, sighs impatiently. "Are you girls fighting again?"

"Of course not." Cassy licks her lips, dropping the fork a little too loudly. The clang as it hits the porcelain bowl reverberates through the room, followed by her hasty attempt to cover it as she picks up her knife and begins sawing into what is left of her steak.

Her dad raises a bushy eyebrow, eyes narrowed and mouth pursed. "Really? Because you seem really upset with her. Would you like to talk about it?"

She grips her knife harder, jumping when Ruin's hand slides across her thigh. His thumb rubs against bare skin, her thin cotton dress sliding up from the movement. Her entire body stiffens, the grip on her knife loosening. What is he *doing*?

"She's mad at Winter for telling me about Ruin, Walter. She didn't want us to know," Lyanne supplies, oblivious to her daughter's sturdy glare.

"Cassy's hard to tie down," Ruin says, reaching out to twist a lock of her silver hair casually. "She doesn't want to commit."

Cassy turns her glare to him now, but the twinkle of amusement in his eyes leaves her feeling deflated. "We aren't together," she says firmly, not turning her stare away from the ghost.

"Sure," Ruin says with a grin, dropping her hair. "Whatever you say, my beloved."

"My beloved," Lyanne sighs, nearly toppling out of her chair. She's had three glasses of wine at this point, and Cassy is certain she needs to be cut off. Wine always affects her mother poorly. "That's so sweet. Cassy, why do you have to be so stubborn?"

Ruin answers for her again. Only, he doesn't turn away from the murderous look in Cassy's eyes as he does so. "She's scared. She doesn't want to commit because what if it doesn't last? What if it isn't real? What if it isn't everlasting? What if the person she chooses doesn't choose her in return? What if they don't like what they find below the surface?"

The pair watches each other for long seconds before he says again, "She's scared."

He won't accept me for who I am. For what I do. He doesn't like it; he wants me to stop. He's a ghost, anyway. It doesn't matter what he likes or doesn't like. We can't be together for more reasons than whatever fear he thinks I hold. Is he scared of anything? Is he scared to initiate something with me? Does he think this is real? It can't be, so it doesn't matter. Attraction is attraction, that's all. I'm attracted to loads of people. It has nothing to do with the thoughtful gestures and kind gifts, with the easy conversations and flowing laughter, or the deeply accurate observations he's made about me in such a short time. I may—It can't—Is he—

Walter clears his throat, staring between his wife and daughter before saying, "Well, Ruin, I think you know Cassy a little too well."

Ruin lets out a soft chuckle, releasing Cassy from his fierce gaze. "I think she doesn't know herself well enough."

Lyanne sighs, waving her hands and tipping out of her chair. Walter is up in a flash, catching her with a lofty huff. Lyanne says dreamily, "Oh, little doll. You picked good this time. You picked *right*. That's clear as day."

"I didn't—" Cassy tries, frustrated and a little awed at Ruin's assessment of her.

Her father interrupts. "I'm going to get your mother into bed, darling. You know how the wine goes to her head." Cassy can only nod as he begins pulling her mom out of the room, adding over his shoulder, "You two have had too many to drink tonight, too. You shouldn't be driving. Your room is all ready for y'all."

She wants to argue, knowing it is a ploy to make them stay. Knowing Ruin has not had a single glass of wine and she has only had one. She sighs anyway, pushing herself to her feet and making to leave.

"Where are we going?" Ruin is on her heels, following her out of the dining room and to the set of steps leading to the basement.

"*I'm* going to my room to read and doom-scroll until I pass out from exhaustion," she snips, the hem of her dress rising as she begins to descend.

"Our room, now," Ruin says playfully, following behind her.

She turns to narrow her eyes at him over her shoulder, grinding out, "No. No, no, no. You can stay anywhere else. Transport back home and pop back in in the morning. I don't care where you go, you just can't stay here."

Ruin laughs at her very serious remark, shaking his head. "I don't think so, C.J."

She pauses, frustration growing. "Look, I don't know what your deal is today, but just…stop, okay? Just stop."

"You asked me to be truthful." The statement is soft and earnest, and her eyes flutter shut as she inhales deeply in surprise.

She stutters out, "Y-You told me you couldn't do that, remember? That you *wouldn't*. I'm not going to forget about that just because you start assessing me honestly." She stalks through the living room downstairs in response, heading straight to the bedroom on the other side of the basement. She slips in the door and shuts it behind her before Ruin can follow, not that it makes a difference in the outcome. He pops up beside her with a growl, rubbing at his large nose in annoyance.

"That hurt, you know. I was solid when you hit me with that door."

"Oh, were you?" Cassy blinks up innocently at him, yelping when strong arms grab her and lift her into the air. She lands on the blue-clad bed flat on her back, gaping in shock as Ruin crawls over her to invade her space.

"You've been doing some wicked things lately, Cassy, and I think you need to be punished." His voice is rich and low, her core throbbing at the idea of being punished by Ruin more than it should. No. No, they can't do this. *They can't.*

"Please," she tries to scoff, but it sounds more like a shaky beg. *Fuck.* There's no way she'll be able to stop if he touches her now. No way she'll be able to turn him away. "You can't *punish* me. I'm not a child you can spank into obedience."

Ruin lets out a low laugh, one hand trailing up her side. Before she can stop him, he's pulling her up again, forcing her to straddle his lap. "Bend over," he grinds out, jerking his head toward the front of the bed. "We'll find out how well spanking works on you, my beloved."

Cassy stops breathing, her voice wavering. "N-No." It's weak and brittle, that word. She never stood a chance.

"No?" he questions, grinning. "Oh, I love your defiance, Cassiopeia." Ruin's lips reach forward to trace a pattern down her neck and across her cleavage, hands scooping underneath her ass and squeezing. And she *knows* this is a bad idea. Knows this is an accumulation of tension and attraction that's built up over the months, but...

"What are you going to do about it?" she breathes, grinning despite the small part of her screaming that this is wrong. She gasps at the sharp nip at her breast over the fabric of her dress, letting out a breathless moan.

"Bend over, Cassy, and find out. Bend over so I know you want this."

She scrambles to do as told, crawling out of his lap and getting onto all fours. She lies on her elbows, arching her back and waiting with a racing heart for what comes next.

Is this real? I must be dreaming. Why would Ruin choose to do this now? I haven't missed his longing gazes and I know he hasn't missed mine, so what changed? Did my near-death experience spur him into action, or is this purely an attempt at getting back in my good graces? Maybe I should be angry if that is all this is to him. But I can't stop. I don't have enough impulse control for it. I didn't expect him to be so domineering, but I love it. Maybe he has a leftover high from the sage. How long does that last on ghosts? I want—He is—I need—

Ruin's hand pushes her dress up to her back, shoving it around her waist to lazily drape down. He groans when he sees she isn't wearing any underwear, muttering something unintelligible under his breath. He's still for so long that Cassy almost says something, almost provokes him, but his hand comes down on her ass at just the right moment. She moans into her comforter, gripping the sheets harshly as he does it again. Again. Again. As it is becoming too much, the skin too tender, his hand slips between her legs to find her clit.

"You're so perfect, Cassiopeia. Your ass is so lovely when my hand is imprinted on it," Ruin grinds out, and she turns to find him watching her ass with fascination. Watching her wetness drip down her thighs as he continues to finger her. She moans, burying her head down as far as it will go and rocking to get more of the sensation. And just when she almost has it just right, just when she is sure she is ready to let go, he stops.

"R-Ruin," she pleads, whimpering. She looks at the smug, heated look on his face and knows she isn't going to like what comes next.

"I told you I would punish you, my beloved. Did you think I would let you come? Did you think you deserved it after what you did?"

Cassy pants, trying to form a single, coherent thought. But it is all too much, too sensitive, too good. "Please," she manages to say, her cheeks red in embarrassment. She has never had to beg anyone to touch her before, never had to beg for her release. And, oh, how she *loves* it.

"No," Ruin says simply, standing abruptly. She can see the erection through his jeans, can tell he is just as turned on as she.

"I have to go before you convince me to change my mind with those devilish lips of yours."

She cries out, sitting up and reaching out all too late. Ruin is gone, and she knows he isn't going to come back. Frustrated, she tries to take care of herself. Tries to pretend it is his hands on her, pushing her to the brink again. But it isn't enough. Release evades her all night, and she isn't able to sleep a wink because of it.

"Sleep well?" Ruin questions the next morning, grinning down at her knowingly.

"Like a baby," she lies, trying to play at being nonchalant. Trying to pretend she isn't angry and frustrated and needy.

But Ruin knows it is a lie. *She* knows it is a lie. And neither one of them acknowledges it, or the reason for it, in the days that follow.

Chapter 14

"Where's your cute roomy?" Winter pops another bubble in her gum, stretching across Cassy's couch to prop her feet in Cassy's lap. She has forgiven Winter for the family dinner trickery last week, but only barely. Like Ruin, Winter is also trying to work her way back into Cassy's good graces, hence her visit.

"Probably working." Cassy bites on the inside of her cheek, wishing she could tell her best friend the truth.

He disappears in the middle of conversations and doesn't come back. He's been pestering me with gifts but not visiting often for the past three weeks because he feels guilty over what another ghost did to me. He punished me in the most delicious way and acts like it never happened.

Another pop accompanied by an incredulous look as Winter moves to sit up. "He works a lot."

"I guess so." What else is she supposed to say? How could she ever begin to explain the situation to her best friend?

"I think you have a thing for him." A calm, pointed statement that Cassy doesn't process immediately.

I am a bad liar. I hate lying, but I especially hate lying to Winter. Does she know I'm lying? She always does. She probably smells my fear. She's so scary sometimes. But so soft and sweet, too. That's conflicting, isn't it? That's Winter, though, I suppose. I love her so much. Does she like Ruin? Does Ruin like her? Does she—I think—I really—

"Cassy, babe, did you hear me?"

"What?" She turns her chillingly blue eyes to Winter, staring into her best friend's familiar, comforting brown ones.

"I said—"

"Oh, no. I've told you that a bajillion times already, Chilly. I don't have a thing for him. The way you described it to Mom was, like, out of a romance novel. You've only seen us together once. I know I talk about him a lot, but...Why would you tell her all that stuff?" Cassy twirls a lock of hair around her finger, a lock that used to be more of a sterling silver and now seems to be an aging white.

She points at Cassy's hand with a quiet laugh, leaning forward with light dancing in her eyes. "Because you avoid every con-versation about him and twirl your hair nervously when you *do* have to talk about him."

Cassy drops her hand, scowling. "No, I don't."

"Alright, I can catch a hint. You still don't wanna talk about it. I'd push harder if you weren' still mad at me for the last time I pushed too hard." Winter rolls her eyes, adding, "What's with the white highlights, by the way? I noticed 'em when I came in, but I didn't want to say anythin' at first because you never mentioned 'em in our calls. I didn't want to bring 'em up in case you hated 'em, but well, I couldn' help myself. It's an odd choice for you, but it's cute."

"Oh, yeah. I just...wanted a change, I guess." The truth is, the white hair appeared after Cassy's brush with the Class Two Soul. She hasn't seen Winter in person since, and she was certain Winter couldn't see the difference in their daily video chats, so…she never mentioned it. She isn't sure if it was out of self-preservation or because she truly does hate the change.

"I like 'em," Winter announces pointedly, grinning. "Do you?"

"I think so." Cassy twirls a lock again, staring off toward the kitchen. Abruptly, she stands, moving toward the dishwasher.

I need to do the dishes today and vacuum. I should probably mop, too. I might do some sewing. Or read a book. Oh, but what I really crave is a good hunt. Not a ghost, though. I'm stuck with this itch to kill someone bad, to dish out justice, but I know Ruin won't approve. It's a bug I got sick with years ago and I can't quite shake it. Should I do it anyway? I don't always have to listen to Ruin. He doesn't come enough to notice my absence, anyway. He doesn't have to know. Death may tell him, eventually, but surely one soul won't bring the scary entity to my doorstep. I want—Does he—I should—

"What gives?" Winter stops Cassy with her legs as she goes to pass by, hands on her hips as she watches Cassy wearily.

"What do you mean?" Cassy pushes past her friend and flees into the kitchen, opening the dishwasher and taking out clean, pastel-colored ceramic plates. If she doesn't do it now, while she's thinking about it, it won't get done. And she already feels like a slob as is, since she constantly forgets to do simple chores (or, most often, gets into slumps where she physically *can't* bring herself to do anything but sit and panic over the chores and other things that need to be done).

"You're bein' really weird. Weirder than normal, Cassy. Cagey, quiet, lost in thought. That's not like you. What's goin' on?"

"Nothing." She opens the drawer full of silverware, placing a few spoons away before noticing the mess on the table. There's an empty cup there she needs to grab, so she'll bring it to the dishwasher when she's done cleaning the table, too. Silently, she drifts over and begins to clear away the sewing supplies, along with the clippings of fabric and thread littering its surface.

Winter approaches from behind, sighing as she picks up where Cassy left off at the dishwasher. *Shit,* Cassy thinks, knowing she always abandons tasks halfway through despite her best efforts. No matter how hard she tries to condition herself, she always starts on one thing and leaves before it's finished; distracted and scatter-brained, according to many teachers from her youth. "You're lyin'."

"Chilly," Cassy whispers, pausing with a stiff back. "Don't strong-arm me right now."

"And why shouldn' I? You're my best friend, Cassy. My only friend. I've never seen you so...so caught up in your head. You almost seem scared."

Cassy's whole body stiffens now, arms and legs tingling with awareness. Her best friend knows her better than she cares to admit. "What would I be scared of?" She scoffs, forcing Confident Cassy to come up to the surface. Confident Cassy always fixes things, always gets herself out of precarious situations. Confident Cassy can get her out of this, too.

"I don't know, that's why I'm askin' you." Winter pauses, sighing softly before spitting out, "If it's Ruin, I can help you get out of the lease. It's not as hard as you might think—"

"No!" Cassy screams, whirling around to face her. So much for Confident Cassy, who fled when faced with a whirlpool of anxiety. "No, it isn't Ruin. He's great. Fantastic, even."

"Then what in the world are you so frightened of? Have you gotten yourself inta some kind of trouble, sweetie?"

"It's just work stuff," she manages out, smiling softly, reassuringly. Winter can't know, because if Winter gets caught up in this deadly game of hide and seek she's playing with Death..."I'm stressed out, and I can't talk to anyone about it because of the whole top-secret clearance thing. It's taking a toll on me, that's all. It has nothing to do with Ruin, I swear. He's a great man." Mentioning work usually makes Winter and her parents back off. Cassy has lied to them for so long about her secretive government job that they know better than to question her about more details. But Winter latches on to the latter part of Cassy's words, clicking her tongue in amusement.

"Oh, I think this has a lot to do with that man." Winter wags a finger at her closest friend, grinning like a fool. "I think you like him and you're scared to admit it to yourself."

Cassy swallows, closing her eyes tightly. Ruin thinks so, too. Had said as much last week, right in front of her parents, before bringing her to the edge of an orgasm and dipping. "I thought you said you weren't going to push anymore." Then a soft sigh as she whispers, "I can admit it, Chilly. I *do* like him. He's hot and funny with a good personality. He gets me like no one I've ever known. It's just...the two of us are an explosion waiting to happen. Any romantic notions between us have been shoved into a bomb that's waiting to diffuse, and once it does...once it does, it'll be *my* heart full of shrapnel while he walks away from the wreckage."

"Don't make it complicated, babe. Can't you two just have some fun? I know you don't do serious, so don't let it be." Winter is attempting to make it sound so simple, so easy. And maybe it would be if Ruin wasn't...well, *dead*. And working with the man hunting her down, the man with an army full of others like Ruin at his disposal.

"Ah, you don't get it. He and I...it can never happen. It would only end in heartbreak." Cassy tries to keep it simple, direct, and to the point. But Winter has never liked *simple*.

Winter pauses, cocking her head and gaping at Cassy. "Oh, no. You don't...you don't actually have feelin's for him, do you? You never catch feelin's! No wonder you're so torn up about the man."

"I..." She doesn't let Cassy continue, her body slinging into Cassy's as Winter holds her and laughs. Cassy carefully moves her head, tucking into her best friend without letting her lips brush against anything more than hair.

"Oh, honey. Bless your heart." Coming from Winter, that's usually an insult.

"Don't do that. Don't pity me." Cassy moves to shove her away, embarrassed. Her cheeks are heated, her neck inflamed.

"But I do. You've never gotten attached to someone before. Never. And now what? Now that you've gotten someone to be involved with you, you don't wanna be involved? I don't get you sometimes, Cassy. I love love. Don't you want that for yourself?"

"Ah, I don't know, Chilly. I've never wanted love. Not...not the romantic kind." She's wanted revenge, wanted retribution, wanted vengeance; never mercy, never hope, *never love*. Maybe...maybe it isn't really a *want*. Maybe it's this deep *need* inside her she chose to tuck away until Ruin came into her life. The ghost brought that need to the surface of her drowning heart, and she doesn't know how she's going to submerge it again.

"Just because you didn' want it before doesn' mean you can't want it now." Winter pulls back, hands on Cassy's shoulders as she shakes her head sadly.

"Ruin and I can't happen," Cassy tells her friend—and herself—firmly. "There are a lot of things that just…don't work between us." He's dead, she's not. He works for Death, Death wants to kill her. Major deal breakers, if she's being honest. Deal breakers she has repeated to herself this entire conversation because if she forgets for even one second what's at stake…

He doesn't even want me anymore. He probably regrets what happened between us the other day. My punishment. I shouldn't admit I want him, not after the way he's been ignoring those wants. None of it matters, anyway, because he's avoiding me. How long will he avoid me? Will this be the rest of my life? I haven't thought past now. What happens in the future? Am I supposed to run from Death the rest of my life? I can't do that. I can't be scared for my entire life. I can't—I won't—I will—

"See? That right there, Cassy! What is that? You're terrified." Winter holds Cassy now, pushing her face close to her best friends. Cassy jerks back, stumbling into the table and clattering to the floor loudly. She is gasping, her eyes wide and full of a deep-rooted fear she can't hide.

"Don't," Cassy cries when Winter comes closer to inspect her; those nurse instincts are always hiding below the surface. Cassy holds her hands up, shaking her head furiously. Her ass aches, her heart's racing, and she feels dizzy with fear, but she still says, "Don't come near me."

"I don't understand what's goin' on. You've never hidden things from me. Never." Winter crouches down in front of her despite the warning. And why wouldn't she? Cassy never told Winter what she is, what Cassy chose to be. Her best friend would hate her if she knew. Winter heals people for a living, even those who aren't deserving. And Cassy...what she does is the exact opposite of healing.

"I..." Cassy struggles to find the words to say because there are none that can make any of this okay, or right, or easy. "There are things in this world..."

"Oh, don't give me a philosophy lesson, honey. I don't care about all that mumbo jumbo. Just the truth."

"I can't do that, Winter. I can't..."

Winter has always seen right through Cassy, and she shouldn't have ever believed she could hide this side of herself from her best friend. And now...now Cassy's going to lose her. What kind of person will condone what Cassy does? Murder is wrong, deserving or not. Even children know that. Telling Winter that she is a killer, that she feels no remorse, that she wants to do it again...she isn't sure her best friend will accept that. She can hope, but why hope when it only leaves you filled with disappointment? Winter will leave Cassy and she will be truly, truly alone. Not that she doesn't already feel alone. Maybe that's why she's so attracted to Ruin, despite their different levels of liveliness. He understands her like no one else can, sees a side of her that she's never revealed to a living soul. Maybe that's why it hurts so badly now that he's ignoring her, why she can no longer hide the pain and fear that's been festering in her heart ever since her brush with death and a Class Two Soul.

"What has he gotten you into, Cassiopeia?" Winter's voice is barely above a whisper, the deadly calm terrifying. She never calls Cassy by her actual name. *Never.* The way she says it...it's not filled with love and sensuousness, not like it is with Ruin. It's full of deadly promise, of worry and rage. Cassy can see it in the twitch of Winter's left eye, in the clenching of her jaw, and in the tightly pursed lips.

"It's what *I've* gotten myself into, Winter. Ruin is trying to protect me from my own stupid mistakes." A mistake she's craving to make again. Just one more time, just one more body...

It's been so long since I killed. So long since I sought out justice. I just want to scratch the itch. I just want to hunt. If I don't kill someone deserving soon, I will go mad. I can't think about anything else. Forget the ghosts. Forget Ruin. I need to do something good, to help rid the world of one more monster. I need it. I need it—I need it—I need it—

"*Tell me what you did, Cassiopeia.* Tell me what you did or I'll—"

"You'll what?" Cassy scoffs at her, crawling over and grabbing her friend's face by the cheeks. "Anything you threaten will be nothing compared to what I could do to you. Nothing compared to what I've done to others. And if I got any closer than I am right now, you would be dead before you fully understood what it meant." She isn't sure what makes her say it, or why her own voice has become a deadly dagger poised to strike at Winter's heart.

Winter's eyes narrow in suspicion, not wide with fear like Cassy expected, or maybe even hoped. If Cassy scares Winter away in a different way, if she *forces* Winter to leave...well, maybe it won't hurt as much as Winter walking out would have. "You sayin' you're going to kill me? Go ahead, Cassiopeia Jaynes. I'll come back and haunt you; then we will see what kind of answers you give me."

"That's the problem." Cassy shoves her away gently, swallowing hard. How did Winter know how to strike back so harshly, so absolutely? "I know what it means to be haunted."

"You're being so dramatic today, Cassy. Just tell me—"

The front door slams open and hits the wall so hard that they both jump, and Winter is the first to turn toward the entryway. She stands to her full height, a slightly intimidating five feet ten, and blocks Cassy's body from view as she addresses the figure whom she assumes is Ruin.

"Ruin, now isn't a good time," Winter says, arms crossing across her chest. But it isn't Ruin who comes into the kitchen.

It *is* a ghost...just not the right one.

Chapter 15

"**W**here is the hunter?"

Cassy freezes at the sound of that voice, at the Southern accent she vaguely recognizes.

"Ruin isn't here." Winter doesn't understand. She doesn't know, and he's going to—

Cassy leaps forward and grabs Winter by the ankles, pulling her best friend as hard as she can manage from her position on the floor. Winter yelps and falls to her knees, letting out a loud *oomph* as Cassy promptly dives into her body and knocks her fully to the ground. A ceramic bowl barely misses their heads as she does so, the crash echoing behind them with a horrifying clarity.

"Get out of here!" she shouts at Winter, scrambling to her feet. She faces the man, the *ghost*, and her face pales until it's almost the same color as his. *Oh fucking* hell.

"Recognize me?" His grin is grimy, his voice dripping with rage as his body flickers with a deep red she'd seen in her nightmares lately.

"Should I?" Cassy *does* recognize him. Oh, boy, does she. Because this isn't just *any* ghost.

It's the ghost of Erron Gates.

I killed him. Has he become a Class Two, then? He must be a Wronged Soul. I'll have to kiss him again. He won't let me kiss him. His lips tasted like liquor. Will they retain that taste? I hope not. I'll kiss his cheek. Winter has to leave. Where's Ruin? I can't depend on Ruin. Why is Erron here? Erron must hate me. I won't—I can—If I—

"Don't play with me, ghost hunter," he snarls, red light flashing so rapidly now that it would give an epileptic a seizure. It's a deep, menacing color, and never before has she felt threatened by a color alone. But the way it flashes and glides across the floor, the way it seems to have a mind of its own as it explodes from his body and wriggles in the space around him...

"I've already called the police, psycho, so I suggest you get out of here *now*." Winter has pushed herself back to her hands and knees, her glare brilliant and terrifying. She hasn't actually called anyone, seeing as her phone is lying on the table, but it's sweet that she's trying to protect them from who Cassy's certain she believes is a psycho intruder wearing strobe lights.

Erron Gates laughs, the sound dark and heavy. A chill runs down Cassy's spine at the sound of it, another bowl suddenly barreling toward her friend. Winter dives off to the side, eyes wide as she looks over to Cassy.

"Stop it, Erron," Cassy hisses, her legs feeling wobbly. *Confident Cassy, Confident Cassy, Confident Cassy.* "This is between us, isn't it? That's why you came. You want me, not her."

"You know him?" Winter whispers, fuming. She doesn't understand yet, but she will. Oh, this isn't how things were supposed to happen. Cassy was supposed to be mean, to scare her off in a harmless way that would hurt Cassy's own heart more than Winter's, but...

"Oh, you know exactly why I'm here." Erron's gaze is back on his target, his anger palpable.

"You wanted another taste?" Cassy teases, hands on her hips as a smirk pulls up the corners of her lips. The distraction works, Confident Cassy works, and Erron snarls at her menacingly. As long as she can keep his attention on her and away from Winter, it will be fine. She can figure this out, can get rid of the ghost somehow. She *is* a ghost hunter, after all.

"Your *taste* is poisonous." The red flashes are becoming so rapid that she can hardly make out his form, his own lips painted in an animalistic snarl that she isn't sure a human is capable of. That light caresses him lovingly, dancing in a terrifying sequence of moves that draws them in and out of his orbit.

She frowns, pouting. "I've never had any complaints." She inches forward as she talks, impossibly slow as his body continues to waver.

A finger at his side twitches, and his head tilts to the side as something lifts into the air above the counter. "I'm sure you would kill any man who did twice over."

She ducks as a plate comes clattering by, followed by an iron pan. She kicks out at that one to avoid being hit, knocking it to the ground and grunting from the pain in her toes.

"You're throwing a fit like a child, Erron. Come on, surely there aren't hard feelings between us?"

"Cassy," Winter warns, watching Erron closely now. Her expression is calm, but Cassy knows the woman well enough to see the hint of fear hiding in plain sight. "Cassy, somethin' is wrong with this man. You shouldn' be…"

"Get out, Winter!" Cassy shouts so loudly, so aggressively, that Winter jumps, and Erron flings another plate in response.

"Absolutely not," Winter hisses, eyes dancing between Cassy and Erron in an attempt to assess the situation.

"Oh, you stupid, brave girl. Just leave before you become a ghost, too!" Cassy doesn't watch to see Winter's expression, much less to watch Winter process the damning words that left her mouth. She turns back to Erron, inching forward again. Slowly, so, so slowly...

"How am I supposed to get out, huh? The two of you are blockin' the doorway!" Cassy flinches, realizing she's right. *Fuck.*

"It's time for you to leave." Cassy points at him threateningly, trying to distract from the fleeting movements of her feet.

"Is this how you treat your guests, Cassy?" The lights are flickering now, and the bulb above them bursts in a violent haze that leaves Winter screeching. A bit of glass slices Cassy's cheek, but she doesn't allow herself to react. "I never did catch your name that night, you know? I never thought I would need it."

She smiles at him, saccharine sweet. "You were just thinking with the wrong head, sweetie. That's not my fault."

Behind her, Winter hisses, "Cassy, now is not the time to have an attitude!"

"It took a long time to find you, you know?" He's stepping closer now, as close as he dares, while that red light bursting from him illuminates the dim room. One particular beam seems to be reaching for her, stretching itself thin as it tries to make contact. The curtains are open, and the setting sun provides enough light to help keep him in their direct sight. His body has a translucent glow, one she's certain Winter must have noticed by now.

"Did it?" Cassy picks at her nails and watches him under her lashes in boredom, feet scuffling subtly. "I heard I'm pretty popular with the dead right now."

Confident Cassy is sassy. Confident Cassy doesn't care about the ghost in her kitchen. Confident Cassy isn't worried about herself or Winter. I'm not her, though. I have to be her. I can't be her. I want to be her. I will be her. Where is Ruin when I need him? My lips are my only weapon here. I have to kiss Erron. I don't want to kiss him. Kissing ghosts is disgusting. I need to kiss someone alive soon. Yes, I want to do that. I want—I need—My lips—

"The Shadow Kisser, they call you. A lame nickname, if you ask me." The other Class Two Soul didn't talk to Cassy like this; it attacked without question. But this ghost has a personal connection to her, and he clearly planned this entire ordeal.

"How rude." Cassy lets loose another pout, dropping her chipped pink nails to her sides. "I earned that nickname fair and square."

"Oh, yes, darlin'. You have. Now it's time I earned myself a nickname. How does the Shadow Kissing Destroyer sound?"

"That's horrible. I knew you were dumb, but come on, Erron." She scowls at him, so close now. So, so close. Just a few more inches and she can dart toward him, plant her lips *somewhere…*

"Ah, it needs a little work. I think Death will be so grateful I found you that he will personally help me pick a fitting name out, don't you?" His smile accompanies silverware flying, forks and spoons shooting like bullets toward them. Winter cries out and shoves the table over, crawling behind it quickly to hide.

Cassy manages to dodge the attack, crouching and crying out when a fork skims past her ear and a steak knife slashes her calf.

Looking up at him underneath her lashes, she hisses, "Send him my regards, won't you?"

She springs forward, wrapping her arms around Erron's legs and pulling him to the ground. Somehow, she keeps a grip on him. Firm and real, screaming underneath her touch. She bends her head down so fast he doesn't see the movement, her lips brushing against his pant leg.

"You missed." His laugh is deafening as she's flung off him, her body flying and crashing into the tabletop. The table and Cassy are pushed into the wall behind it, trapping Winter between its legs. Winter yelps and Cassy groans, holding her throbbing side with a scowl as warm blood drips from her leg onto the floor.

Why are ghost clothes allowed to act as real clothes? That's a stupid fucking rule. Who comes up with these rules anyway? Maybe it's Death. It's just one more reason for me to hate the guy. I don't—Why do—What rules—

"Come hide with me, Cassy," Winter whispers from behind the table, her head popping up briefly to display a flash of black and electric blue before ducking back down.

"He'll just come through the table." Cassy waves her hand dismissively, carefully pushing herself to her feet. She's going to have to be smarter about this, which is very unfortunate because she is *not* a planner. Especially not in circumstances where her panic won't allow her to think past rapid plans and useless hopes.

"I'm sorry...he's going to do *what*?"

"He's a fucking ghost, Winter. Catch up already!" she snaps, watching Erron wearily. Did Winter not hear her ghost comment earlier? Did she not notice the translucent sheen around Erron's body? A dark grin adorns his face now, a butcher knife floating in front of him. "Oh, fuck."

Cassy dives to the side just as the knife catapults forward, burying itself to the hilt in the table. Winter screams behind it, scrambling to get out. "I didn't think you two were bein' serious! I thought he was a nut job who broke in; I see injuries from those types of situations every day!"

There isn't anywhere to hide in the small room, and certainly nowhere a ghost wouldn't come to find them. Erron still blocks the only exit, besides the window, and she doesn't see herself and Winter finding a way to shatter it to escape under Erron's careful watch. The knife begins wiggling around in the wood, pulling and tugging as Erron attempts to get it free with whatever ghostly powers he possesses, and Cassy tries to form a plan.

How do I escape this situation? What would Ruin do? Where is Cerci? I can't die. I'm not ready to die. Oh, Death will have a field day with me. I wonder if he's as beastly as I pictured? No, no. I can't worry about that. I have to worry about him punishing me or sending me somewhere horrible. Can he do that? I bet he can, as further punishment. I will—I don't—Will he—

As quietly as she can, Cassy whispers, "Okay, Winter. Here is the plan: You distract him, and I'll give him a big ol' kiss." They are both crouching now, partially hidden by a cabinet. Not that it matters. Erron's eyes haven't left Cassy, and she doubts they will anytime soon.

"Distract the ghost so you can *kiss* him? Cassiopeia Jaynes, I could just throttle you right now!" The glare Winter sends her way confirms those heated words as truth.

"Ah, I'd appreciate it if you'd wait your turn in line, Chilly. No jumping ahead, asshole."

Seething, Winter hisses, "And just *how* do you expect me to distract him?"

"With your beauty and grace." Cassy flutters her lashes at her best friend expectantly, sending Winter a sultry smile that can, and has, brought men and women alike to their knees.

"Oh, don't you start with me!" Cassy earned the slap to the back of her head. "I don't understand what's happenin', Cassy. I mean, I believe in ghosts, I just…"

Smiling sadly, she whispers, "You just didn't think they would do things like this?"

"I suppose. And I suppose I didn't think they would be actively searching for my best friend." She sends Cassy a look that could crumble mountains.

"I will explain, Winter. I promise. Just—right now, I need you to distract him, okay? Act cool. Play nice. We will figure out the rest later." Cassy receives a barely perceivable nod in reply.

Winter huffs and puffs as she stands to her full height, running her hands down her wrinkled black band t-shirt before strutting forward. Cassy's heart drops when Erron's gaze turns toward the beautiful woman, eyes roaming down to her short jean skirt with a lascivious smirk. Her fishnet tights were ripped in the frenzy, a hole on her upper thigh showing bare skin that he licks his lips at.

"Sorry, Erron, is it?" Winter smiles at him flirtatiously, hands on her hips as she approaches. Her accent is as thick as his, something familiar, and he watches her with fascination.

"Yes, darlin'. Don't worry, I'm a gentleman; I won't kill you. I only want your friend. She owes me, you see."

Winter laughs heartily, holding a hand to her chest. "Oh, sweetie, that's reassurin'. You're too cute to be scared of."

Cassy crawls behind her slowly, quietly. Erron is distracted by the pretty face, a fact that is not news to her. It isn't a stretch to think he'd act the same way in death as he did in life. She watches as Winter reaches a hand out, one he takes and brings to his lips. She shivers from the touch, and Cassy's certain she felt the cold chill in her own hand. A chill that she's become accustomed to thanks to Ruin.

"Ah, but I like them scared." Hatred boils through Cassy as Winter moves to drop Erron's hand, but he clings on, their intertwined hands falling between them. Cassy leaps toward those clasping hands, not giving Winter a chance to move before she's shoving her best friend as hard as she can. Winter's hand is ripped away, her body stumbling back as Cassy's lips brush against the palm of Erron's hand.

Erron screams, silverware, plates, and bowls exploding around the room. The entire world flashes red as deep, angry, evil words leave his lips in a demonic lilt. "I'm not the only one coming for you, Shadow Kisser." Then he is gone, his body flickering out of existence as though he were just a hallucination the two women had conjured together.

"Oh, I'm so glad he's gone," Cassy breathes, turning to Winter and letting out an embarrassed laugh. But Winter is gaping at her, those dark brown eyes wide and panicked. A hand clutches her thigh, red spilling down her tanned skin and across her fishnets.

Winter is hurt. She's hurt because of me, because of what I am. Is she going to die? She can't die. She's a nurse; she can tell me how to fix her. I will fix her. I'll fix all of this. No one else I love can get hurt because of me. I won't allow it. I should have pushed Winter away before it came to this. I should have known this was inevitable. I can't—I won't—I should—

"No!" Cassy rushes to her, grabs her, and helps her to the ground.

"It's not deep," Winter murmurs, hissing in pain under her breath. Cassy gently moves her hand to see the steak knife sheathed inside her skin. It's not buried to the hilt, but it is a few inches deep.

"What do I do? *What do I do?*" Cassy's shouting in a panic, but it's really not her fault; she's panicked a majority of the time, anyway.

"Calm down, Cassy. Jesus. Just call an ambulance, okay? I'll need stitches."

"Are you joking? Those things are crazy expensive. I can—"

"Well, it's a good thing my best friend—no, my *sister*—offered to pay my medical expenses, isn't it?" Winter squints her eyes, round cheeks puffing up as she sucks in another pained breath.

"How kind of her." Cassy huffs, pulling her phone from her pocket and doing as told. "I can't believe you're playing the sister card right now. You know how that makes me feel." Winter only calls her sister whenever she wants, or needs, something because she knows how much Cassy loves the term of endearment.

She's never been able to tell her no once the sister card has been played.

Winter squints her eyes, ignoring Cassy's attempt to distract her from asking about ghosts. "Don't think I'm gonna just brush past this whole mess, Cassy. I'm just in too much pain to think about ghosts being fuckin' real and you kissin' 'em right now." She tilts her head back onto a cabinet, groaning as Cassy gives their location to the operator. She hangs up promptly after, pinning Winter with a sad smile.

"I know you won't, Chilly. I'll explain. It's just—"

"Cassiopeia!" Rough hands are pulling Cassy away from Winter, running over her face, her arms, her legs. Warm again, not cold like she had come to expect. "Are you okay?"

"Me? Sure. Winter? Ehhhhh."

Ruin glowers at her as he holds up a hand, showing her the blood he found oozing from one of her wounds. "Erron Gates was shouting about the Shadow Kisser and I—"

"You saw Erron Gates?" Cassy's shocked expression alerts him, and he instantly scrambles away from her.

"No, of course not. I just heard about it and ca—"

"That's where you've been, isn't it? You've been with *him*." He's been hanging out with Death, the man who wants to kill her. How horrible is that? She can't believe he would leave her here, alone, just so he could hang out with her soon-to-be murderer. A man he's been lying to. A man he's been hiding secrets from.

"That's preposterous." He clears his throat, looking over to Winter in an attempt to avoid Cassy's gaze. "It doesn't look deep, if that's helpful. I'm familiar with what death looks like; this isn't it. I don't think she'll die."

"No, but you might be dying again if you don't look me in the eyes and tell me you weren't just hanging out with Death." Cassy watches him carefully, expecting him to deny it again.

He doesn't.

"You have to understand, C.J., that my job isn't just a job. Death and I are friends, you know that. Very old ones. I can't just—"

"I don't understand you," she whispers, allowing the hurt to show. "I don't get you at all. You approached me, you know? You came to me and said you wanted to help me, to protect me. I didn't ask you to do that. I didn't *want* your protection. But I took it, and I accepted the friendship that came along with it. I craved it. I craved *you*. But this? Abandoning me after what we did, leaving me defenseless so you can go hang out with your buddy who has an army searching for me? The one you claim not to like all that much? That's low, Ruin. More than low. It's…humiliating, and downright cruel."

"You're never defenseless," Ruin tries, pointedly staring at her lips. He pivots whenever he sees the rage-filled glare she stares back with. "You don't understand…"

"Then make me!" she screams when he stays silent, jabbing a finger into his chest.

How could he do this to me? How could he betray me like this? I knew they were friends, but to abandon me for him? To ignore me after I bared my body to him, after I trusted him to do such wicked things to me…how could he? How could he—How could he—How could he—

He grabs her hand, holding it to his chest gently, firmly. "I can't. I just need you to trust me."

"I do." A tear slips down her cheek, surprising both of them. "And maybe that's the problem. I think I jumped into this friendship a little too quickly. I was too desperate for someone to understand me fully, to accept me entirely. I wanted you and everything you had to offer so badly that I didn't think things through. And...I let my impulse control take over. My need for you has been so consuming that I haven't been thinking straight since the moment I met you. I think trusting you has cost me a lot more than it's cost you."

"My beloved..."

"Don't start with that bullshit. You don't mean it, anyway." Cassy glances over when she sees flashing lights outside the window, a loud knock following shortly after. "Now, if you'll excuse me, I have to take my real, *living* friend to the hospital."

"Cassy, that's harsh—" Winter starts, seeming to grasp the tiniest bit of the situation, but she ignores the injured woman just as fully as she ignores the shocked ghost.

He wants to hang out with Death? That's his prerogative. But he doesn't get to play double agent. He doesn't get to whisper sweet words in her ear, make her long for him, and also get to hang out with the guy he's supposed to be protecting her from. One of them is going to get caught, and Cassy refuses to be a fly trapped in a spider's web. Especially when that web is being woven by a man she should have never allowed into her life in the first place.

Chapter 16

Winter needed six stitches, which she claimed was really good for a stab wound. She spoke with every nurse and doctor at the hospital, laughed off the stab wound as Cassy's clumsiness, and no one asked any probing questions beyond what Winter provided. It was odd for Cassy to see her in that environment, to watch Winter interacting with people who weren't her. She, herself, never interacts with people who aren't her best friend, besides the weekly phone calls and monthly visits to her parents, or people who she doesn't plan on killing. Not that she's been interacting with her best friend lately, anyway. Winter's proudly ignoring her after the entire ghost fiasco and subsequent hospital trip—probably because Cassy admitted she was preparing to cut Winter off because she was scared the news about her...extracurricular activities wouldn't go over well. Winter, in fact, didn't seem all too concerned that Cassy is a ghost hunter with lips that banish lingering souls to Death. She is, however, *pissed* that Cassy thought she couldn't trust Winter with such life-altering information. Cassy's mother found out Winter is giving her the cold shoulder and has gone so far as to berate her during their most recent phone call for causing another "squabble". She deserves it, to be quite frank. She wouldn't be all that angry if Winter took the information she was given and posted it online for the fakes in Cassy's field to find and harass her over; that's the least amount of punishment Cassy deserves for not trusting the only person she knows will never betray her

Ruin left Cerci at Cassy's house that first afternoon and the dog has stayed by her side in the days since. Cerci doesn't appear to be very concerned about her missing owner, seemingly as happy and laid-back as ever. But tonight...tonight, Cassy won't need the dog to stay by her side. Tonight, she's sneaking out and kissing someone who deserves it.

She hasn't had time to do any research or to stalk and hunt as she prefers to do. But that's okay. She knows exactly where to go to find someone deserving, and she knows exactly what to look for in her victims. And what does it matter, anyway? If she gets caught by the police, Death will catch up to her sooner rather than later. She'll be a bird trapped in a cage, and jail time won't matter when she's dead. Despite all the risks, all the what-ifs, she knows she will do it. *She needs it.*

Cassy slips sharp brown heels onto her feet, shoving her lucky taser into her bra with a grin. She steps back, examining herself in the mirror. She looks paler than usual in the blush pink dress, her white and silver hair tied up in a knot behind her head which is covered by a brown bob wig. Her icy blue eyes are green today, the contacts itchy and irritating. She smooths her hands down the soft chiffon dress, adjusting the hanging sleeves so they fall just off her shoulders. She looks dreamy, innocent, *gorgeous.* She'll attract exactly the right type of person, and more importantly, all the wrong types, too.

She uses an app to direct a taxi to her house, waving bye to Cerci before stepping out and locking the door behind her. Out of the corner of her eye, she sees the dog slip through the back wall, that giant body disappearing into the trees behind the house. Probably to snitch on her, if she had to guess. Cerci and Ruin have some kind of weird repertoire going on, a secret language she is not privy to. Not that it's any of her business how they communicate. Not that she cares.

I do care. I shouldn't. I shouldn't hope that Ruin comes running back, begging me for forgiveness. I shouldn't want to give it to him. He deserves my anger. I deserve to be alone. I should—I won't—I deserve—

"That dog is giant," the driver remarks as Cassy bends to click her seat belt into place, jerking his head toward the back of the house. "I only saw its back paws, but...wow. You must feel really safe with that thing around."

She grins, tilting her head up as the buckle clicks. "She's a big baby. *I'm* the bitch everyone has to worry about."

"Oh..." The man has the good sense not to say another word for the forty-five-minute drive into town.

The bar Cassy waltzes into is dark and grimy, the smell overwhelmingly horrible. Not zombie perfume, like the ointment that now resides in her first aid kit, but...still horrible. She makes herself ignore the smell because there are plenty of bodies inside, plenty of victims to choose from and hide among. She swings her hips as she walks to the bar on the far right, waving at the bartender with a shy smile. The look she receives in return can best be described as an annoyed snarl, a finger rising to tell her to wait.

"She's always this grumpy," the woman beside her says with a light laugh, a hand reaching out to touch her side boldly. "Why don't you sit with me?"

Cassy is pulled down onto the stool beside the woman, her gaze falling onto the beautiful specimen before her. The woman's dark red hair has this entrancing, messy look, the curls brilliant and wild. Her dark eyes are enchanting, drawing her straight to them. It's almost enough to distract her, almost enough to have her missing the feeling of that hand attempting to roam lower.

She laughs, taking the woman's tanned hand by the wrist, moving it away from her waist, and raising a brow. "You haven't even bought me a drink yet."

"What do you prefer?" The grin that greets her is infectious, almost a replica of the one Cassy sends all her victims. It's a red flag for her, and her guard raises immediately in response.

"Something...sweet," she purrs, leaning forward to subtly reveal more of her chest while forcing a blush to her cheeks

"Don't worry, you'll love this." The bartender actually approaches when this woman waves, her words lost in the blaring music before the bartender disappears again. Her lustful gaze falls back on Cassy, heated and sultry. Cassy allows her eyes to roam down that curvy body, allowing her gaze to linger on the generously sized breasts covered in the thin blue satin of the stranger's dress. It's not a difficult chore; she's always been one who loves to admire.

"Are you a local?" The woman's question is simple and conversational, as though she's actually interested. It's a question most scammers ask before stealing from their prey; easier targets are only here for the weekend.

"Oh, no. Just visiting for the weekend. A little getaway." Cassy emits a shy laugh, wondering what her game is. Cassy knows she must have one: she can tell from the way the woman's eyebrow keeps twitching. Nervous tick, she assumes.

"How fun." Cassy's drink slides in front of her, and she takes a small sip to appease the stranger. The woman watches her lips closely before continuing. "So you're here alone?"

"As alone as I've ever been." Cassy pouts, as though this is upsetting.

Maybe I should be upset. I really have been entirely alone for far too long. I had Winter. Kind of. But do I have her now? Will she forgive me? Will she care that Death is hunting me? I think she will. Will she ever text me again? Will she ever let me fully explain? She shut down after I told her how long I've hidden my secret, after I admitted to deceiving her because I wanted to protect myself from an emotional loss that was never coming. Ruin is gone, too. I don't know if he will come back, either. Will I—Does she—I can—

"I'm single, too." She misinterprets Cassy, sighing loudly. Cassy doesn't think she is really alone, though. There's a ring imprint on her left hand, exactly where a wedding ring would go. She wonders if this woman's partner is hiding around here somewhere, waiting for her to snag their next victim. She wonders if this is some fun game they like to play on the weekends, foreplay of some sort. If she had done some research on the woman beforehand, she would have known something like that.

"I only asked because a guy is staring at you, over there by the pool tables?"

Cassy frowns, turning over her shoulder to glance in that direction. Sure enough, a strange man is staring her down. He's watching her as though she's dinner, as though he's about to eat her whole and refuse to spit a single bone back out…in a literal way. A shiver runs down her spine, and she shakes her head as she turns back to see the woman's elbow tucking back into her side.

"Just some creep. I'm used to it, unfortunately. What did you say your name was?" Cassy picks up her drink again, bringing it toward her face and subtly sniffing. Nothing smells different, but the surface is a little foggy. *The fucker tried to roofie me,* she thinks haughtily.

"I didn't." A classic line from someone like her: a trickster, a cheat, a thief. Oh, this kill will be so fun.

"How mysterious. I'm C.J." Cassy pretends to be shy again, sucking the drink up the straw but not allowing any in her mouth or down her throat. The woman seems satisfied with the performance, her posture relaxing. She must have marked Cassy as a rich target, with her designer dress and expensive jewelry. To be fair, this outfit *did* cost her over five thousand dollars, mostly because of the jewelry. It looks more expensive than it really is, though. That's why she bought the set in the first place.

"C.J." She says the name with a hint of humor, as though it's comical.

"Don't like it?"

"What does it stand for?"

"Nothing." Cassy shrugs, feigning ignorance. "My mother just liked it."

"She sounds like a smart woman, to do things because she likes them and not letting anyone convince her otherwise." Another purr, followed by her eyes dropping down to Cassy's barely sipped drink. "You don't like it?"

"It's delicious, but I'm a slow drinker. And a lightweight." Cassy lets her eyes glimmer with playfulness, smiling flirtatiously. "I think I'm already feeling it." She forces her body to sway, forces a bubbling laugh from her throat. "She pours heavily."

"That she does!" A wicked laugh now, one that fades as the woman hops down and gestures that she'll be back. Cassy takes the opportunity to pour half the drink in the sink on the other side of the bar, leaning forward and splashing it out quickly before anyone looks her way. She slides back down on her seat moments before the woman returns, the man from the pool tables by her side. Ah, so she *does* have an accomplice.

"This is Shane! Isn't he cute?" Cassy nods enthusiastically, pretending to be more out of it than she is. Though, to be honest, she's not sure how, exactly, a roofied person would act. She's kind of winging this entire trip, after all.

"Very," Cassy shouts over the music, slurring the word.

"Do you want to go somewhere quieter with us? We have a room at the hotel next door, if you want to join?" His voice is rough, like a smoker's. He shoves his hands down into his ripped jeans, boots poking out from underneath. He doesn't don a cowboy hat like most men flaunting around town do, but it's clear by his rugged look and the deep, country voice he possesses that he's a Tennessee native.

"Sure!" Cassy giggles and hops off the stool, stumbling into his body. She lets her hands graze his backside, her eyelashes fluttering innocently. It's a dangerous game, but it's one she enjoys so dearly.

I could die. I could live. I could get the itch in my brain scratched. Death could find me. Screw that guy. I won't give up the things I love because of my fear. These people deserve it. They were going to take advantage of me. Probably. Or steal my money. I can't wait to kill them, to end their lives and save many more in exchange. Will Ruin be mad? What would Winter think of this? What if—I could—Ruin is—

They each take Cassy by an arm and help her out into the cold night's breeze, chuckling at their success. She finds herself wishing for the coat she left in her room in her rush to sneak out.

She pretends to drag her feet and to be completely delusional as they drag her through an abandoned alleyway toward the back door of the place they claim is a hotel. She's inclined to think otherwise, considering how rundown it appears from the outside. Come to find out, the inside isn't much better.

The inside reveals aging wallpaper and narrow halls, the permanent smell of cigarette smoke mixed with mold hanging in the air. The ceilings have splotched watermarks, and the carpet is torn in so many places she loses count. She even thinks she spots rat droppings in a few places, but those can also be weirdly dark colored stains. Hopefully not blood. She doesn't let her gaze linger as they lead her to the third door on the right, pulling out a key to open the wooden door that looks like it's been kicked in a few times.

She's been in this situation so many times before that fear isn't a consideration at this point. She doesn't worry about what's going to happen to her or the repercussions of her actions. Why would she? It's all a fun, deadly game to her. A sick, twisted one, she's positive Winter would say. Well, fuck that. This brings her so much joy, eases so many aching thoughts, that it doesn't matter what Winter *might* say about it. She needs it more than she needs Winter to text her back, more than she needs her friend's acceptance. More than she needs Ruin's, too. This is for *her*, and she won't back down just because those two may be judging her for it.

"You are so pretty, Cassy," the woman purrs as Cassy is pulled through the doorway, the door slamming shut behind them. Cassy only giggles again, mind spinning. Did she tell them her name was Cassy? No, she's fairly certain she didn't.

"I can see what he likes about you," a new voice says from the corner, a woman with black hair and green eyes. No, not just a woman. *A ghost.*

"Fuck," Cassy hisses under her breath, dropping the roofied act. She yanks her arms away from her captors, managing to free one and using it to lunge at the woman who holds the other. Her lips make contact with the woman's hand and her gasp is the last noise she makes before collapsing to the ground, dead. Shane cries out in outrage, surging for Cassy so quickly that she can do nothing but brace for impact.

She hisses as he makes contact, his body landing on top of hers as she's knocked to the floor and onto her stomach. She should have known it wouldn't be this easy to find a target without doing any research beforehand. She should have known that she was not safe on her own anymore. Not after Erron Gates found her. Because if a newly departed soul like his hunted her down, why wouldn't one who's been hanging around a little longer? One who wants to stick around on this earthly plane?

I'm stupid. So, so stupid. They say blondes have more fun, but I think that's bullshit. Blonds just get into more trouble. I should dye my hair. This brown wig didn't save me, though. Maybe just shave it all off, then. Would I still, technically, be considered blonde, since my natural color faded to silver long ago? Oh, I never got to tell Winter I'm sorry. I'll never see Ruin again. I can't die like this. I won't—I can't—If I—

Cassy jerks underneath the weight of the heavy, very real body above her. The man isn't large, but he is strong. He has a lean sort of look, the muscles underneath the arms pinning her down pulsing. She has no chance, and they both know it.

"Now, now, Cassy, where are your manners?"

She jerks again, crying out when she feels something stabbing into her side. A syringe, she thinks. What did he inject her with? Poison, maybe? Oh, she hopes not. She really didn't plan on dying today.

Whatever is inside her works quickly; her limbs are suddenly heavy and incapable of lifting themselves. She thinks...she thinks she's paralyzed. She can't even move her lips, can't rely on the one precious weapon she possesses.

A boot lands in her side, her ribs aching as she's pushed onto her back. Somehow, the thought, *At least they weren't steel-toed boots*, rings through her buzzing mind. "Don't worry, honey. We aren't going to kill you yet." Shane grins, glancing over at the female ghost.

I wonder how they met. Does he realize she's a ghost? Can I only tell because I've been around them, because I recognize the slight hue to their skin? The man isn't dead, so what does he get out of this? He doesn't seem upset about the dead woman I presumed to be his wife. Will she come back as a ghost? Oh, I don't want to be haunted. Or hunted down again. Will Ruin help me? Did Cerci go tattle like I suspected? Will I—Can he—Maybe if—

"We are waiting on our special guest to show up," the ghost confirms, sighing as she looks down at the body on the dingy carpet. Pale, lifeless. "Ruin, you call him, I think?"

No. They aren't here to cash in their prize to Death. They're here for Ruin. Are they trying to blackmail him? Did they find out he is double-crossing Death? Do they think he can offer them a better deal?

Her mind races with jumbled thoughts, the only thing it can do as they sit in silence and wait for Ruin. She doesn't want him to show up, even if they kill her. Even if she's stuck like this forever. She'd rather be stuck like this than know it's her fault Ruin was found out by Death. She doesn't know what kind of punishment Ruin would undergo, but...it would have to be truly horrible, coming from Death. Even if they are friends. *Especially* because they are friends. His betrayal won't go unpunished, and he'll be made an example of so no one else thinks to follow in his footsteps. The thought of Ruin being tortured, or worse, leaves a cold, slimy fear running through her veins.

"Maybe he won't show up," Shane says after an hour passes, shrugging nonchalantly. "And none of those damn reapers showed up to take Lara's soul."

"That's because she kissed Lara, idiot. Her soul wasn't on any of the lists; all the reapers will feel the shift that an early soul brings. That means Ruin knows exactly who we have, and he has instructed the others not to come collect. But if he doesn't want to show up willingly, then we will make him." Something glints in the dim lighting, something sharp and long. Cassy feels it before she sees it, the blade sinking into the soft spot just below her ribs where a needle punctured not long ago. "She won't die immediately, but..."

She can't even shout, can't twist and plant her lips on the ghost and send her off to whatever plane she deserves to be on. She can only watch as blood trickles out of the wound, as the ghost yanks the blade back out and allows the blood to pool. *As if the carpet wasn't dirty enough,* she thinks bitterly.

Within seconds, Ruin appears. At least, she thinks it's that quick. She feels a little lost between the shock of the stinging stab and the way her mind has become so addled from whatever she was injected with. Not that she can properly tell time on the best of days anyway, considering the time blindness her ADHD has gifted her.

Ruin and Cerci flicker into existence in the doorway, his face calm and deadly. Cerci growls lowly under her breath, no longer the sweet, innocent dog Cassy knows. Ruin radiates a dark energy, a scythe gripped tightly in his hand. It's taller than he is, dark and shiny. A pattern of vines wraps around the handle, the blade itself carved with the words "don't fear the reaping". His long brown hair is pulled back today, the silver streak stark amid all the darkness. His tall form looms over Shane, his shadow seeming to take up the entirety of the room.

Why is he holding a Scythe? I've never seen him look so...hot. I like this version of Ruin. He'll probably destroy these two idiots in the time it takes me to blink. I hope he saves me. Not that I need to be saved. I'm an independent woman, after all. This situation just got a little out of hand. I am bleeding kind of badly, so I hope he does it quickly. I wonder if he is going to slice them in half. That would be a little sickening. I wish—I hope—If he—

"You called?" His eyes meet Cassy's briefly, flickering away quickly to focus on the two threats lingering in the room. She tries to focus on the smooth copper skin of his face, staring at his cheekbones and jawline to avoid meeting that gaze again.

"We did." The ghost's green eyes dance with excitement and anticipation, her body involuntarily drifting closer to the dark cloud that is Ruin. "We have a proposition."

"Do you?" Those hazel eyes are on Cassy again, hardening as they fixate on the slick blood leaking from her side. The usually subtle golden ring around his irises begins to shine, illuminating his striking face in a way that makes him look positively frightful.

"We found the girl, as requested. We didn't kill her, as requested. But we want more than just survival in our ghost forms."

"Our? One of you is still very much alive. Let me fix that for you." He swings the scythe so sharply that Shane doesn't have time to move, the blade cutting through him in one harsh movement. But his body doesn't split in half. It only collapses, a lifeless shell. Shane's ghost doesn't appear from it, apparently sent off with the cleave of the scythe. Hopefully, to find Death and submit to crossing over.

"Okay. Okay, I see we've upset you." The ghost drifts backward, wavering in and out of existence. She moves to retreat through the walls, but her body is blocked by some unknown force. She can't go anywhere. Cassy would laugh in amusement if she were capable.

"Oh, no, dear. I'm not upset. *I. Am. Livid.*" Ruin pounces, his fingers elongating with nails sharpened to a point, and hisses in her face, "You dare insult me? You dare bring me this prize and try to request more? The offer is generous enough. I will not tolerate any attempts to negotiate."

"But all I wanted was—"

"I care not what you wanted. You've practically killed the Shadow Kisser. What use is she without her life? Her power? *You fool.*" Ruin grips her by the neck with those scarily long fingers, angling his scythe up to her neck. Then he grins, the sight so wickedly evil that a chill runs down Cassy's spine. And, to her utter horror, it isn't fear she feels but *delight.* "I think, as a reward for your poorly executed plan, you will receive a very special prize. *A kiss.*"

"No! No, you swore!" She's screeching now, howling and kicking as he drags the ghost toward Cassy's immobile body. Shallow tears run down the ghost's flickering face, noises of panic and fear escaping her lips. Ruin shoves her down to her knees, pressing a foot on her back and pushing her down. Cerci steps forward to growl directly in her face, sharp canines on display.

"Go on, Christina Zavala. Kiss her goodbye."

Christina weeps heartily, her face bending over Cassy's. Her dark hair falls across them, the long waves brushing against

Cassy's cheeks and disappearing over and over again as she shakes her head.

"Please—" Christina tries to beg, hands on the floor on either side of Cassy. Her chest brushes up against Cassy's, her face so near that Cassy could lean up and do it herself if she could only move. Wait...she can, she thinks. Her toes are wiggling. Her fingers, too.

"Why should I listen to your begging when you did not listen to hers? Why should I care for your last wishes when you did not give her the option to voice hers? You made a choice when you stole Cassiopeia Jaynes from me. *It was the wrong one.* I do not tolerate ghosts who try to steal what is rightfully *mine*." That scythe is now on Christina's back, threatening her once more. Whatever that thing does, the ghost is terrified of it. Maybe it doesn't *just* send them to Death? Maybe it damns their souls.

I hope that scythe brings a fate worse than death. Even if it means that Ruin is a liar. Even if it means I've been betrayed by him again. He loves to hide things from me. To pretend he isn't something that he is. I do that too, though. Maybe we aren't so different. Can he see that between us? Does he care? He must, if he's claiming me so boldly. Should I be upset that he's being so possessive when we aren't even together? No, how can I be mad when he came to rescue me? I could kiss him right now for saving me. I could not kiss him so he will do it again. I could—I would—Even if—

"I thought that you would want this," she weeps, hiccuping. "I thought this was the best way to get what I wanted. My daughter has passed on, and I thought she could be brought back. I just wanted to see her again."

"Dearly departed souls do not just *come back*, you fool. And I would not dare ask one to do so. You'll see why soon enough. Go ahead, Christina. Kiss—"

With a hesitant, scratchy voice, Cassy interrupts, "Kiss me and *die*."

Chapter 17

Wet, salty tears hit Cassiopeia's cheeks as Christina's lips brush against hers, soft and resistant. She smiles into the kiss, feeling satisfaction as the ghost's body disappears. Christina's weight is lifted off her chest, her tears sticking to Cassy's face. And then Ruin is replacing the ghost, leaning over her and holding her cheeks in his hands. One roams down to touch her wound, coming back seeped in warm blood. He purses his lips, and just like that, she knows it's bad.

"Your nurse friend." The words are choked, barely coming from his lips as Cerci whines nearby. "Can she heal you?"

"Maybe." It's an effort to get out the words, an effort to breathe properly with him looking at her like this. Like she's his entire world, and he was about to watch that world crash and burn before him.

She watches as he pulls something from his pocket, a jar of green paste. He sticks two fingers inside, swallowing so hard the veins in his throat pulse. "Eat this."

She opens her mouth obediently, closing it around his fingers as they push inside. It tastes like chocolate mint, and she absent-mindedly licks around his fingers to get every bit she can. It's not like the disgusting ointment he presented her with last time; this was entirely pleasant. She lets out a tiny, appreciative moan, the noise a small hum in the back of her throat. Ruin ignores it, quickly pulling his fingers out, resulting in a small *pop* that feels too dirty for either party to acknowledge. "So good," she whispers on an exhale, breathy and full of pain, in an attempt to nullify the awkward moment.

He only nods, jaw ticking as he clenches his teeth. After a small pause, he says, "This is going to feel strange. So just-just bear with me, okay?"

Cassy is scooped up into his arms, a cry of pain unwillingly leaving her lips. How do they always find themselves in this position? Her injured because of a situation that *he* put her in? Why does she keep doing this to herself? *Why does she like it?*

She isn't sure how she knows, but she's certain they fade out of existence. Exactly the way he always does, only this time, she is along for the ride. Her body pinches and pulls, the sensation not painful but horrifically uncomfortable. She groans in discomfort as she's stretched and twisted, as she's pulled apart and put back together in a matter of mere moments. Before she can blink, they are sitting in Winter's dark apartment. Cerci didn't travel with them, either left behind or directed to go somewhere else. Hopefully, to distract Death so he doesn't sense how near she came to joining him permanently. *Again.*

The lights flicker, revealing Winter sitting at her computer with a pair of black headphones over her ears. She looks up at the lights, frowning when her computer game flickers, too. Then she turns her head over her shoulder, screeching when she spots Ruin illuminated in the brief flashes. The screams come to an abrupt halt when she beholds Cassy in his arms, coated in blood.

"*What did you do now?*" She stands, tossing the headphones down and racing over. She's only in a large t-shirt, one shoulder exposed.

She always looks so cute like this, messy and relaxed. She's usually so tense because of her job, because of the way her parents treated her growing up. She always feels this need to be perfect, to be put-together. I wish—She is—Her parents—

"It's not his fault, Winter." The words are soft and slow coming from Cassy, a blatant lie that Winter has the courtesy to ignore.

"Lay her on the couch," Winter directs, glaring at Ruin so intensely that Cassy is sure he would keel over and die if he wasn't already dead. She leaves to go out of the room, veering off into a hallway that Cassy knows leads to a bedroom with a conjoined bathroom.

"I'm going to bleed all over it," Cassy says lowly, weakly pushing on Ruin's chest. He ignores her, laying her down as instructed anyway. He has the decency to settle her so her wounded side is hanging off the edge, more likely to bleed onto the carpet than the couch itself. "What did you give me earlier?"

"Something to help clot the blood. You could have bled out."

"I think she missed all the important bits. If she hadn't, I *would* have bled out by now."

"You don't know th—"

"Hold this." Winter is shoving something into Ruin's face, a giant bowl of water, by the looks of it. He takes it, scowling at her, then glances back at Cassy. He doesn't say a word, though, probably because he knows it wouldn't be very wise of him to do so.

"I love you," Cassy tells her best friend, hoping she understands the apology.

"I love you, too, idiot." She can see the sterile cloths Winter pulls from a small box, probably a first aid kit she's created. She has given dozens of those to Cassy over the years. "I've not been ignoring you because I'm mad about the ghost huntin' stuff, you know. I just needed time to process that. I've been ignoring you because of the implications. Because I don't think you fuckin' trust me and that *hurts*. Because I'm positive you're hidin' more secrets and I think you still aren't willin' to let 'em go. You're my sister, and I'd do anythin' for you. I don't know what made you think otherwise."

Cassy hisses as a wet cloth hits the wounded skin, the pain bearable but annoying. "You could have just said so. We could have talked it out. We could have—"

"You just popped up in my house with a hot ghost and are currently bleedin' on my couch, Cassiopeia Jaynes. I don't owe you shit." Winter pauses her diligent moves, looking up at Ruin with her eyebrows scrunched together. "It's clotted already. This is too deep to be clotted already."

"It'll start again if you don't stitch it up," Ruin warns behind the bowl of water, his face a mask of deadly calm.

What is in these weird concoctions he always has? They work like magic. Alchemy, I think he said once. Does he make them? Does he know someone who does? Does he get them from Death? Why do they stink so bad? I don't really care where he gets them from; I just appreciate how well they heal me. I don't—Why does—Does he—

"Right. I probably don't even want to know," she murmurs under her breath, going back to her work. Cassy's not sure how many cloths it takes to clean the wound, how many dips into that water, but Winter gets it done. She disinfects the site with alcohol, which burns like hell and leaves tears cascading from Cassy's eyes like a waterfall, before pulling out a needle and dental floss with a grin. "This is all I have, so...we're going to make it work."

The needle digging into Cassy's flesh isn't as horrible as she imagined it would be. She doesn't watch, though. She doesn't want to see how many stitches it takes, and she certainly doesn't want to see how large the wound actually is. She decides to let her friend take care of it all. Winter's steady hands are a comfort and a relief.

"What did you two get up to this time?" Winter's question comes after a long bout of silence, as though she was working up the courage to ask it.

"I was ghostnapped." Cassy turns just in time to see Winter's face, a priceless reaction she wishes she could have caught on camera. Shock, awe, and most importantly, flabbergast.

"You went willingly," Ruin snaps, glaring at Cassy. The look is full of deep irritation, and she can practically see him thinking of proper punishments for her actions. She shivers as she remembers the last time she received a punishment from Ruin, briefly distracted until he hisses, "You took a risk that didn't pay off."

"I had to! If I hadn't—" Cassy snaps her mouth shut, realizing all too late that Winter has no idea about her extracurricular activities.

Will she care? Killing is different from ghost hunting, even if it is for a good cause. Will she be upset? Will she turn me in? Will it matter to her that I've saved more lives than I've taken? Will she—Will she—Will she—

"You didn't have to do *shit*," he seethes, bending so he can stare directly into her soul. Something dark dances behind his hazel eyes, ominous and bone-chilling. "You did it because you're a selfish, entitled brat. You did it because you have no self-control."

Cassy swallows, wishing he could see inside her mind. Wishing he could understand how she isn't *any* of those things, but no one ever believes her when she voices the thought aloud. Teachers, friends, her parents—everyone has voiced to her before that she has a deeply selfish side, that she has very little impulse control, and those things will always negatively impact her. It never hurt from them, but from Ruin...it's *excruciating*. "You don't understand. It isn't like that. *I had to.* If I hadn't, my mind would have—"

"I don't want to hear your pitiful, weak excuses." He bends over to tap on the lip print on her arm, his touch cold and harsh. "We had a deal, remember?" He had asked her to stop killing for a while, to hunt ghosts instead, while she hid from Death.

"I didn't say I would stop forever," she whispers, hating herself for feeling like she owes an explanation to the man. The ghost. The...whatever he actually is.

He smacks his lips as though tasting disappointment. "No. I suppose you didn't."

She turns that anger at herself onto him, glaring harshly in challenge. "And it's not like you've been very good at protecting me, Ruin. Those ghosts were trying to bait *you*, not Death, who is getting closer to me every day, by the way. What are you planning on doing about that, because I really don't want to be stuck in another situation like this because of you."

Ruin doesn't say anything, only watches her with a careful neutrality for a long time before setting the bowl down and disappearing.

"Will he be back?" Winter is putting away her tools now, apparently having finished while the two of them argued.

"I'm sure. He's like a bad rash that no ointment works on." Cassy glances down at the red, puckered skin on her side, impressed with Winter's handiwork. She would hope it was good, with Winter being an E.R. nurse and all.

"You two seem to be havin' a lovers' spat," she remarks, strutting over to her sink to dump the bowl of red-tinted water and wash her hands.

"We aren't lovers, remember?"

"Eh, one can only dream."

"I'm not allowed to dream it."

Winter turns to watch Cassy over her shoulder, a sad smile on her lips. "You never let yourself loose, do you?"

Cassy stiffens, running her fingers over the new stitches in her side absentmindedly and doing her damnedest not to pick at them. "I'm not a dog on a leash, Chilly. Ruin is…Ruin is good. Fun. Different, like me. But it can't happen. I don't think he wants to be attached to someone like me, and I can't let myself be attached to someone like him."

"Someone dead, you mean?" Winter shuts the water off, slamming her hand towel down and spinning toward Cassy with fury dancing in her brown eyes. "Not that bein' dead is a requirement for you to shove people away. You do that to your livin' friends, too."

"That isn't fair, Chilly. I—"

"Don't call me that right now. I haven't forgiven you yet, Missy. I won't until you tell me what in the blazin' *hells* is going on. I have *tried*, Cassy. I have tried to think of logical reasons for what happened that day. But I can't find a single one. I'm missin' a piece of the story, and you need to give it to me."

Cassy sucks in a deep breath, refusing to meet her gaze. "I can't te—"

"You can't tell me? *You can't tell me?* I'm your only friend, Cassy. If you can't tell me somethin', then who can you tell?"

"No one." Cassy releases a small sob, her lips quivering as she tries to rein everything in.

"No one but Ruin, you mean?" Winter's in front of her now, crouched down and grabbing her by the knees. "He knows whatever this secret of yours is and that's why you're mad, isn' it? Because you think he won't accept it—won't accept *you* fully. Or maybe you two are caught up over the kissin' stuff? I know it sucks, but surely you two can work around that?"

"It's more complicated than that. The kissing is just the tip of the iceberg, Winter, and it's so much more than not accepting what I am. I don't think he minds it, actually. He's just being protective. That's why I'm so mad, Winter. Because what right does he have to be protective of me? What right do I have to let him? The friendship, or whatever we have, is temporary. He can't protect me forever; that's become clear over the past few weeks. I'm being hunted, Winter, and not even he can change that."

"You're…bein' hunted? What did you *do*, Cassy? Is it the police? The F.B.I.? Or is it a ghost thing?" She looks so worried, so scared, that another sob escapes Cassy. And that look of determination, of fierceness, tells her everything she needs to know. Winter won't turn her in to whoever is hunting her, no matter what she's done. She'll stay by Cassy's side no matter what happens. No matter who comes for her in return. She should never have thought otherwise, should never have let her fear keep her from trusting Winter with the truth.

I don't deserve a friend like her. I should have told her already. I shouldn't have lied. What does it matter if I lied when I murdered, too? They say one sin is no less than another. Killing, lying, thieving: It's all the same. When Death catches me, will I go to hell? Will Ruin stop him? Will I be a ghost? I don't want to be a ghost. I don't want to stick around. Maybe if—Will I—I should—

Cassy sucks in a deep breath, gripping Winter's hands tightly and tilting her head up to meet her friend's eyes. Slowly, she opens her mouth and tells Winter the truth.

Chapter 18

By the time Cassy makes it home, it's nearly a full day later. Winter let her stay and sleep on the couch after confessing her darkest sins and bawling her eyes out for hours. Winter held her and let her release it all, not saying a word until she had finished. Then, and only then, did her best friend say, "They deserved it. You did the right thing."

Cassy whispered back, "Death doesn't care about that."

"I'll drag him back by the ears and give him a good talkin' to, honey. Don't you worry about that man." And that's all she would say on the matter. After seeing ghosts (and Ruin holding a scythe), Cassy supposes Winter didn't think it was too much of a stretch to believe that Death is a real, literal figure, too. Considering Winter's dark tastes, she is probably thrilled about the notion.

Cassy fell asleep not long after that conversation and was woken up by Winter, who practically shoved Cassy out the door so she wouldn't be late for her night shift at the nearby hospital. She deserved more than the brief hug Cassy was able to gift her, but that's an issue for later.

Cassy groans as she enters the cold rental house, wincing with each step. The pain isn't horrible—Winter managed to find some painkillers she had stashed in her medicine cabinet from a wisdom teeth surgery three years ago—but it's not nonexistent, either. And the deep cold brought on by a Southern January doesn't help things, either.

"Hi, sweetheart," she purrs to Cerci as the giant dog comes bounding up, sliding to a stop at her feet. Cerci's heavy tail pounds against the floor, her tongue hangs out, and her mouth tilts in a dog's version of a smile. "Thank you for coming to save me last night. You're such a good girl. Yes, you are."

Dogs are more loyal than humans could ever dream of being; this one in particular. But even she would not pick me over her master. Does she only protect me because Ruin commanded her to? Does she only stay out of loyalty to him, not me? Does she love me the way I love her? I should never have let her in. Animals sucker me in too fast. I don't—Does she—Dogs are—

"I helped, too. Does that make me a good boy?"

She reaches to pet under Cerci's chin, ignoring the man in her bedroom entryway—and the fluttering, breathless feeling his words ignite in her stomach—entirely. After a few heartbeats that she uses to calm her breathing, she says, "I'm not entirely sure what you are anymore, Ruin. Ghost, reaper, boy? All of the above, maybe?"

"Does it matter what I am? I'm asking sincerely."

She glances up to meet those hooded hazel eyes, his expression that of someone who is bracing themselves for defeat. "I—" *Does* it really matter? She likes Ruin. He's...he's like her. Complicated, morally corrupt, and most importantly, understanding. She thought he was judging her before, that he didn't want her to kill because he thought it was wrong. But she understands the truth after repeating his little outburst from yesterday in her head over and over for the past twenty-four hours. Ruin wanted her to stop because he *knew*. He knew something like this would happen and he was trying to keep her out of trouble. Too bad she tends to find trouble, anyway. Or maybe it just has an unhealthy attachment to her. "No. It doesn't. But I would like to think that you trust me enough to tell me."

"It isn't a trust thing." She watches him dip his head solemnly, that tense stance of his slowly easing. "I don't have a choice in the matter."

"Because of Death, right?" Just saying his name leaves a chill down her spine, has her blood freezing from the inside out in fear, in sadness, in anticipation. "Will he...will he know what happened? Will you be punished?"

"You're worried about me being punished?" A scoff, followed by a hand running down the stubble on his cheek. Then he pulls out a cigarette, something she hasn't noticed him doing lately. After a singular puff, his face contorts into a frown and he continues. "No. No, the only one who will punish me is myself."

"It isn't your fault. I jumped into that situation head-on. I dived off the cliff of my own volition. Nothing you said would have stopped me. I know I was trying to put all the blame on you, but...my poor decisions aren't your fault."

"It *is* my fault!" His fists slam into the trim on the doorway, shaking the entire wall. "I should have locked you inside this house and never let you out."

"Should you have now?" Her pounding steps echo as she approaches, steam practically leaving her ears. "Maybe you should have handcuffed me to my bed, too. Maybe you should have duct-taped my mouth shut so no one would hear me scream. Maybe you should have—"

He leans forward, puffing smoke in her face and barking, "That's *enough*, Cassiopeia."

"I'm only offering helpful suggestions. You know, since you seem intent on locking me up like a prisoner. And killing yourself all over again with these disgusting things." She is so angry, so vengeful, that she plucks the cigarette right from his lips and flings it to the floor. She promptly steps on it, lips twitching as she watches him try to hide his irritated snarl.

If he locks me up, I'll never forgive him. I'll never forget. Ruin wouldn't do that, though. He's only saying it because he's angry with himself. I'm angry with him, too. And myself. I'm angry with the world. I'm angry with Death. I'm angry—I'm hurt—I'm bitterly—

"I tried to quit, you know. I tried because you said it was a disgusting habit, and I didn't want you to be disgusted with *me*." Cassy's breath stumbles and rolls, and she barely has time to retrieve it before Ruin grabs her by the shoulders. The move is so sudden, so forceful, so *urgent*, that she gasps as he pulls her into his strong body with little hesitation and snarls out, "If I hadn't dragged you into my life, yours wouldn't be in danger."

"We all die." She swallows hard, tilting her head up defiantly. He wants her, has wanted her from the very beginning. She has been trying to lock it all away, and it seems he's been doing the same. "Even Shadow Kissers."

His eyes shutter close as he flinches, as though the idea of her dying is painful. "Your time isn't up yet."

"I suppose a reaper would know, wouldn't he?"

"I can't—" A deep inhale and exhale, a sharp click of his tongue as his eyes flicker back open to stare into her own. His hands move from her shoulders to her waist, fingers clenching into the fabric of her t-shirt. "I take souls where they need to go. Send them to the right place. It's why I—it's why I never stuck around for your ghost hunting adventures. They all know my face. And if they don't, then one look at me and they will know. Ghosts don't see the same thing you do when they look at me, Cassiopeia. I'm an ugly, abhorrent beast. Ghosts see my true form."

Cassy reaches out to touch that supposedly abhorrent face, running her thumb along his stubbly jawline softly. His hands clench tighter around her waist, his entire body shaking underneath her touch. She isn't sure if it's out of fury with himself or because he is struggling to maintain his composure when she's touching him so bravely, so openly. "You aren't ugly or abhorrent. Not to me. I've met a lot of people in this life, Ruin. Most of them are more monstrous than you can ever dream of being."

He swallows hard, licking his lips and watching her with drawn-in brows. "You don't hate me for dragging you into this? You aren't terrified of what I can do to you or your friends or your family?"

"A teddy bear like you?" She clucks her tongue as he chuckles softly under his breath, shaking his head roughly at her. "Why would I ever fear a reaper? You are the hand of Death, you aren't the act of dying itself."

"I'm so sorry." His words are a whisper in the still air, a confession to a priest who isn't there.

"Don't be. I started this journey. I *earned* Death's wrath. But you haven't earned mine. You have stood by my side, tried to help me, even when you couldn't be here. Even when you were at the beck and call of the very person who is trying to kill me."

Death, his friend. Death, whom he works for. Death, whom he lies to. Does he lie to me just as easily? Does he keep the truth for me and me alone? Does he want me to know him just like I want him to know me? I don't want to die. I don't want to lose Ruin. I don't want to hide the rest of my life. I want—Does he—Death is—

"Look what I've done to you," he murmurs, twisting a lock of her white hair. The beautiful silver is almost entirely gone now, leeched into white after the latest near-death experience. "You were too close to death."

Cassy smiles bitterly, whispering, "Too close to Death and not nearly close enough to you."

Ruin pauses, a pained look on his face as he lifts a hand to rub a finger along her bottom lip. A reckless move he's done more than once lately. Will her kiss hurt him like it does the others? Will it send a reaper to Death's doorstep? She isn't sure, and she doesn't want to risk the reaper in front of her to find out. But Ruin...Ruin is leaning in, anyway. He's leaning in and he's—

His lips are warm and soft, his hands pulling her impossibly close. Her own lips move on instinct; the self-restraint to pull back is non-existent. She greedily takes his kiss, greedily presses herself into his body. She practically melts into him, his strong hands gripping onto her hips to keep her upright. It isn't a slow and tantalizing kiss; it isn't a test to see what she can take. It's a whirlwind of movement, a direction of passion, and it's everything she has dreamed of for years. She's missed this intimacy, missed the way it feels to just...*make out.* Missed not worrying about her lips killing her partners.

She can't help but let out a little moan when his teeth skim over her bottom lip, nibbling softly before pulling her back into another furious kiss. Her hands are pressed against his chest, her body lifting as he scoops her up and spins to pin her against the nearest wall. Her legs wrap around his waist instinctively, her arms moving to loop around his neck. She can feel every inch of him pressed against her now, evidence of how much he wants this. He wants this, despite it being so very wrong of them to exist in this moment that shouldn't have been allowed to come to fruition.

"*Fuck.*" The word is a pant as Ruin jumps back suddenly, a screech leaving Cassy's lips as she falls. She manages to get her legs underneath her but still tumbles, falling to the hard floor on her good side. "I'm sorry. I'm so sorry, I just couldn't handle any more."

Cassy glances up, eyes wide, not understanding his deeply apologetic, gasping words. At least, not until she sees his blistering lips. They are bleeding and raw, skin peeling and burning in several small patches. Did she...Did she do that? Is *that* what happens to a reaper who kisses her?

"I shouldn't have let you do that," she whispers, scrambling up to her feet. "I should have known..."

Ruin puts a hand on her cheek, snarling. "I don't regret it, my beloved. I'll heal in a few hours, and the second I do—"

"We can't do it again," she interrupts firmly, pushing at his chest softly and holding a hand over her lips as though to block him from their dangerous, seductive ways. "My lips are deadly."

"Not just your lips, darling." The heated gaze he sends her way...it sets her body aflame.

I want to get hot and heavy. I want to drag him into my bedroom and continue. I want to show him ways we can have fun without using my lips. I want to—I want to—I want to—

Cassy practically sprints into her room, slamming the door shut behind her. Not that it matters, since he can walk right through the thin border if he wanted, but...it's the point that matters. Her entire body shakes as she sinks to the floor, her voice broken as she calls, "Never again!"

The thought is depressing, heart-crushing, inevitable. She can't be with anyone romantically, but especially not Ruin. It's too complicated for both of them. They are too entangled in secrets and lies for it to ever work out. And that *kiss*...it felt more intimate than their moment at her parents' home. It felt more real. And for that alone, she knows she has to end this.

Never again.

Chapter 19

"I thought you would have moved out by now," Ruin remarks playfully as he slides through the front door, severe gaze boring into Cassy as she slowly lowers the book she is reading. "What in the blazing hells are you reading?"

She quickly slams the book shut, hiding the giant monster holding the tiny girl on the front by shoving it under a pillow. "I'm not one to run *or* hide from my problems. And what I read is none of your concern." She can't stop the blush that pours into her cheeks, can't look into his eyes; not only because of the book, but also because of what happened between the two of them last night.

A sad smile stretches across his long face. "No wonder you like me so much. You might be the only person in the world who would prefer me in my other, more monstrous form." The words are quiet, solemn. A reminder to them both of what he is and what she can never be.

"Depends on how monstrous it is." She swallows the confession rising in her throat, swallows the words that threaten to tell him exactly how much she doesn't care about whatever secret form he is hiding behind the handsome mask. She's obsessed with him, despite every reason there is not to be. Despite the fact that they can never be together. The lies building a bridge between them shouldn't be an encouragement to cross over it.

He takes a hesitant step forward, shoving his hands down into the pockets of his usual dark jeans. He's wearing that dark red button-down again, the one Cassy had inwardly complimented him on when visiting her parents. She has to forcibly jerk her gaze away to stop herself from admiring his form in it again as he speaks. "Hmm. I didn't realize the monsters had to be cute."

"Well, I do have standards." His barked-out laugh is abrupt, filling the small space with a warmth she desperately needed.

She blurts out, unable to help herself, "This is awkward. I don't like it."

He smiles softly, head ducking. His hair covers his face, the silver streak glistening in the dim lighting of the rental house. "I feel like this is a consequence of your actions, my beloved."

She sighs sadly as she shuts her eyes, wincing. "Don't do that. Don't blame this on me. Our situation is..."

"Unfortunate?"

She nods in agreement, flickering her eyes back open to admire him once more. "Among other things. I need you to be understanding, and I need you to put that kiss behind us. We both know lingering on it will lead to no good." She still can't meet his gaze when his head lifts, her hands clamped together and twisting tightly. She has to move, has to twitch, but...it's all so much worse when he's staring directly at her as though he can see her every thought. As though he can tell she's thinking all too intently about the kiss she just told him to forget. She bravely glances at him out of the corner of her eye, the twitching increasing when she sees the heat he brazenly stares her down with.

"I *want* to linger on it. I've replayed it over and over, Cassiopeia. I've thought about it all night. I don't often sleep, but if I had last night, I would have dreamed about it, too. I tried to get rid of the thoughts by using my own hands, but the entire time, I had to tell myself it was you. Even release did nothing to ease the burning ache you left behind. So, *no*, I won't be understanding. I won't put it behind us."

Cassy tenses as he strides over to her, crouching down in front of her and grabbing her by the chin. She lets him force her gaze toward him, lets her eyes clash with his. The thought of him touching himself, of him thinking about *her* while doing it, has heat building up deep inside her core. Now she can't stop picturing it, can't stop imagining what it would have been like if it *had* been her hands. It almost distracts her enough to miss him leaning in, to miss the desperation in his gaze as he does so.

I wish this could be real. I wish I could be with him. I wish he wasn't dead. I wish his boss wasn't hunting me down. I wish I could let him ease my own heat. I wish—I wish—I wish—

She jerks her head just as Ruin's lips reach her, forcing him to kiss her cheek instead. The low growl he emits is inhuman, the sound pulling a gasp of surprise from her lips. Her body is suddenly being flung down, and she finds herself flat on her back on the couch. Ruin is on top of her in a matter of moments, his hands pinning her down harshly. She jerks underneath his hold, but he doesn't budge an inch.

"Why are you doing this?" His face is hard and unflinching as he asks the desperate question, his cold body chilling her to the bone. She has started to theorize that it's purposeful, the cold touch. She thinks it's a punishment, or a reminder.

"Have you thought past your own insatiable thoughts? Have you given this consideration beyond what it would be like to get in my pants?" The words are hissed barbs, a veiled insult that he doesn't miss.

"You think that's what this is about? You believe that I'm thinking with the wrong head? That's not what this is, Cassiopeia Jaynes, and you know it."

She's made him angry now. So, so angry. His eyes are practically blazing with it, attempting to set her on fire with the ferocity of it all. "Well, what else am I supposed to think, Ruin? Because clearly, I'm having to do the thinking for both of us. You work for Death. You remember him, don't you? He's the one who has a hit out on me. The one who has the entire ghost population on the hunt for the Shadow Kisser. What happens when he finds out that you've been helping me? What happens when he discovers that you're *sleeping* with me? He's going to destroy you, Ruin. I don't know what happens to reapers, or if death is even a thing for you, but...I can only imagine the kind of torture you will endure because of me.

"And what happens after I'm caught? Because that's inevitable, Ruin. I *will* be caught. *I. Will. Die.* And I'm pretty sure Death is going to ensure I won't be a ghost. Not that I want to be one. So what happens then? We will both be miserable in two entirely different realities. It isn't feasible, Ruin. The two of us just aren't meant to be." The truth that escapes her is a jumble of words, ones that leave her in a fast and furious brigade. It's every thought she's had on the subject in one condensed speech, every worry voiced in a simpler context.

His frown is infuriating, his confusion written across the scrunch in his brows. "You're really that worried about me?"

"Of course I am!" she shouts, wishing she could jab a finger into his chest. It's her turn to be angry, her turn to burn him with her furious gaze. "I'm worried about you. I'm worried about myself. I'm worried about us. I've never *not* wanted a fling. Never cared about having an emotional connection. Not until you. We can't just have fun with each other. We can't just have sex and move on. I know it won't be the same with you. I know that one time in bed with you would leave me desperate for more. And I'm not ready for that. I'm not ready to miss you for the rest of my miserable life. I'm not ready to pine over you for my entire afterlife. *I can't do it.* I won't."

"You'd rather have that 'what if' for your entire life? You'd rather close this door than walk through and see what lies beyond?" His anger is gone, his eyes empty and distant.

"What other choice do I have? The things Death could do to you..." She shivers underneath him, not wanting to consider it.

"You act as though you know him."

"I think I am an extension of Death, and if I'm as twisted as I am, then...then how horrible is the one who made me?"

He dips his head down and groans into her neck, his lips brushing against her skin delicately. "That's not fair, Cassiopeia."

"Why not?" She clenches her eyes shut as his lips trail a path down to her collarbones, moving so one hand pins hers down and the other skims up underneath her shirt.

"You don't understand the circumstances behind your creation, you don't know—"

"Then enlighten me!" She jerks as Ruin nibbles on her neck in caution, a low growl leaving his lips as if warning her not to go down this path. "If you know so much, then please, explain. I understand it was an accident. I understand that I am a mistake that Death is just now getting around to cleaning up. I just don't understand *why*. Why now? Why me? Why lose control at that moment in time? Make me *understand* Ruin!"

"I am willing to risk whatever wrath you think is coming down on my head. I am willing to defy every principle I've held for thousands of years for you. Does that not matter to you? Is it not enough of an answer to know that I lov—"

"Do *not* say that to me right now." Cassy's eyes shoot open as she hisses the words, physically recoiling. And did he...did he say thousands of years? "We hardly know each other, Ruin. If you've truly lived thousands of years, then you know this is a passing thing. A fleeting one. I don't do love. I don't do lasting. It's the exact point I've been trying to make—"

Ruin's face is vicious and wrathful as he pulls away from her slightly, her words striking somewhere deep within him. "I've watched you for years, Cassiopeia Jaynes. Did you think that our meeting was a coincidence? Have you stopped to think for even one second that Death hunting you is no fault of your own? That I am being punished for falling in love with a mortal from afar?"

She blinks a few times, mouth opening and closing pitiful-ly. Because *no*. No, she hadn't thought that for one second. Why would she have? Ruin acted as though their meeting was planned, sure, but not for *years*. He was constantly leaving her, constantly abandoning her in times of need. That isn't what someone in love with her would do. Especially not someone who had loved her from afar and finally had a chance to make her fall in love with them, too.

Does he mean it? Is this something more for him or a bit of fun? Does he get a kick out of playing with the mortal girl? If he loves me, why does he leave me? If he wanted me so badly, why did he stay away? If he—If he—If he—

"If you are in love with me," she starts, licking her lips and trying not to stutter as she attempts to get the worst of her thoughts out. "Why would you leave me? Why stay away so often? Why hold me, comfort me, make me want you? Why do any of it when you planned on abandoning me afterward? I'm not a boomerang, you know. You can't throw me away and expect me to come barreling back into your arms."

Ruin's breath is heavy and hot against her face, his head tilted down so he can stare into her eyes. The hand that had been roaming her body mercifully stops just below her breasts, the skin below it tingling but not on fire enough to make her stop thinking entirely. "I've been hiding things from you, my beloved. Lying to you about things. And I want to tell you about them. I *want* to confess all of my darkest sins. But my tongue is tied, and some secrets just aren't mine to share. There are oaths I swore that I cannot break. I thought leaving you would be better, that not being around would hurt less than being next to you and knowing you would never be mine. But it wasn't. I managed to contain myself after that night at your parents, pulled myself together enough to break away. But when I kissed you yesterday, something inside me broke. Something told me I couldn't hide from you or my feelings anymore. I'm sorry if I hurt you. It wasn't intentional, I swear it, Cassiopeia. I tried my hardest to stay away, to keep you safe, but my hardest wasn't good enough."

"Why do men always think they know what's best for women?" Her voice is a thing she pulls from her darkness, cold and defiant. A testimony to what lies inside her, waiting for her to draw it out. The thing Death put inside her. "I needed you, Ruin. I had practically no one before you. I couldn't tell Winter about my dark side because she wouldn't understand, and I had convinced myself that she was going to walk away from me because of it. I convinced myself she would have thought I was insane for believing my kiss was deadly. Some days I thought I was, too. But when you came into my life, I knew you were different. I knew you were like me. That we were equals. But I suppose I'm inferior in your mind, aren't I? I must be, if you think so little of my decision-making capabilities."

His face drops, his features panic-ridden. "No, my beloved. No, that isn't—"

"How did he find out?" That dastardly darkness is still present, her eyes cold and distant as she watches him squirm above her.

His scoff is dismissive, angry, and hurt. "Does it matter?"

She smiles bitterly, making a broken noise in the base of her throat. "I guess not. What did he threaten you with? What did he say he would do to you if he found out you had been with me romantically?"

"He promised unimaginable torture," Ruin whispers, swallowing hard. She watches the movement like a lioness watching a wildebeest she plans to devour.

"And you came to me anyway." No change in her expression, no sign that she cares or that it matters in the slightest.

He leans forward and glares, words coming out wild and passionate. "Of course I did. Of course I came anyway! From the moment I found out you were changed, I began to watch you. I was worried about what a gift like yours could manifest into, worried about what kind of monster had been unleashed upon the world. And I quickly found out that you weren't a monster at all. That you were trying to do something good. You have not once tried to use your abilities selfishly. You didn't let people hire you as an assassin and you didn't kill anyone who didn't deserve it." He pauses, panting so he can catch his breath. His glare has disappeared, replaced by a look of vulnerability and tenderness. "You were trying to do something *good*. I didn't understand at first why you would do something like that. But I watched you from the in-between, and I quickly realized that you didn't have a reason for being good. You just *are*.

"I fell for you so fast, Cassiopeia Jaynes. I have always worn my heart on my sleeve, and you took it without ever knowing. So, yes, I came to you. I couldn't stop myself. I couldn't risk the 'what ifs' that you dismiss so readily. Whatever happens to me now isn't on you, my beloved. Every bit of this is my fault."

Ruin looks so ashamed, so wrecked, that she allows her darkness to retreat inside. All that is left now is a creeping sadness for the reaper above her. "Was Death ever hunting me?"

"Oh, yes. I didn't lie about any of that, Cassiopeia. You're in terrible danger. I was just arrogant enough to believe I could protect you from it." His eyes flicker shut, his long lashes fluttering.

"You're right," she says suddenly, glaring as she breaks from his hold and reaches up to grab him by the hair at the nape of his neck. "This *is* all your fault."

Cassy leans forward and kisses Ruin harshly, briefly, surprising him into being unable to move. She pulls back and stares at him, unable to continue knowing it will only hurt him. Quietly, she whispers, "That's the last time my lips will touch you, Ruin, but will it be the last time yours touch me?"

The sound that leaves him can only be described as a desperate plea, his hands ripping at her shirt unceremoniously. She clings to him, clawing at him, drawing him into her. He's warm now, and she can't stop herself from once again considering why.

I've always thought that he chooses to be hot or cold. Is it based on emotions? Does he even notice? Is it a reaper thing, or do ghosts do it, too? Reapers and ghosts share a lot of similarities. Does he do it on purpose, as a punishment? That's my theory. I think he was trying to remind himself, or me, about the reality of our situation. I think it was a way for him to keep control. Does he—Is it—I wonder—

"What's running through your beautiful mind, my beloved?" Ruin murmurs against her skin, licking his way up to her breasts. Her bra clips in the front, a clip that comes undone with a single flick of his nimble fingers. She shudders underneath him, arching up as his mouth covers one of her rosy buds. His free hand grips her other breast, squeezing, pulling, tugging.

"Do you control it?" she breathes through the sensations, her stomach fluttering violently, uncontrollably. "The hot and cold touch?"

He grins widely. "Mmm. Yes, sometimes. Around you? Hardly ever."

"So it *is* an emotional thing," she murmurs to herself, gasping as his teeth find the side of her breast.

"Only with you," Ruin admits lowly, looking up at her under his lashes with a wicked grin. "I've had a lot of firsts with you."

"I thought you said you've tried it all?" she counters, the corners of her lips ticking up when he barks out a laugh.

"Devious woman," he murmurs, the stubble on his cheek brushing against her as he leans up and purrs into her ear, "I may have a lot of experience, but I have never experienced *you*."

Cassy licks her lips, struggling to contain them, as she whispers playfully, "I'm just a notch in your bedpost, then."

"I don't sleep, remember, my beloved? I have no need for a bedpost." The devilish grin on his lips has her toes curling, the twinkling in his eyes a promise and a commitment.

What kinds of things does Ruin like in bed? Will I be enough? I'm certain he has tried things I've never even dreamed of doing. I have experience, but not as much as he's implied he has. Not the kind that thousands of years would provide. Can reapers get STDs? Definitely not. I doubt he can get me pregnant. Maybe I should ask. I'm on birth control, though, so it isn't important right now. Will I be able to live up to his standards? Does he have high standards, anyway? Will he care if I'm not into the same things he is? Will we be compatible sexually? Will he—Does he—I don't—

"It's so interesting to watch that mind of yours at work," Ruin says as he tugs on her shorts, removing everything as quickly as possible. His hands roam down her thighs, leaving goosebumps in their wake. She can't stop herself from lifting her hips, from offering herself to him eagerly. Ruin chuckles at her impatience, taking her by the heel and lifting her leg lightly as he begins trailing kisses from her ankle upward.

She swallows hard, her eyes glazing over with lust as she watches him slowly approach her sex. "It's annoying."

Ruin begins to lick, to bite, to suck the closer he gets to her core, and she curses him explicitly under her breath for teasing her so greatly. "I would love to be inside that mind, watching every thought unfold. I would love to know how you view the world because I already know how it views you."

She shuts her eyes tightly as he *finally* reaches the apex of her thighs, placing slow kisses there, too. "And how is that?"

Ruin pushes her legs farther apart, his pupils blown out as he stares down at the wetness waiting for him there. "Beautiful. Powerful. Confident. *Sinful.*"

"Do you like that about me? That I have a perfect outer appearance, but inside I'm rotten to the core?" She watches him for the truth, not particularly sure if she wants to know his honest answer. But answer honestly, he does.

"*I love it.*" Those lips are upon her, her back arching violently at the first lick, at the first suck, in a way that will likely leave her aching tomorrow. Cassy's mind empties so quickly that she didn't know it was possible, experiencing a pleasure that she's never had before. Is the pleasure because of his experience or just because it is *Ruin*?

Ruin hooks her leg over his shoulder, pressing it forward as he leans into her. She feels his fingers collect her slickness, pushing into her shortly afterward. It's all she can do not to scream out, all she can do to contain herself as he pumps into her. Everything is so wonderful, so overwhelming, that she doesn't realize she is on the brink of release until it hits her like a freight train. She never understood when her books claimed the women would see stars when they orgasmed, but she understands exactly what they meant now. Because this...this perfect, mindless moment brought the stars to her. She doesn't even have time to make a wish to them before it happens all over again and her mind goes numb once more.

When she finally comes down from her high, Ruin is waiting patiently for her. He's watching her intensely, his eyes gleaming with a lust so ferocious that she begins to shake. During one of those back-to-back orgasms, he had stripped himself entirely, and she is finally able to take him in completely. His chest isn't that of a bodybuilder or an athlete, but that of someone who works out but isn't rock hard all over. Of someone who eats well but doesn't say no to dessert. It is perfect, and human-like, and makes her forget what he really is underneath it all. Not that it matters. She would still be falling in love with him if he didn't look like this at all. If he looked like the monster he claimed to be.

"I need—" Cassy starts, her eyes flickering toward his sizable member. It is large, larger than most of her partners before, and thick.

Do reapers have bigger dicks? Or was this what it was like when he was human? Was he ever human, actually? I kind of assumed he was a ghost first, reaper second, but that may not be true at all. Was he built by Death to be this perfect? Was he created or born? Is his dick this thick because that's how Death wanted it to be, or did Ruin get to choose? Is his—Was he—I wonder—

"What do you need, Cassy?" Ruin's voice is low, a small noise of pleasure leaving him when she leans forward and grips him by the hilt, guiding him inside her.

"I need *you*."

He grins, letting out a shuddering groan. He pushes fully inside her, bending down to press his forehead against hers while her body adjusts. "You already have me, Cassiopeia Jaynes. You always will."

Then the stars come back to life as he begins to move inside her, granting the only wish she would ever ask of them. Giving her this moment with Ruin she dreamed of but never imagined to be possible.

Chapter 20

The morning light had barely begun to creep in through Cassy's bedroom window when the door flung open, clothes landing in her face only seconds later. "Get dressed, you two. We needed to be gone yesterday." The voice is rich and sweet, coated in a timelessness similar to Ruin's.

Cassy jolts up in panic, holding the sheets over her chest like she's in a cheesy romcom. The woman standing in her doorway is unfamiliar, her wild, dark curls flying around her as she continues to scoop up clothes and fling them at the couple still lying in bed. She is tall—nearly as tall as Ruin himself—and her eyes are a deep, unnerving black that Cassy recognizes, though she doesn't know from where.

"Ruin." Her hard voice shakes, and she licks her lips as she tries to think of the best plan for kissing the...wait, no. It isn't a ghost. There's no slight sheen to the body, no flickering colors or wavering in and out of existence.

"Five more minutes," Ruin says on a sigh underneath the comforter, unmoving and unconcerned.

"It's not like you were planning on doing much more sleeping anyway," the woman snarls, her teeth snapping in a dog-like manner. "So get up and move. Do you think I *wanted* to come in here and watch you two continue fucking like animals?" Before

Ruin can answer, the woman snaps, "No, you imbecile. I didn't. I came in here because the reaper council is coming."

That gets Ruin's attention, and he jumps into action as a result. He leaps out of Cassy's bed, not bothering to show any consideration for the strange woman as he strolls around naked. "Ruin!" Cassy cries, watching him with hungry eyes despite herself.

"What? Oh, yeah. Cerci doesn't care, my beloved. She's seen it all before and hates every inch of my body with a veracity not even a viper could possess. Isn't that right, my darling?"

"In other words, I'm taken," Cerci, the woman, sighs as she flips her long, dark hair over her shoulder. It nearly reaches her waist, the wildness of it enchanting Cassy entirely. That, and the woman's body. She is curvy and blessed in all departments, her loose cotton dress unable to hide the beauty underneath. Her skin is tan and smooth, and Cassy finds herself undeniably jealous. It's a feeling she isn't quite accustomed to. She isn't entirely sure if it is because the woman is beautiful or because Ruin is so familiar with her. Both, more than likely.

How does he know her? Is she an ex? Is she a family member? Can reapers have family members? Is she a reaper, too? Did he name his dog after her? Why is she here? Has she been watching us? If so, why? Who is she? Why did—Why should—Who is—

When Cassy is finally able to form words, Ruin is already dressed again. "You…did you name your dog after her?" She blinks at him wearily, unsure about what is happening. He had never *mentioned* this other woman to her. Never hinted at having friends other than Death. "Is she a reaper, too?"

Cerci laughs inexplicably, amusement gleaming in her eyes as she tilts her head toward Ruin. "You are so pathetic, you know that? You should have told her ages ago. I would have, if I were you. Lying isn't an attractive trait."

"I wasn't lying, *pet*. I just omitted some details." He says "pet" as though it's an insult, glaring at Cerci with a look that promises death.

"Lying," Cassy seethes through her teeth, siding with the strange woman, her own glare hitting Ruin now. "What else have you been lying about, Ruin?"

"Get dressed, Cassiopeia, and I'll tell you." She ignores his lingering stare as she stands upright, not bothering to hide her body from Cerci since Ruin hadn't. She has never been shy about herself, and she has always loved her body. It isn't perfect by any means, but it is *hers*. It had gotten her this far in life, and it would be with her for all time. She might as well love the thing that fuels her. She might as well embrace it.

She just finished slipping on a pair of clean leggings when Ruin says, "I didn't name my dog after her because she *is* my dog." That causes her to pause, her brows wrinkling together in confusion. Then she plucks her bra from the bed, turning toward her drawers to find a shirt silently as she tries to process the information. Ruin waits patiently, knowing her too well to disturb her processing delay.

Finally, after she is completely dressed, she says, "I've been snuggling with a woman this entire time and you didn't deign to tell me? Either of you?"

"I like to snuggle," Cerci says in her defense, as though offended. "You're warm."

"Okay." Cassy clenches her jaw, head tilting to the side as she tries to keep herself calm. "Okay, I'm ignoring you right now, pup. Why the *fuck* do you have a...a shape-shifter as your *pet*, Ruin?"

"She volunteered for the job a long time ago, my beloved. I only treat her as a true pet when around company. Any other time, she's just my friend. Sometimes a horrible one, but a friend nonetheless." A non-discrete look of irritation flashes toward Cerci.

"And...and how does one become a shape-shifter? Did she...Did Death do that to her, change her like he changed me?" Ruin clenches his jaw at her question, nodding only slightly. Cassy turns to Cerci with a new look in her eyes, an understanding that runs between the two women like electricity.

"Reapers are coming," Cerci reminds them, breaking eye contact as she turns to Ruin again. "They are here to claim Cassy on your behalf."

"Oh, fuck." Ruin groans into a hand that swipes down his face, sending an apologetic look to Cassy. "I can explain this. I swear, I can, I just—"

"On your behalf?" Cassy whispers, lost.

"It's not what you think." He swallows, ear tilting to the side in a familiar move as he listens to something in the wind. "They're near, we need to go."

She takes the hand he extends to her, letting him whisk them away. A creeping nausea has entered her throat, threatening to overwhelm her at any second. She feels as though her mind is swimming through a fog, as though every part of her body is detached and she has no control over anything. Reapers are coming for her. Had almost reached her. Did Death know, somehow, that she and Ruin crossed a line they can't uncross last night? Did he decide that enough was enough? And what had Cerci meant, on Ruin's behalf? He told her last night he was still hiding things from her, and had proved that this morning, so can she really be mad at him for omitting things? Can she be angry for his lies, for being "pathetic" as Cerci called it, when she knew there was more to him than she had yet to discover?

She supposes it depends on what the omission is.

Cerci being a human is a shock, but one she is trying to manage subtly. She keeps sending Cerci discreet looks as they flicker from one location to the next, never stopping for more than a full minute. But each time they arrive somewhere new, Cerci is still there, still human-like, still a woman. Her sharp nose and soft jawline, her widow's peak and the mole on her right cheek...it is all inexplicably *human*.

Ruin finally stops transporting her when they stand inside an old, abandoned house, windows broken and weather deteriorating what was once someone's home. Battered curtains sway in the breeze, leaves and dust stirring on the molded wooden floors as it rushes through. The yellowing walls also show signs of molding, littered with black spots and oozing areas. The trio stands in front of an aging door, the stairs across from them missing a few steps. From the looks of it, they had rotted a long time ago.

"Where are we?" Cassy questions as she finishes taking in her surroundings, anger rising so suddenly to the surface that she changes her line of questioning abruptly. "Actually, I don't care where we are. What the *fuck* is going on, Ruin? Your dog isn't a dog, reapers are chasing me on your behalf, and apparently, you are *still* lying to me."

But Ruin is not next to her and Cerci anymore. He has already exited through the front door, scythe in hand as he breezes across the small front porch and hops over the few steps leading to the yard.

"This is my childhood home. Kind of," Cerci provides an answer to Cassy's original question, placing a hand on her shoulder. "It's safe here."

"How did they track me down? *Why* are they tracking me down?" Is it usual for reapers to hunt? Not only that, but hunt in *packs*?

I am so fucked. Can Ruin do anything about this? Is it finally my time to die? Who will tell Winter? Will she report me missing or assume I ran off with Ruin? I should call her, say my final goodbyes. My parents, too. How long ago did Cerci live here? This house is ancient, practically falling apart. How old is she? How did—Why is—Who will—

"Your scent." Cerci turns and runs her hand down the stairs' banister, sighing wistfully. "Death has marked you, and you smell just like him. His scent surrounds you; any reaper who stumbles within a hundred miles of you will recognize that scent. And as of late, it's been a lot more intense." Cerci reaches out to twirl a lock of Cassy's white hair, smiling sadly and with little comfort.

"My power increase." Cassy swallows, glancing down at her arms, at her hands. She had formed wrinkles and aging spots overnight, as though she were entering her forties and not her mid-twenties. She hasn't had time to inspect the rest of her body, but she suspects she'll find much of the same elsewhere. Hesitantly, she reaches up to touch her face. Flinching at what she feels there, she quickly drops it. "That's how they found me. Last night, for some reason, my power must have changed again. What do you think it will be this time?"

"There's no way to truly know." Cerci chews on the inside of her cheek for a minute before adding, "When Death passed powers along to me, I was finding new abilities for months. But your progress has been faster than mine these last few months. There was enough separation between you and Death when you were first gifted powers that the new things didn't progress, but...well, you've had too much exposure as of late, I believe."

"Did you age like this, too?" Cassy watches the shifter carefully, eyes squinting in suspicion. Cerci looks...well, young. Around Cassy's age, actually: in her mid-twenties.

"I was already dead when I inherited my powers." No hidden emotions there, no remorse or sadness.

"Oh." It's all Cassy can think to say. She doesn't want to comfort Cerci because she doesn't think that's what the shifter wants or needs from her. "And...shifting was what he gifted you with? It was purposeful?"

"My gifts were intentionally given," the shifter confirms, taking a deep inhale before saying, "I'm not sure how much I should tell you, considering it's not my place to. But I can tell you that the intention matters. Death needed a friend when he made me. He needed something different when he made you."

Cassy stumbles back as though she has been slapped, eyes wide and pleading. "No. No, no, no. Tell me the pervert did not give me kissing powers because he...because he *wanted* me."

Was Death attracted to me? Is that why I was chosen? Did he kiss me when he gave me his powers? Did he—Was he—Why did—

"It's not like that, Cassy. Death's job is lonely. I know Ruin has told you that before. Sometimes it gets to be too much. Sometimes, when he longs for something, there are consequences. This time, when he longed for companionship..." Cerci trails off and shrugs, sharp black eyes watching something behind Cassy.

"I was the consequence." Cassy swallows the bile rising in her throat, closing her eyes tightly and wrapping herself in her arms. She doesn't want to think about Death craving her, craving love, craving more. It is unimaginable. Sick. Unforgivable.

"The house is secure," Ruin says from behind her, grabbing one of her hands. She numbly allows it, following dutifully behind him as he drags her outside and over to a cellar off to the side of the house. Ripping the doors open, he growls lowly, "Get in."

"I don't want to go in there." She peers down at the darkness inside, a singular swinging light bulb visible from her position. She watches as Cerci descends the stairs gracefully, pulling the string to turn it on and turning to watch her with a raised brow. As though saying, "Is that really so hard?"

"You have to. It's warded against reapers, Cassy. They can't get you as long as you are inside." Ruin looks pained as he admits it, his face contorted and the knuckles around his scythe turning white. With a sudden clarity, she realizes why.

"That means you can't come with me." She watches him swallow, Adam's apple bobbing as he nods in confirmation. She is angry with him, unbelievably so, but she doesn't want him to get hurt. She doesn't want the others to attack him because of her. "What are they going to do to you?"

"They are going to demand a price for your continued safety. Cerci will stay with you, Cassy. She'll protect you with her immortal life."

"She's loyal to you," she says slowly, mind spinning. "But wasn't she created to be loyal to Death? Didn't that ghost say it would be owed a prize from Cerci's owner?" That ghost had also labeled Cerci a hellhound: Is that what she shifts into when she changes? Not a dog, but a hellhound.

"She was." Ruin's smile is sad, as though realizing a hard truth is about to come out. "You'll understand why soon enough, I suspect. I can't tell you, but I can show you. I can only pray you won't hate me afterward." With that, he is gone, flickering out of existence as though he were an illusion she conjured. As though he were the ghost she always believed him to be.

With a shaky breath, she turns, taking one step at a time down the stairs. Descending into the damp, dusty cellar, she prays she doesn't meet her demise here.

Chapter 21

"They won't attack him, will they?" Cassy questions Cerci, staring up at Ruin's back. He doesn't bother to close the cellar doors, as though he wants her to watch what happens.

"They wouldn't dare," Cerci replies, watching along with her. Cerci's tone is one of certainty, but it does little to calm her growing nerves.

"And…Death? Will he come? Will he hurt Ruin?"

If Death hurts Ruin, I'll tear through him with Ruin's scythe. I'll cut him until he bleeds. I'll destroy him if that's what it takes. I'll allow the entire world to succumb to ghost attacks if it means Ruin is safe. I'll hunt them all down later, kiss them into submission, if it means I can keep him for myself. I'll fight—I'll hunt—I'll submit—

Cerci lets out a boisterous laugh, resulting in Ruin turning to glare down at her over his shoulder. The sound rings out like a charming bell, gorgeous and joyful. The kind of laugh that comes from someone who doesn't laugh often. "Oh, sweetie. Death hurts Ruin daily. Tortures him, I dare say."

"Cerci," Ruin grinds out above us, slamming his scythe down onto the ground. A wave of quakes shudders the ground and the walls around them, shutting Cerci right up for a few precious seconds.

"Too close to home?" Cerci pushes Ruin, an amused gleam in those pitch-black eyes.

Cassy tries to warn the shape-shifter. "Cerci, I don't know if—"

"Ah, he won't do anything to me, Cassy. Not while your life is at risk. Now, once we get out of here, on the other hand…" Cerci winces, as though she knows exactly what happens to someone who crosses Ruin Morrigan.

"Remember that, Cerci, while you protect my beloved's life," Ruin calls, a strong wind kicking up around him outside.

"What's happening?" Cassy whispers, chewing on her bottom lip and wringing her hands nervously. That anger for Ruin has faded, replaced by worry and anxiety. They can address the Cerci thing later, can fight it out whenever they are safe. For now, she will have to let it go so she can focus on the situation at hand.

"They're here," Cerci says simply, her gaze sharpening and her body stiffening. Then, right before Cassy's very own eyes, she shifts. The giant dog she had begun to love is now before her, snarling and snipping threateningly at the staircase.

"This is where she fled to," a male voice from nearby announces, not far from Ruin. "I smell her."

"I suggest you forget that smell," Ruin says darkly, his voice low and menacing.

The footsteps she thought she heard stop abruptly, hushed whispers passing through what seems to be a small group. "Boss," the man says eventually, and she can make out a large, imposing form in front of Ruin. "I—*we* didn't realize you were here."

"Could you not scent me as well?" Ruin's question is innocent enough, but his tone holds dark implications.

"We thought it was just the Shadow Kisser's way. She's always smelled so similar to you, we thought—"

"I care not what goes on in your mind, Braxton. I think we can all agree it's a nasty place to be." Ruin is joking with these people as though he knows them. As though they are friends. Maybe they are, for all she knows. She knows so little about him, after all. It's why she won't admit to how strongly she feels, why she refused to reciprocate when he admitted to being in love with her yesterday.

Braxton, appropriately humiliated in front of his comrades, releases a loud sigh. She can see a few pairs of feet surrounding the cellar, but she isn't sure of the exact number. As the seemingly leader of the group, he begins to try to explain their presence again. "We knew you were looking for the Shadow Kisser, and when we realized we found her, we planned on bringing her to you. I swear, boss."

"Last time you found one of my chosen, you mauled her and left the pieces for me to find," Ruin growls, slamming that ominous scythe onto the ground again. Cassy watches in amazement as the group tumbles back as one, only shadows visible to her now.

"That was five hundred years ago!" Braxton whines, letting out an impatient huff. "Last we heard, we were supposed to kill the chosen. How were we supposed to know that you liked that one?"

"Words spoken like a true toddler," Ruin bites back, snarling lightly. She can see the muscles in his back rippling as he struggles to contain himself.

"Alright, Ruin, that really isn't—"

"I am ordering you to leave," Ruin interrupts, holding out a hand to stop him. "This chosen one is mine to keep."

"Ruin, you know we can't just leave. Your previous orders override this one. You told us that if you ever found another chosen one that we had to vet her *and* you. You said that we needed to ensure this one dies or becomes one of us. There is no ordering around that, unfortunately. We can't leave until we are satisfied with your decision. You know we have to get her testimony and—"

"All of you are useless," Ruin barks, the cellar doors slamming shut unexpectedly. Cerci's transformation afterward is quick and precise, her slim hands suddenly on Cassy's shoulders.

"Listen to me, Cassy. I am going to break the wards and one or more of those Reapers are going to come down here now. They are going to say some things that you won't understand, and you're going to have to piece things together yourself because Ruin isn't allowed to tell you anything. Do not be scared. They will deem you weak and unworthy if you show any fear. Just...just be yourself, okay?"

"I already don't understand." Cassy hugs herself and licks her lips unsurely, trying to find the right words to explain her thoughts to Cerci. "Is this a trial of some kind? And what does that mean, one of his chosen? And why do they think I have to become one of them? Why does Ruin get to order them around? Why does—"

Her questions are interrupted again as the cellar doors fly back open, revealing a dark-skinned man in a form-fitting black suit. "Can I come in, gorgeous?"

"Only you," Cerci bites out, glaring at Ruin. "And I suppose I'll allow you in too, Ruin." She bends down and begins writing something on the ground, but Cassy isn't sure what the symbols are or what they mean. And...and she is writing them with blood. *Cerci's* blood. Her wrist is bleeding, cut by her own volition.

Cassy's heart plummets as Braxton strolls down the steps casually, smiling gently at her. He's handsome, with eyes a molten silver that stare right into her soul. She watches with faint amusement as he rubs a hand over his bald head, as though he is thinking, before he opens sensual lips. "I hear you have a thing for Ruin."

"Shut the fuck up, Braxton." Ruin's words are accompanied by a slap to the back of his head, and Braxton, despite his large and muscular body, stumbles down the rest of the stairs like an uncoordinated baby deer.

"Okay, okay! Geeze. No need for violence," Braxton hisses back, though his voice sounds more merry and less like a summons for said violence.

"No need *yet*," Ruin snaps back, hardly appeased.

Cassy watches the interaction intently, lips unwavering.

Should I answer his questions? What is happening? Is Ruin a captain of some sort? Head of the reapers? Are these his lieutenants? I don't know what I'm supposed to say or do. I don't know what Ruin expects. I don't know what this man, Braxton, expects. I don't know—I don't know—I don't know—

"Cassiopeia Jaynes," Ruin says abruptly, his voice thunderous in the tiny cellar. "You are under trial as ruled by the Reaping Council. From this moment on, you will be detained until your loyalties are proven and your testimony received. Braxton has been elected as the sole representative for the council and, therefore, will be the judge who decides your fate. May Death be in your favor."

"May Death be in your favor," Cerci repeats solemnly, spine straight and arms crossed in front of her chest as she stands next to Cassy.

Braxton smiles sweetly, innocently, despite his devilish nature as a reaper. "Let the trials begin."

Chapter 22

Cassy lets out a surprised noise as her arms are ripped behind her on a phantom wind, a rope unwinding from the corner like a snake. It slithers toward her and climbs up her legs, binding her hands together tightly. She feels the itchiness, the roughness, of the material the entire way up. With a shudder, she tries not to think about the way it wriggled up her like it was a living thing.

"Don't speak yet," Cerci whispers into her ear despite not moving, as though the very molecules inside the still air carried her voice to Cassy. "Braxton has to ask you something directly before you speak. Once the first question is asked, you can speak freely."

"Hello, Cassiopeia. Can I call you that?" His smile is meant to disarm her, but she isn't fooled so easily.

"No, you can't," she says plainly, watching him with a suspicious gaze. "But you *can* call me Cassy."

Braxton laughs good-naturedly, eyes sparkling with delight. "Alright, Cassy. Do you know why we are here?"

She opens her mouth to lie but somehow finds herself unable to. "Death gave me a gift, and he wants my privileges to use it revoked." Braxton tilts his head curiously, clicking his tongue as he begins to pace. She can't tell if it is because he is nervous or because he simply wants to.

"Have you met him before? Death?"

I must have at some point. He was the one who gave me my powers. I haven't seen him, though. So it doesn't count, right? Two people have to talk and introduce themselves to truly meet. So I haven't really met him. He has met me, I guess. I can't lie. Why can't I lie? What is—Why can—I have—

She wiggles her fingers nervously behind her back, shifting around on her feet. "Not that I'm aware of."

"So, as far as you are aware, you have never seen him? Never sensed his presence?"

"No. Ruin has been distracting him, I think. Keeping his attention on other things."

Braxton clicks his tongue again, pausing to look up at the ceiling before sending a sly smile to Ruin. "Oh, I think Death's attention has been heavily fixated on you, Cassy. Ruin hasn't distracted him at all."

"Maybe." She shrugs, trying not to look over at Ruin. She doesn't want him to discover the fear inside her that is threatening to overcome her and all of her good senses. "Maybe not."

This situation, this group of reapers...she can't comprehend it all. With a mind like hers that runs so quickly, the explanations should be readily available. But her mind is failing her. The only thing she can think about, in rapid, paralyzing thoughts, is Ruin. About *his* safety, *his* fear, *his* worry. He's told her many times she doesn't know anything about the supernatural, and she's realized far too late that he is right. This is clearly some kind of tradition or rule these people have to follow. It is even clearer that Ruin has been trying to keep her away from this. The only thing she doesn't understand is *why*. She fears she will find out soon, and she isn't entirely sure if she will like the answers she desperately needs.

"You took a different approach this time, Ruin. You never even hinted? Never tried to make her understand?" Braxton watches Ruin with something akin to pity, those sensual lips turned down in a sad frown.

"That's never worked before. Why try now? And Cassiopeia…she's different. I didn't want her to make the same choice that all the others have made. I selfishly want to keep her. I love her too much not to try." Ruin has deflated, she notices, when she risks a glance at him. He can't even look at her, can't try to explain through his own eyes or expression or body language. He seems to have just…given up.

Braxton abruptly turns to Cassy again. "Cassy, you've been dubbed the Shadow Kisser. So, in your own words, what ability have you been gifted?"

She licks her lips, a nefarious smile creeping across her face as she says simply, "Kiss me and die." She had said the words to Christina the ghost, and they had never felt more right. Even Braxton takes a step back at her words, at her expression, at her conviction.

"Right. Right, well, I suppose that's the problem, isn't it? You've been a little free with your kisses."

Ruin growls, jumping at Braxton and gripping him by the collar of his shirt. "Are you implying that she is not free to do so? That she is little more than a common whore and not a cunning woman using her abilities for good?"

Braxton stumbles back and the two hit a wall, Ruin's face full of wrath and pure rage. "No, sir! I'm sorry, I didn't mean it that way. I swear!"

"Apologize to her!" Ruin lifts him and slams his head against the wall, shaking the interior of the cellar.

"I'm sorry," Braxton says on an exhale, looking over at Cassy with wide eyes. She can only smile sweetly, demurely, and blink her eyelashes innocently at him. "I hope you didn't take my words the wrong way?"

"Of course not," she answers, smile still resting on her face. "I know how good I am with my lips. It's not an insult to acknowledge it."

Braxton chokes, looking over to Ruin pleadingly before blurting, "It isn't like you can blame me for bringing it up, man! You ordered us to put out a hit on her. We didn't realize that you stuck around after you finished making her. We thought you had left and wanted us to clean up your mess. For years, you've complained about her being a problem, and we thought you had finally had enough. The council all agreed that this is an issue we need to resolve. We thought you wanted her dead until we got here!"

What does that mean? Is he being truthful? Ruin looks so angry; Braxton must be telling the truth. Did...did Ruin set the hit out on me? Did Ruin create her? If he did...Did he—Is he—What happened—

Ruin shoves a knee into Braxton's gut, violence dancing in his eyes. That golden ring begins to glow around his irises, his fingers extending into the long claws she had seen when Christina attacked her weeks ago. "If you kill her, I'll rip out your intestines and feed them to Cerci." From Cassy's side,

Cerci waves innocently, licking her lips as though the thought is tempting.

Braxton wheezes, "The trials. You can't hurt me as a result of the trials, or during them."

Reluctantly, Ruin lets him go. "Consider this your only warning, underling."

Braxton rolls his eyes, straightening his suit jacket before murmuring, "You've always been so temperamental." But Cassy can barely hear him over the ringing in her ears, over the truth searing in her brain.

Ruin had ordered the hit on her. Ruin had created her. And if those things are true…if those things are real…then Ruin isn't a reaper at all. He is *the* reaper.

Ruin Morrigan is Death.

Rage, pure and unbridled, suffocates Cassy. Her insides melt with the force of it, her skin suddenly too tight to hold it inside. And she tries. She really, really tries to keep it in. Tries not to explode into fiery debris in front of the strange reaper before her. But she's never been good at holding in her thoughts, never been good at not blurting things out the second they pop into her head. So she lets the rage overtake her.

"How dare you?" Her words are low and venomous as hot, heady tears hit her cheeks. She has always been an angry crier, and she briefly worries that Ruin will think she is crying because she is sad. And she *is* a little sad. But mostly angry. So, so angry. Her vision blurs with it, her body temperature spiking.

"Cassy." Cerci reaches out and touches Cassy's shoulder, but she jerks away from the touch with little effort. She only stares at Ruin, his head bent low and long hair covering his face in shame.

"How dare you?" she repeats, wishing her lips could do more damage from this distance. For now, her words can be her only weapon. For now, she can only make him hurt as greatly as she does. "I can't believe you. I can't believe the *audacity* you had to lie to me in the way you did. What was the point of it all, Ruin? What was the point in hunting me down, warning me, *threatening me*, when none of it was real? Or maybe it was, since you seemed to have ordered your underlings to hunt me down. Was that before or after you met me, I wonder? Before or after you supposedly fell in love? How did it feel, knowing you tricked me into sleeping with you? Knowing you had me so terrified of *you* that I crawled straight into your arms? Did you get off knowing you had fooled me so deeply?"

Ruin's head snaps up to her now, those hazel eyes filled with sorrow. The unearthly glow is gone, the long claws retracted. Braxton takes a step away from him, looking between the two with wide eyes as though he hadn't quite grasped the situation between them until this very second. "I never lied to you, my beloved," Ruin says, quiet and steady in a way Cassy is not. "You made assumptions, and I let you believe them. And I *never* wanted to trick you. You know me, Cassy. What kind of man do you think I am? Do you think I would lie so readily just to get a taste of you? Hurt you so deeply just to come out on top?"

She tries to think back to the past, to the moments she was certain Ruin had lied to her. But her memory has always been shotty at best, and she can't recall a single conversation. She can barely process the thoughts racing in over the ringing in her head as it is.

Had any of it been real? Does he actually love me? Why do any of it? Why drag this out? Why not tell me? Why lie and omit any of it? Why come around at all? Why not let his reapers kill me? Why did he want me to fall for him? Why sleep with me? Why—Why—Why—

"What else do you need from me, Braxton?" Cassy questions, turning her fiery gaze onto him. The reaper flinches, unable to stop glancing over at Ruin fearfully.

"I didn't mean to start a fight," he says, clearing his throat awkwardly. "You know that, don't you, Ruin? You know I would never try to take away anything that made you happy."

"Braxton," Ruin seethes, that sorrow transforming into something much, much more terrifying. "I think you should stop while you're ahead."

"Right. Right, boss. You're totally right." Braxton wipes sweaty palms on his pants, turning back to Cassy with an easy, awkward smile. "Well, I do have one more question for you, Cassy."

"Ask it and let me be free. I'm not having fun anymore." She keeps her glare pinned on Braxton, thinking it unwise to look at Ruin right now. If she does, her wrath might just burn right through the rope binding her. Maybe it wouldn't be such a bad thing if it did.

"Are you in love with Ruin Morrigan?"

"N—" Cassy lets out a noise of distress as her tongue is pulled from her mouth by some invisible hand, as though two fingers have pinched and pulled it forward. She tries to answer again, her tongue remaining stubbornly outside of her mouth. And the feeling inside her gut, swarming and nose-diving within, leaves her sick. She knows, then, that the truth is something she can't hide from. She can't lie to Ruin to hurt him. She can't lie to Braxton to save him from Ruin's wrath. She can't even lie to herself to make this entire situation feel less catastrophic.

With a sudden inhale, her tongue snaps back in her mouth, the word, "Yes!" leaving her lips in a breathless moan. Cassy pants as she looks over to Ruin, swallowing hard as she waits for him to react. But Ruin's face stays painfully calm, his arms crossed across his chest as he watches Braxton intently.

"Well." Braxton glances back up at the cellar doors, jerking his head toward them. "I'm going to discuss my decision with my colleagues briefly. I'll be—"

"You don't have to discuss shit with them," Ruin argues, stopping him with a hand. "You were the elected official here. *You're* the judge. This is your choice."

"Is it?" The question is light and airy, yet somehow leaves a stone inside Cassy's gut. It lands with a thud, weighing her down suddenly. She stumbles slightly, falling to her knees with a groan. The concrete below her is not gentle, and she feels the scrapes stinging her skin as they are formed. Her chest aches painfully, the reality of the situation a burden she didn't anticipate. And it *hurts.* It hurts so bad to know just how much she is losing. She opened up, she let herself fall in love, and for what? For this heartache? For this betrayal? She lets out a noise of distress, wishing desperately she could reach out and clutch it to ease the pain.

"What did you do?" Ruin howls, racing for her. But she leaps away from him, using her feet to push her back, back, back.

"Don't touch me, *Death*," she spits, turning her cheek to him.

"I'll be back," Braxton repeats sadly, fleeing into the warm air above them.

"You must understand why I did it," Ruin breathes, falling to his knees before her. "You must listen to my reasoning—"

"I don't have to listen to anything you say," she hisses, tears still streaming down her face. It's painful to speak, to breathe, to *exist*. "Doing that is how I wound up here, isn't it?"

"Cassiopeia, I didn't do this because I took enjoyment out of it. I didn't do it because this was a game. When I created you…" He tugs on his hair, looking slightly unhinged and entirely distressed as he tries to put his explanation into words. "When I created you, I was lonely. I've been lonely my entire life. That's why I've surrounded myself with these people who have put you on trial, why the reapers were created in the first place. Why Cerci was created. I'll never forget the first time I saw you. *Never.* Do you know why?"

Does it matter why? Should I even bother listening to this? This could all be lies, too. Is he held to the trial's rules of telling the truth? Probably not, since he isn't on trial. So every word that comes out of his mouth could be a lie. I shouldn't listen to this. I want to, despite myself. I'm such an idiot for hearing him out. I have to stop him. I can't—I won't—I'm so—

Cassy can't help herself; she shakes her head. Ruin takes it as encouragement to continue, his words rapidly escaping his mouth. "I came to collect Trisha. She was on my list, and I showed up expecting to collect her soul and move on to the next location. But then there you were, touching her, holding her in her time of dying. When I looked at you, I knew you were the most beautiful woman I had ever seen. Not necessarily because of how you look, but because of what I saw inside you. You weren't scared of death, and you weren't scared of watching someone die. And you had this intense look in your eyes, like you understood that Trisha was an abominable person without even knowing her. You looked at her and saw what was inside, and it baffled me. It intrigued me. I knew then that you were different."

His expression shudders, jaw clenching and unclenching while trying to decide how to tell her the truth. "I reached forward to touch Trisha as her soul rose to the surface, but she spoke to me before I could. She said, 'Don't take that one yet. She's special.' I just smiled and agreed, then took your hand. I crouched down to kiss it, patting it to show Trisha that I was respecting her wishes. Spirits come more easily like that, you see? And I *wanted* to touch you, just once. I remember this…longing in that moment. I remember this wish that I could act out on my attraction, that I could get to know you and ask you out like any other man might. My loneliness was deep and brutal, and it appeared without me realizing. I can't always control my powers, and sometimes…sometimes they escape me without my knowledge. Not long after that reaping, souls started showing up who weren't on my list. After the third one, I knew it wasn't a coincidence. I knew what I had done." Ruin hangs his head again, swallowing hard as he awaits Cassy's answer to his admission.

"Stop," she says quietly, her voice quivering as she tries to make her heart stop swelling in despair. "Just stop."

She has wondered many times about her creation. She has always believed herself to be chosen, but she never knew why. She just knew she was different: She had been born that way. The quiet girl who observed, the one everybody liked but nobody loved. The girl who could get away with murder. But now...now she knows she isn't special. She wasn't chosen. She was an accident, a concept that had never occurred to her before. Ruin had mentioned it before, sure, but she hadn't taken much merit in the sentiments. She will now, though. She won't let herself be fooled by Death again.

"So I came to find you," he whispers, continuing despite how adamantly she shakes her head to dissuade him. "And what I found was more than I had bargained for. I became attached to you so fast, and I—"

"That's so fucking creepy," she snarls, snapping her teeth at him in an animalistic way. She has never acted so viciously before, so primal. She knows it's the piece of him inside her coming out to play. "You stalked me for years, watched me do who knows what during that time, and you expect me to find it romantic? Because I *don't*, Ruin. Stalking women is so predatorial."

"I *am* a predator," he snips back, jumping forward to hiss into her face. She stares head-on into that angry hazel gaze, lips pursed as she refuses to turn away. "I was created to reap the souls of the dead, Cassiopeia Jaynes. If you saw my true form, you would run away crying from pure fear. Looking at me is like seeing a reflection of the darkest beasts the world has to offer. A monster like that is not created to be prey. You can call me all the vicious names your wicked little brain can summon, but know that none of that matters to me. My behavior is predatorial because I am an *animal*, my beloved. I'm sorry that I fooled you into believing otherwise."

"I wasn't the one you were fooling," she retorts, icy blue eyes cold and hard. Ruin jerks back as though she slapped him, his fury overcoming him. But before he can respond, before he can deny her accusations, Braxton is strolling back down the stairs.

Ruin's entire body stiffens, that burning ire turning to his friend. Braxton seems smart, though, and stays a healthy distance away. He doesn't approach Cassy, either, which seems like another smart move on his part. Cassy braces herself, unprepared for what a sentence from the reapers may be.

Will they order me to die? Will they want me to be one of them? Will they make me immortal? If I become immortal now, will I look like myself again? Why is my body changing so rapidly, anyway? Why did it change whenever I first inherited my gift? Can they fix this? Do I want them to? Will they take my powers away? Will they—Can they—I don't—

"Cassiopeia Jaynes," Braxton says, his voice suddenly serious and hard compared to the light playfulness from before. "The Reaping Council has sentenced you in accordance with our laws."

From beside her, Ruin drops his head into his hands as though he already knows exactly what his friend is about to say. But Cassy has no clue what laws he is referring to, so as she stands fully once more, she questions, "And what sentence would that be?"

"We leave you with two choices: Allow Death to grant you immortality—without your powers but with the chance to form new ones—and swear fealty to stay by his side and loyalty to his person. Swear a blood oath that can only be broken by a true death—something that can only be granted by Death himself—in which you will receive no afterlife and you will forever live alone in darkness."

"And my second choice?" she whispers, her entire body shaking. She can't swear loyalty to Ruin. Not after what he did, not after all the lies he told. She won't swear loyalty to a man who holds no loyalty to her.

Braxton sends her a sad smile, saying only, "Die."

"What?" Her word is a breathless lilt, her entire world spinning on its axis.

"Your death will be sanctioned by the council, and Death himself will be the one to swing the scythe. You *will* get an afterlife, but your powers will not remain."

She stumbles back into a wall, the impact leaving a rush of pain racing through her arms and shoulders. She pays that no mind, though, as small, hiccuping breaths escape her unwittingly. Her two choices are no choices at all.

Cassiopeia Jaynes must swear loyalty to the man she loves, to the man who she just found out has been lying to her about who he is from the second they met, or allow that man to gift her a death blow.

"You have one week to make a decision." Braxton disappears, along with the shadows that were hovering at the cellar door. And Ruin, damn him, disappears along with them.

"Fuck," she whispers, sliding down to the floor. Her hands have come unbound on their own, the rope slithering off to the corner it had come from, and she brings them to her wet cheeks with a hollow laugh. "Fuck, fuck, *fuck!*"

Chapter 23

"**R**uin has asked me to keep you here," Cerci says quietly from Cassy's side, looking over her with worried eyes.

"Of course he has. And you'll do exactly as he says, won't you? Like the good little bitch you are." Cassy hadn't meant to spit out the words, hadn't meant to poison them with her vicious venom. But they strike true, leeching into Cerci's blood and rattling her to the core.

"You know what? *Fuck you*, Cassy. Maybe you haven't realized it yet, but I'm your friend. I saved your sorry ass multiple times. Times when I should have let you die. And you know why? Because I'm a *good little bitch* and I ran to my master. So maybe stew on that for a while, if you ever get out of this self-pitying episode, that is." With that, Cerci changes; the beautiful woman becomes a terrifying dog. Hellhound, according to the ghosts. Watching her now, snarling angrily and leaping up a whole flight of stairs, Cassy can understand why she earned the title.

"Self-pitying," Cassy whispers to herself, scoffing. As if she shouldn't be reeling from betrayal. As if Ruin hasn't been lying to her their entire relationship. If it can be called that, anyway. They slept together once. Fooled around once. *Truly* kissed once. But what she feels now, what makes her bones heavy and her soul weak, is something she isn't entirely sure she can recover from: heartbreak.

Cassiopeia Jaynes spent her first day in the old house curled up on a dusty couch, unable to bring herself to move. She got up to relieve herself, ate the food Cerci dropped at her feet three times that day, but...she didn't have the motivation to go anywhere but to the bathroom that surprisingly still had working pipes. She suspects the place has been taken care of for a long time, if the dated eighties-style kitchen is any indication.

When she woke up the next morning, her entire body felt weak, and she spent hours vomiting. Her face was paler than normal, her wrinkles more prominent, and her hair...her hair was starting to fall out. She wept for so long that a puddle formed beneath her, soaking the couch pillow she had been using to rest her head upon. When Cerci showed up that night with her food and noticed how sick she looked, the shape-shifter finally broke the silent treatment she had been giving Cassy.

"You know what you need to choose," Cerci said quietly, chewing on her bottom lip. "You know what will end this."

"Killing myself will end this," Cassy spat back, suddenly angry. The sadness was fading as she stared at the woman, anger and bitterness slamming into her like the force of an atom bomb.

"They won't let you die, Cassy. You know that." Cerci seemed sad when she said it, as though she herself knew what it was like to crave death and be unable to have it.

"You chose this, right?" Cassy questioned, swiping at her eyes furiously to clear her tear-filled eyes. "You chose to stay with him? Made a deal of some kind?"

"I did," Cerci said, watching her wearily. "I had my own agenda when I made a deal with Death."

"And what of that agenda now? Did you ever accomplish it?" Cassy watched her carefully, a plan forming in her mind.

"No. I've considered giving up many times, actually. But I'm still here. Still serving my friend loyally." Cerci paused, opened her mouth, paused again. "I don't stay because I have to, Cassy. I don't stay because I'm duty-bound. I stay because I love him. I stay because he is my best friend. I stay because I choose him over all else, even when I hate myself for it."

"Yeah? And you want me to choose him, too? You want me to obey him for all eternity?" Cassy turned away then, feeling too bitter to have a productive conversation. If she chooses to bind herself to Ruin for eternity, he's the only one who can release her from that oath. She doubts he will ever do such a thing, even if she begs for it.

"No, Cassy. I want you to choose happiness. I want you to obey yourself and stay true to your heart. I gave up a lot of things for love. Every day, more is taken from me because of it. But I'm obeying my heart. I'm listening to it. This bitterness? This fury?

It won't last forever. But a permanent death like the one they're offering? *That* is for eternity."

Before Cassy could think of a proper response, Cerci had changed back into a hellhound. She looked at Cassy with those eerie black eyes as though pitying her before lying down on the carpet where she stood. And the next time Cassy leaped up to go puke, Cerci followed, changed back into a woman to hold her hair, rubbed her back, and whispered reassurances. The second she had recovered, Cerci was a hellhound again. It was a pattern the shape-shifter followed all night and into the following days.

Day five of being a captive in Cerci's old home has arrived, and Cassy hasn't gotten any better. Truthfully, she is much, much worse. She has bald patches in her hair now, the once shiny, smooth hair brittle and weak. Her skin looks like that of an old lady, her body weak and unable to move without help. Her bones are frail, a fact proven by the snapped ankle she received when she tripped over Cerci on her way to the bathroom last night. It aches horribly now, but Cerci has done a wonderful job of wrapping it up. Her vomiting is still prominent, and her stomach constantly feels hollow. Some hours, it feels as though it is eating her from the inside out. Looks like it, too, with the way her stomach caves in and how her skin has glued itself to her bones. The only thing that sags now is her breasts, but she can hardly bring herself to care about her appearance anymore. She is too sick to worry about much else.

"Cerci," she whispers, her voice that of a weak, broken thing. "I need to—" But she vomits before she can request help walking to the bathroom. The hellhound becomes a woman in an instant, her tan hand rubbing Cassy's back and encouraging her to get it all out.

Am I going to die before the seven days are up? Why am I so sick? Why am I aging so quickly? What is happening to me? I need Ruin—no, I don't need him. I can make my own decisions. I need to make that decision quickly, though. But how can I think when I am this sick? I need to be myself again. Will I ever be that again? If I accept the deal, will I return to normal? Will I—Will Ruin—Why am—

"My beloved." Ruin's voice is choked, as though he can't believe what he is seeing. Cassy could hardly believe it, either, when she looked into the broken mirror this morning. She has aged horrifically; no grace involved whatsoever.

"Ruin." She can't stop her voice from sounding relieved, can't help herself from wanting to fall into his arms. And, oh, how she hates herself for it.

"I'm so sorry," he whispers, face cracking as he watches her painfully. "I'm so sorry I've done this to you."

"You should be," she croaks, waving a hand at him slowly. A move that makes her wrist ache, her skin pulling against it painfully. "Why...why is this happening? *What* is happening?"

She has always loved her body, but it is failing her now. Failing her spectacularly, and she has no idea why. Is it the power eating away at her? Is it some kind of punishment sent by the council? Do they have that power? Can they do that without Ruin's permission?

"Because of me," he says simply, nodding thankfully at Cerci, who is cleaning up the vomit. "Because of what I am."

"I-I don't understand." In the first two days, Cassy told herself she would never speak to Ruin again. She was so upset, so vindictive, that she would have followed through. But now...now she is dying. Truly, awfully, dying. And she needs to know what it is she is dying for before she makes her final decision in two days' time.

Ruin sits gently beside her on the couch, reaching out as though to touch her and jerking his hand back abruptly. Cerci disappears after a few minutes of silence, and Cassy hears paws tapping against wood as she exits the house entirely.

"I am Death," Ruin says eventually, swallowing as though struggling to form the right words. "Where I go, death follows. And you, Cassiopeia, are beautifully alive. You are a prime example of your species, brimming with life and joy and fulfillment. Only...only those things wilt around me, like petals from a dying rose. And so...so the longer I am at your side, the sooner death will claim you."

"I—" she pauses, thinking back to the past. When she first gained her powers, her hair turned silver, her skin paled, and her eyes turned to an icy blue. Then, not long after Ruin showed up, her appearance began changing again. It only took a few months, actually. The wrinkles, the white highlights...it was all because of him?

"Yes," he says, as though reading her thoughts. "Do you understand now? Do you see why I had to stay away? Why I couldn't allow myself to be with you?"

"Oh," she breathes, eyes wide in realization. "Oh, Ruin." *Damn it all to hell.* Ruin had truly been in love with her, then. It wasn't something he had said just to make her stay, like she was inclined to believe the last few days. He loves her, and he left because he loved her too much to stay. Because he didn't want her to face the choice she has to make now. Because he was putting her needs above his own.

"I couldn't tell you," he whispers, head drooping low in shame. "I'm not allowed to admit what I am. I don't know why, but…I've never been able to tell anyone who I am until they guess for themselves. My tongue does the thing—you know, the thing that happened to you during the trial when you tried to lie? For me, it's impossible to tell the truth. So all those times when I let you believe I was things I am not…it was easier that way. Easier than trying to make you understand. Easier than hoping you wouldn't hate me after you found out."

"Why did you order the hit?" She licks her dry lips, her words shaky and slow.

If he loved me before I knew him, why order me to die? Why send a ghost army after me? Why warn his reapers? Why watch me for years if he wanted me dead? He could have done it himself. He probably should have. Maybe he couldn't bring himself to do it. Maybe it was the only way he knew how to break free. Maybe he—Why did—Why tell—

"Because I hated myself for loving you. Because I put us in a situation that could not end well for either of us. I thought…I thought pushing you away was the right thing to do. The *only* thing to do. But the moment I sent that order out to my underlings…" He flinches, taking a deep breath before staring into her icy blue eyes. "I regretted it immediately. I hated myself for it. But I couldn't take it back; it was too late. So I sought you out instead. Introduced myself, despite knowing it would only end badly for you. It was my only option. My scent would hide yours for a while, until I could figure out what to do. But then you started falling for me, too, and I started to hope for a better future, and I..." Ruin groans, sliding his hands through his hair and shuddering as he closes his eyes.

"Why send me after ghosts?" She licks her lips again, unable to keep them moist. Her entire throat feels dry, too. Her skin is itchy, or maybe it's her bones that itch. She isn't sure how to tell the difference anymore, the way they cling to each other like lost lovers.

"I was trying to distract you. To keep you from killing anyone else. Those deaths were drawing attention to you; anyone who knew what to look for would have been able to find you. And, selfishly, I was stopping you from killing people who were not on my list. It's wrong to take lives early like that, even if those souls don't deserve to stay on this earthly plane. Even if they are evil, withered things that are far beyond salvation."

"And then I went and killed anyway," she says, sighing softly at her own incompetence. "And that had reapers on my tail immediately."

"I was so angry with you that day," he admits, watching her intently. "All my carefully laid plans were ruined, and I didn't know what to do with you. I didn't know how to save you anymore. I still don't."

"Only I can save myself now," she murmurs, coughing into her hand abruptly. When she pulls her hand away, a small patch of blood lies there. Subtly, she wipes it on the dark couch and hopes he doesn't notice. "It's my choice: stay with you or die."

"To die like this..." He looks her over, shaking his head sadly. "It's brutal, C.J."

She smiles lightly, weakly. "I'm C.J. again, huh?"

"You are many things to me. Some are more important than others."

"I have another question," she states, erupting into a coughing fit again. Will she even manage to get it out at this point? "Braxton mentioned others. I just…how many? How often? Is this—us—even *real*?"

"Of course it's real." With the way Ruin jerks back in pain as though she sucker-punched him, Cassy feels a bit of regret for asking the question. But she had to. She has to *know*. "There-there were others, yes. But the circumstances were much, much different. They weren't accidents."

"You chose them," she says plainly, her voice merely a croak.

"Yes. But *they* didn't choose *me*." He stares into her soul as though to make her understand, to make her see the truth. "I knew you were different when you left a mark on me, too." He fingers the silver streak in his hair, a near-identical match to what hers used to be.

"How many?" She turns her head away, not wanting him to see the rippling jealousy that has risen to the surface. She doesn't want him to think she cares, to know that she still loves him, despite it all.

He sighs, and she catches him placing his head in his hands. "Six. The first time I tried, I was beyond lonely. I spent centuries on my own, centuries without anyone by my side. I craved companionship. I craved love. I had a few reapers, but…that wasn't what I wanted. What I needed. I chose an Egyptian queen to be my bride, chose her for her beauty and nothing more. She was…stunning, to say the least. As remarkable as history paints her to be. She had many lovers in her lifetime, and I wanted to be one of them. And she took me willingly, wantonly. I didn't realize until it was too late that she was playing me for a fool. When I gifted her some of my power, she didn't realize that it came with a caveat. She didn't want to rule by my side for eternity. She wasn't in love with me and didn't want to be tied down to me for the rest of time. When given her ultimatum, she decided to die. Killed herself using a venomous snake."

"You're talking about Cleopatra," she breathes, head spinning back to face him with a mouth gaped open in surprise. "You're trying to tell me that you dated her? That you...That you *fucked* her?"

"Jealous, my beloved?" Ruin smirks down at her, a thumb reaching out to trace her bottom lip. "You have always had a crude mouth."

"Who else?" she demands, outraged. He can't *really* want her, not if he has been with someone like Cleopatra.

"Amelia Earhart." He pauses, letting that sink in. His expression turns wistful, his smile light and sad. "She was brilliant. I was attracted to her mind and to her motivation. But she didn't want to stay with me, either. She hadn't made a choice yet when she went up in that plane. But her seven days were up, and..." He shudders, opening and closing his mouth before adding, "Marilyn Monroe. I didn't realize she was in love with someone else. I didn't know...I didn't know that her time with me was a distraction from her life. When the time came to choose, she chose death."

"You have expensive taste," she says, licking her lips again, again, again. "The other three...were they famous, too? Is that your type? Famous women in their late thirties?"

I am beautiful, sure, but I'm not anything like those women. How can he want me when he's been with women like that? How can he love me when he's had them? I've never been jealous like this, never felt inferior to anyone else. Why did—How does—Is he—

"No, Cassiopeia." He laughs heartily, his hand dropping down to her thigh. "The other three were ordinary women. A beautiful woman from South Africa who would not leave her people to join me. A daring, dangerous woman I found in a circus in North America. A shy, nervous woman working in a library in Ireland. Those three were in their twenties. But none of them were willing to sacrifice their eternities to be with me. None loved me enough for it. They wanted fleeting fun and nothing more. They wanted the same things as you. I thought it was a mistake, at first, choosing you. I thought I had repeated history by mistake. Now, I'm not so sure."

"Were you in love with them?" She turns away again, unsure if she can look him in the eyes if his answer is yes. Unsure if she can say anything without confirming to him that she isn't a repeat of his past.

"At the time, I thought I was. I was head over heels for Cleopatra, obsessed with her, until I found the next woman. Then she was my true love, until I found another. I mourned and I pined, but…I don't think any of it was real. I don't think I felt more than a profound attachment. My loneliness dominated me for a long time, Cassiopeia. It controlled me. Meeting Cerci, allowing her to join me at my side…that changed things. It healed me, if only slightly."

Cassy flinches, forcing herself to ask, "And you and Cerci…you two never…?"

Ruin laughs again, shaking his head adamantly. His gaze trails to the open door, watching a spot in the distance as though knowing exactly where she is out there. "No. No, never. When Cerci offered to stay by my side, it wasn't because she loved me, or even because she held any affection for me. I had just collected her husband's soul after a Class Three attacked him in front of her; she wasn't ready for a relationship. She still isn't. She died soon after him, heartbroken and desperate to see him again. She offered to stay with me because she thought I would lead her back to him, that I would revive his soul for her. But I can't. *I won't.* She understands that, I think. She still searches for answers on her own, and I allow it, but…"

"That's horrible," she whispers, a tear slipping down her cheek for her newly found friend.

Would I risk an eternity without Ruin if I knew I had the chance to get him back? Would I bind myself to someone if it meant I could find a way back to him? Would I still be able to hold onto that love after hundreds of years have passed? Yes. Impossibly yes. I don't know how I know, but I do. I don't—Would I—Would he—

Ruin nods along sadly, his grip on her thigh tightening as he turns back to her. "Yes, it was. It pains me to see her so saddened over a loss so tragic."

She purses her lips, understanding lighting her eyes. "That's why you won't tell me about Class Three Souls. Because you and Cerci have a history with those, and you don't want her to get upset." It makes sense. She wouldn't want poor Cerci relieving that, either.

"Do you understand now, Cassy? Do you see why I lied, why I tricked, why I hid? I didn't have much of a choice. And look at you. Look what being with me has done for you." His whisper is pained, his face strained as he looks her over. Reaching up to cup her cheek, he says, "I love you more than I ever knew I could love. You've awoken something in me that I've been searching for for years. You are the one I have been waiting for my entire, eternal life. In the morning, when it comes time to choose, I need you to choose me." Ruin gets down on his knees before her, bowing his head low as tears slip down his cheeks. "I am begging you to choose me."

And before Cassy can answer, before she can tell him she doesn't know what or how to feel about any of this, he's gone. But that touch on her cheek lingers, her lip tingling from the brush of his thumb. Something else stirs in her chest, though, something foreign and painful. She opens her mouth, crying out, "Cerci!" just as her hands fly to her chest and she collapses.

Chapter 24

"**S**he's not doing well, Ruin," a quiet voice murmurs nearby, followed by the rustle of clothes and a sharp exhale.

"I know," comes his ready answer, the quiet following palpable.

"She won't make it," the voice says again, someone Cassy vaguely recognizes to be Cerci.

"I know," he says again, agitated and afraid.

"She has to decide *now*," Cerci tries again, imploring him to make some sort of decision. Cassy recognizes the angry tilt in her voice: fear.

I already know what to do. I've been thinking of the right words to say for days. Will I be able to get them all out? I feel so weak and inhuman. I feel so alone. But I have to tell them. I have to tell Ruin. I need—I want—I have—

Cassy opens her mouth, closes it again. Licks her lips once, twice, and tries again. "I—" The words die on her tongue, a shadow looming behind her closed lids. It takes a lot of effort to open her eyes, and even more to stare into Ruin's terrified gaze.

"My beloved," he breathes, relief filling his features upon seeing her awake.

"I've already decided," she says hoarsely, attempting to lift herself. Cerci laid her down on the couch and covered her with a hole-ridden blanket, but she feels undeniably cold. She can feel that cold in the marrow of her bones, in the very cells that are the reason for her existence. It feels too familiar, too foreign, too inevitable. It feels like death.

"You have?" She can tell that Ruin is trying not to be hopeful, but the glimmer in his hooded eyes gives it away.

"Yes," she croaks, paper-thin eyelids fluttering close before lifting again. "I want to make a deal, Death."

Ruin leans back, brows furrowed. She has to close her eyes again; the weight is unbearable. "Oh?"

"Your others...they were gifted powers, too?" The darkness behind her lids is comforting, is reaching a hand out and offering her a place inside its depths. So she opens her eyes again, forcing herself to reject the offer despite the horrific heaviness that makes her so willing to accept.

"They were. Not as...useful as yours, but powers all the same." Ruin still seems confused, his hands shoved down in his pockets. Turning away from her, she sees him sneakily slip a cigarette from one and a lighter from the other. He told her he is trying to quit, but she can only imagine how stressed he is seeing her like this. Because, truly, she is no longer a woman. She is a skeleton being inhabited by a woman's soul. And she's certain he can sense how close that soul is to being collected by his hands.

"And if they had accepted your offer to stay by your side, they would have lost their power," she confirms, drool slipping from the corner of her mouth unwittingly.

"Sure, but they would most likely have gained something new. Not nearly as powerful, a party trick compared to what they had, but…" Ruin's eyes sparkle, a grin lighting his features. "Oh, you brilliant, wicked woman."

"My offer," she croaks, barely containing her smile, "is this: In exchange for staying by your side for eternity, for agreeing to be Death's bride, I ask to remain the Shadow Kisser. I ask to be your equal, to continue to share the burden that living in the darkness brings to you. I ask that you give me a task. I ask that I not be a reaper, but a collector. I ask that you allow me to hunt the souls who have been roaming the earth, that you allow me to kiss them and return their spirits to you. I ask that you be as loyal to me as I am to you, and that no matter how many miles separate us, we never truly part. I offer my lips to you, Ruin, and you alone. I offer myself to Death."

"I—" Ruin pauses, excitement thrilling through his veins. "I accept your offer, Cassiopeia Jaynes."

Cassy's weak smile is followed by, "And you won't have to bring this to the council, correct? Deals are for you to make alone."

"Yes." He bends to his knees beside the couch, leaning his head over hers. "And that means you won't have to worry about living through the night."

"I know," she says simply, her wrinkled hands shaking. "Shall we seal it with a kiss?"

Ruin's only reply is a tiny chuckle, his lips hovering over hers for precious seconds before they close the small space. He kisses her softly, slowly, surely. He lets his lips linger over hers as his dark power flows into her, a shadowy wisp that curls from his mouth into hers like a long tongue. It laps around her lips, her mouth, her teeth. Then it dives down her throat, her back arching as it pierces through her heart. She gasps as it does so, her entire body erupting into an electric current. Ruin backs away from her, watching her with a confidence and smugness that has her fear of the pain ebbing away entirely. He knows what it means to become immortal, and this pain is part of the process; there's nothing for her to be scared of.

"I love you," she manages to say the words aloud for the first time as her body erupts into dark flames, igniting from within. She screams, the pain intense and insatiable.

How long will this last? How much more pain does the process demand? What will Ruin tell the council? When can I get Ruin alone? What will—Can I—If it—

Her screams end abruptly, the fire fanning into falling embers. The couch is covered in scorch marks, blessedly saved from erupting into flames. And thereupon it she lies, her body *hers* again. She can see her silver hair, and she reaches up to touch it with a soft sigh. Her hands are smooth once more, the sickly skin back to its normal ivory hue. She no longer feels like vomiting, no longer feels weak and unable to move. She pushes herself into a sitting position in one fluid motion, marveling at the way she fills out her own body again. Turning her head to look at Ruin, the breath that had just returned flees from her again.

Ruin's eyes are full of dark promise and immeasurable love, his gaze stripping her to her core. And as she stands, she sees Cerci flee the house entirely. Cassy takes that as an invitation to pounce onto him, wrapping her arms around his neck and pulling her to him. Their lips meet in a frantic, desperate motion, a kiss so normal she wants to cry tears of joy. There is no punishing pain for Ruin, no burning and peeling skin. They are equals now, as per their deal. Her lips belong to him. Nothing she does to him will hurt him. And, *oh*, the things she wants to do to him.

"I thought you were going to leave me," Ruin whispers against her lips, pressing his forehead against hers lovingly.

"I thought I was, too." She swallows, wincing at her own words. "And then I realized, why does it matter how many secrets you held from me when it was for a good reason? You protected me, just like Cerci protects you. And why does it matter how many exes you have? They were using you, just like you were using them. Just like I used every person I've ever had sex with. You lied about a lot of things, sure, but I lied to myself, too. I was so desperate, so lonely, that I fell in love with a ghost. I despised my attraction for you, tried to convince myself that it was only physical. Truth be told, I'm grateful you aren't a ghost. I'm grateful you are an immortal being."

"Most people hurl at the thought of being immortal," Ruin murmurs against her cheek, but she feels the upward tilt of his lips against her.

"Being immortal means I'll never have to give you up. Never have to give *this* up," she says simply, blinking up innocently at him.

Her hand trails down his chest to the belt looped through his dark jeans, masterfully pulling it apart without looking down. She can feel Ruin's breath hitch at her touch, can feel his heart racing underneath the palm she places on his chest. Then his lips are on her again, devouring her very soul.

I want this. I need this. Why did I ever think I could live without this? Why did I ever want to give this up? I can have this every day, multiple times a day, and it will never get old. I could never be tired of being in love with him. I could—I won't—Why did—

Their clothes come off in rapid succession, starting with Ruin's pants and ending with Cassy's. They tear at each other like rabid dogs, desperate to be together in the way their souls yearn to be. She trails kisses over every inch of Ruin's skin, marveling over how perfect he is for her. Relishing every taste she never dreamed of receiving. And Ruin lets her, for a while. He lets her kiss and lick over soft muscles, lets her get down on her knees and take him into her hands before saying a single word.

"Cassiopeia," he moans as she pumps him once, watching him from underneath light lashes. "I can't...you can't—"

"Why not?" The lick that follows leaves him speechless, the light kiss to his head followed by her teasing laugh. She couldn't do this before, though she had pictured it too many times to count. It's positively thrilling to be able to pleasure him in this way, to have the chance to watch him come undone from the power of her lips alone. "Is something wrong?"

"Quite the opposite," he chokes out, curling a hand into her hair to hold her still. "It's too right. I don't know if I'll last with you—"

"Who said I wanted you to last?" Another one of her seductive laughs follows when he attempts, and fails, to sputter out an answer. After teasing him a bit more, she adds, "Are you telling me the almighty Death hasn't learned his limits? Hasn't mastered his own release? Surely you aren't the type to spill early. I doubt Cleopatra liked that very much."

Cassy has a teasing glint in her eye, but Ruin still becomes defensive. "She was not *you*," he pants as she takes him partway into her mouth, and chokes out, "A single look from you has me spiraling, my beloved. I've never felt as out of control as I do with you. I think that much was obvious when I accidentally imbued you with my powers after a single touch."

"Mmm," she hums as she takes him deeper, swirling her tongue around his tip before pulling out with an audible *pop*. "Good," she says simply, grinning devilishly. "I want you out of your mind when you're with me, Ruin. I want to see you desperate and on the edge. I want you to crave me like you've craved no other." Then she is on him again, licking and sucking and stroking him until he has no words left to give her. Until he is unapologetically coming down her throat, allowing her to swallow everything he has to offer greedily.

"Cassiopeia," Ruin growls out once he has a second to recover, to breathe through the release that had almost made him tumble over. "Stand up."

Her heart flutters dangerously as she slowly stands, wiping at her lips with the back of her hand with a mischievous grin. "Something the matter?"

"Such a wicked woman," he murmurs, watching her with a predatory gaze. He jerks his head toward the wall behind him, saying only, "Put your hands there."

She considers disobeying his orders for a moment but quickly decides against it when she sees the dangerous gleam in his eyes. She knows what is hiding in those hazel depths, knows that he would love to punish her for disobedience. So she simply does as told, feeling vulnerable as she bares herself to him.

Ruin's hands slide down her body, calloused fingers leaving trails of goosebumps in their wake. They trail down her spine, across her hips, down her thighs, and back up. Then he's tracing circles around her clit, and her every thought flees from her mind. Ruin knows exactly how to touch her, as though he has already memorized the motions. She doesn't even need him to penetrate her to chase her release, coming undone from his touch alone. And when she feels like she can breathe again, when her throat is dry from crying out his name, he reaches up with his free hand to knead at her breasts. Between the two sensations, she is coming again, harsher and faster than the first. And her mind...her mind is blessedly numb, just like he knows she wants.

"Ruin. I can't—" she pants out, her legs feeling like jelly.

"Something the matter?" he repeats her earlier sentiments, and she can practically feel him grinning behind her.

"Yes," she says matter-of-factually, turning to look over her shoulder with a lustful gaze. "If you don't stick your dick inside me right now—"

Ruin lets out a barking laugh, cupping her ass and giving it a harsh squeeze. "I should make you beg for it," he says in that domineering way she so enjoys, pushing his head against her entrance. "I should punish you for the way you've made me suffer this week."

"Punish me later," she pants, arching her back in an attempt to push it in. "Fuck me now."

Ruin laughs again but obliges, pushing inside her in one brutal stroke. She groans against the pain and the pleasure, panting and blubbering nonsense until he begins to pump into her in lazy strides. Ruin grips her by the hips, leaning forward to nibble on her earlobe and whisper, "Your wish is my command."

She doesn't know how long it takes her to come apart again. Every second of having Ruin inside her is utter bliss, every pump granting her wish. By the time she comes twice more, he is spinning and lifting her, shoving her into the wall. This position offers him a way to get deeper, and she swears she can feel him in her stomach. It is the perfect mix of pain and pleasure, mixed with the feeling of his mouth on her breasts and the occasional strokes of his thumb against her clit. She doesn't know right from left at this point, doesn't know her name. But she knows his. She cries it out every so often, pleading and begging for *something*. And Ruin will change something slightly, going harder or faster, squeezing or teasing. And those changes have her erupting again, again, again. Until he finally comes crashing down with her, unable to hold on any longer.

Gently, Ruin lowers her to the ground, holding her steady when her legs wobble like a newborn calf. "You'll stay now, right?" she questions lightly, arms still wrapped around his neck.

"Forever," he says back, guiding her to the couch.

"Let me pee first," she laughs, peering at him under her lashes lightly. "Immortals can still get UTIs, I'm assuming?" She leaves him for only brief minutes, but every second away feels painful. There's a tugging on her chest, a pull demanding she return to him immediately.

"What is this?" she questions upon her return, holding her bare chest and frowning.

"Our bond," he reaches to cover her hand with his, chewing on the inside of his cheek worriedly. "It's just formed, so it will be strong for a while. It will get better, eventually."

"Is it like this with Cerci, too?" Cassy crawls over Ruin, where he lounges on the couch, pulling the thin blanket over their bodies. She props her arms up on his chest, holding her chin and staring into his beautiful face.

I can't believe I get to have this forever. Being immortal doesn't feel different from being mortal. Will my parents notice? Will Winter? I'll tell her, of course. She already knows about Ruin. Mostly. Oh, I've missed my parents' weekly call and the monthly dinner. They are going to kill me. I'll tell them Ruin brought me on a surprise trip. That'll be fine, I think. I need—They are—Winter will—

"To a degree." He takes a strand of her silver hair and twirls it thoughtfully. "But ours is different. It was formed out of love, out of an agreement to be bound together in a way that only soul mates possess. Cerci already has one of those. I felt it when our bond formed. Hers and my bond is completely platonic, not nearly as intense. It was hard for her, at first, though. She wanted to protect me so fiercely that it hurt. Luckily for her, I wanted her by my side. Needed her. And luckily for you, I won't let you leave my side anytime soon."

"Why didn't my appearance change when our bond formed?" she questions as he continues to twirl her hair, gesturing to her skin, hair, and eyes. "I wasn't like this before you."

"You wanted to be the Shadow Kisser. This is who she is." Ruin smiles, flipping them so she is pinned beneath him. "And isn't she marvelous?"

She laughs, a blush rising up her neck and to her cheeks. "Don't tell me you aren't sated?"

"You were the one teasing me about long learned limits. Don't you want to test them?" He leaves a trail of kisses down her neck, sucking on one particularly sensitive spot that leaves her breathless.

"I'm not sure I can make it through another round," she admits between soft moans, gripping onto his strong shoulders tightly.

Ruin leans up, grinning down at her with a sinful gleam in his eyes. "Then let's find out."

Chapter 25

Cassy wakes to the sounds of creaking footsteps and Cerci's low warning growls, the noise startling her into consciousness. Braxton's returning grumble follows Cerci's growl, accompanied by his voice hissing, "You know I have no choice, Cerci. This isn't up to me; not anymore."

Before she can wake Ruin, before she can do more than open her eyes, Braxton is standing next to the couch that their bare limbs still stretch out upon. Cassy, blessedly, is covered by a thin blanket, but she seems to have stolen the thing entirely from Ruin. He is utterly naked, like her, but everything is out for Cerci and Braxton to see. His large member stands completely upright, catching not only her attention, but Braxton's, too.

"Oh, come on, man! Cover up, for Death's sake!" Braxton covers his eyes dramatically, waving a hand around vehemently.

She hides her giggle under a cough, icy eyes turning to Ruin as he slowly blinks his own open. He looks at Cassy first, taking in her covered body before turning toward his reaper. With a husky bite, he grinds out, "You could have knocked first."

"I tried to warn him," Cerci pipes up from behind them, watching Braxton with an amused expression.

"Growls and bites are not warnings," Braxton snaps, waving his hand at Ruin again. "Come on, Ruin! I don't want to see it!"

Ruin sighs, standing and giving her a full view of his rounded backside. He pads over to the pile of haphazardly discarded clothes, pulling on his pants before turning back to Braxton. "You've seen it all before, Braxton. Why complain about a perfect view?"

"Don't...just don't," the reaper grumbles back, pulling his hand from his face. "I came to see what Cassy's decision is, but it seems she's already made it." He turns his gaze to her, sniffing the air harshly before squinting his eyes in suspicion.

"She has," Ruin agrees, pointing at him threateningly. "And if you stare at her any longer, you'll no longer possess a completed set of eyes."

Cassy tries to hide a laugh again, failing spectacularly. Ruin casts her a scalding glare, not nearly as amused as her. "Sorry. So sorry. Please continue having your pissing contest."

"You smell," Braxton tells her abruptly, taking a step forward.

"Rude," she mutters at the same time Ruin says, "Mind your damn business, underling."

"You know how demeaning it is to be called an underling?" Braxton pauses his calculated steps forward, narrowed gaze now on Ruin. "I'm your friend, you bastard!"

"My friend and an *underling*." Ruin's arms are crossed across his bare chest, smooth copper skin on full display. She sees the hint of a smirk hiding on those wide lips, a teasing glint in his eyes.

"You changed her," Braxton accuses, spinning toward Cassy with wide eyes. "I smell it on her, so don't deny it. Damn it, Ruin, you know the rules—"

Ruin's scythe appears beside him, materializing from thin air as he points its sharp blade toward the reaper. "Rules don't apply to me."

"Rules were *created* for you," Braxton bites back, still watching Cassy wearily. She tightens the blanket around her before standing, striding toward Braxton with a confidence she has only ever faked before.

I don't need Confident Cassy anymore. I am Confident Cassy. I was always Confident Cassy. With Ruin by my side, I can be myself. With Ruin by my side, I won't have to hide anymore. I don't have to be scared. I don't have to be hunted. I don't—I won't—With Ruin—

"No rules were broken, reaper," she says calmly, coming to stand directly before him. He may be a good half foot taller than her, but she still manages to look down her small nose at him. "I made a deal with the devil."

"You made a deal," Braxton repeats slowly, blinking steadily as though processing the information. "And what, exactly, was granted to you in this deal?"

"Kiss me and find out." Ruin's low growl of warning leaves her laughing in joy, her own smirk twisting her lips now.

"Nope. No way, Shadow Kisser. Not happening today." Braxton scrambles back from her, scratching his bald head wearily. "So...you aren't going to become a reaper, then?"

"No, she isn't," Ruin snaps, putting himself in front of Cassy to block her from view. She rolls her eyes at the action, giving Cerci a "Can you believe this?" look.

"Okay. Okay, this is okay. This is fine, actually. Cassy's sentence was to die a permanent death or pledge loyalty to you and become an immortal, type not specified. And she has...certainly shown her loyalty, I think. She's clearly been turned into an immortal...something."

"She's like me," Cerci pipes in, watching Cassy with a seriousness that jars her. "She's a companion to Death."

"You made Cassy a hellhound, too?" Braxton blinks at Ruin in surprise, as though unable to picture her as such a beast.

Cassy chuckles, poking her head out from around Ruin's side. "Oh, I'm not a hellhound, underling. I'm something much worse."

Braxton groans, running his hand down his face and mumbling something unintelligible. Then, loud enough to clarify, he says, "You sure know how to pick them, Ruin."

Ruin attacks, tossing his scythe to the side and tumbling into Braxton to force him to the ground. They roll around for a few seconds, punching and kicking, before Cassy fully comprehends the situation. "Cerci, should we...do something about this?"

Cerci leans forward and places her elbows on top of the couch, letting her arms dangle off the front with a sigh. "No. They do this all the time."

"Right. This is...normal then?" She takes the opportunity to slip into the bathroom with her clothes, listening for Cerci's reply as she changes.

"Yep. These two are like brothers. They argue, they fight, they kiss and make up. It's a process, you just have to let them get through it."

"Alright. Want to go outside with me, then? I haven't felt the sun on my skin in days." Cerci obediently follows her outside, the two women sitting on the front porch steps while listening to the thumps of the men wrestling around inside.

After a few minutes of silence, Cassy sucks in a breath and says, "You've seen me naked. Before today, I mean."

Cerci laughs, shaking her head full of wild curls playfully. "You thought I was a dog. I was respectful and looked away."

"Ruin said something once about you telling him things. I brushed it off and forgot about it, but then, when you came striding into my room...I remembered the comment not long after. And even though you were just a dog, that's not all you were to me. You were a friend. You *are* a friend. I loved you then, and I love you now. So...well, I guess what I'm getting at is you can talk to me if you want. You can tell me things that may be too embarrassing or difficult to tell Ruin."

"Ah. That's where this is going." Cerci turns away from Cassy, the wind blowing in the scent of wildflowers. Or maybe that's just what Cerci smells like when she isn't in dog form. "You want to know about my husband."

"Not if you don't want me to know," she is quick to say, tapping her fingers on the porch in anticipation.

Cerci turns to look at her, eerie black eyes hard and flat. "I don't want you to know."

"Okay." Cassy swallows, opening and closing her mouth before deciding that it is better not to say anything at all.

What happened to him? Why is she so determined to get him back? She had to have died young, which means he did, too. How horrible is it to watch someone die at the hands of a Class Three Soul? It can't be good if it resulted in her declaring loyalty to Death to help fight them. I can help her fight them, too. Join her in her mission to destroy them. I can—If she—Maybe I—

Cerci's nose twists, a brief flash of devastation crossing her face. "I've been with Ruin for nearly two hundred fifty years, Cassy. I've held on to my husband the entire time, and I will continue to do so for all of eternity. I've held on to this home to remember him, despite it not really being my childhood home. My home was destroyed and rebuilt by an ancestor; its floor plan was replicated, and the inside was ever-changing. And yet...I hold on to it. There are memories here that I don't want to forget, and there are others I wish had left a long time ago. I appreciate your generosity and kindness, but I will not place the burden that is my pain upon you. This wound is mine and mine alone to heal. This is all I will say on the subject, okay?"

"Okay," she echoes again, a deep sadness creeping into her. She can't imagine the emotional torment Cerci must be in, or the loneliness her loss has encompassed her with.

"Sorry about that, ladies," Braxton voices his apologies behind them, panting and grinning when Cassy turns her head to look at him. "Congratulations, Cassy. I hope I'm still invited to the wedding." With that, he takes his leave, evaporating into the air like a droplet of water on a hot day.

"Great. Glad that's over." Cerci stands, dusting dirt off the back of her flared pants. Cassy watches as she enters the house and listens as a few words she can't make out are exchanged with Ruin. Then a giant hellhound is bounding out, taking off at a sprint into the nearby wheat field.

Ruin's steps are light as he exits the house, pausing to lean on his scythe as he steps onto the porch with Cassy. "Welcome to the family," he says with a sly smile, staring off in the direction Cerci ran.

"I feel very welcomed, actually," she says, watching him under her lashes. "I can't wait to spend the rest of my life like this." And it's true. She wants nothing more than to have Ruin by her side, nothing more than to protect the people he cares for. She may not know them all yet, but she will meet them soon. Befriend them. Care for them. Love them just as fiercely as him. Because through all the snarling and dick measuring, she saw plainly how dearly he cares for Braxton. Saw how much he prioritizes the rules they created, despite having no obligation to follow a single one of them. He does it out of respect and love for the family he has forged.

"What will you tell your family?" Ruin won't look at her, probably because this subject is something they have not discussed and is too late to reconsider.

"I travel a lot for a new tech job, still with the government but much more important. I look so young because I get Botox." She shrugs nonchalantly, placing her head in her hands and propping her elbows on her lap. "We have a weekly phone call and a monthly dinner, Ruin. I'll be sad when they are gone and I still live as a twenty-four-year-old, but it won't devastate me. And Winter...that will hurt more, but she knows my situation. She'll still call me every day. She'll harass me until the day we come to reap her soul. I'm not worried about the after part."

"Cerci hasn't forgotten the after part," Ruin admits, finally turning away from the spot in the distance to look at her. "She is hung up on the past, and no amount of reasoning will ever bring her out of it."

Cassy nods, feeling guilty for bringing up the subject with the shape-shifter. She had only been trying to help, but… "Not everyone gets a happy ending," she remarks, a sad but sure truth.

Ruin nods, a silent agreement. "Cerci's story is a horrible one, and every time she pleads for him, my heart shatters a little more."

She opens her mouth, closes it, then says, "And you can't do it? You can't bring him back?"

Ruin purses his lips, shaking his head gravely. "It's not about can't, it's about won't. It's a horrific imbalance of nature. Bringing someone back from the dead…it would have cataclysmic consequences. My job is to collect souls, not to drag them back into existence."

"Cerci still loves him."

"She will always love him," Ruin says quietly, shuddering. "She loves him in a way that cannot be replicated, in a way that renders her soul broken without him. I know because it is the same way I love you. To have felt you slipping away from me, even so briefly…it was torture. My heart hurts for my friend knowing she's endured centuries of that pain."

She smiles sadly up at him, her own heart squeezing painfully. "I want her to have a happy ending, Ruin. We are lucky to be in this position. She wasn't afforded that luck."

"Don't ask it of me, my beloved. There aren't many things I would say no to if you asked, but this is one of them." His face is so grave, so solemn, that she can only nod. With a light sigh, he says, "We are happy, Cassy. One day she will be, too."

"She isn't...upset about this development? It's been the two of you for nearly two hundred fifty years. This isn't...affecting her negatively?"

Ruin smiles, white teeth flashing at her. "No, Cassy. She's thrilled to have you here. She loves love, whether she wants to admit it or not. And I love you for worrying about her."

"What comes next?" she questions, pushing herself off the ground. Ruin gathers her in his arms when she approaches, leaning down to kiss her softly.

Pressing his forehead against hers, he says simply, "We live."

Epilogue

Cassy bounces on the heels of her feet in trepidation, glancing at the clock hanging on the wall of the church foyer. It is half past five, and the wedding should have already begun.

What if Ruin changed his mind? What if he decided he doesn't want eternity after all? Is he in there, waiting? Is he just running late? Is he—What if—Why does—

"Relax, Cass," Cerci laughs softly at her side, looping her arm through Cassy's. "You know Ruin. He comes and goes as he pleases."

That, at least, is true. Cassy has never known him not to appear and vanish at will, which is the nature of his job. He can't determine death times, and he mustn't leave a single soul behind. Sometimes, it is impossible to gather every soul. Sometimes that means he is leaving ghosts to wander the earthly plane. That's where she comes in, though. She hunts down the souls left to wander, kissing them goodbye and sending them back to Ruin to pass on. The past six months have been the most productive of all time, according to the Reaper Council. It fills her with pride to know she is making such a huge difference in the world. Such a huge difference in *Ruin's* world.

"Well, he did give all the reapers an hour off to be here," she sighs, understanding Ruin is probably tying off loose ends to be here on time. That he is trying to ensure no more ghosts are created so she doesn't have to clean up the mess afterward. But, as much as they hope otherwise, she knows better than to believe they'll catch every departing soul. There are too many too often for even a minute to go by without the need to catch one, much less the hour Ruin is trying to grant them all. For the next week, while they are on their honeymoon, the reapers are being assigned extra work to ensure that that exact situation won't come to pass. Not a single one complained, of course. They are all ecstatic that Ruin and Cassy are getting married; something about him being in a better mood all the time.

"Yeah, and that hour is almost up," Cerci grumbles, glancing at the clock herself now. Cassy has dressed her in a deep navy-blue dress to match the colors of their simple wedding, the cut a revealing V-neck with a large slit in the side to reveal an inch of Cerci's thick thighs. Cassy decided to go with the navy and French blue their wedding planner had suggested, mostly because blue is her favorite color and she has no qualms about having it in her wedding. Her bouquet has an arrangement of white and blue roses, their fresh scent filling her senses and calming her.

"I—" Cassy starts, the sound of a piano abruptly ending her train of thought.

"Finally!" Cerci pulls Cassy into her side, grinning as the doors to the sanctuary fling open. And there, at the end of the aisle under the gorgeous arch covered with fresh flowers and greenery, stands Ruin. He is dressed in a navy suit, his French blue tie draped loosely around his neck. The buttons of his jacket are uncuffed, pushed up past his wrists. And despite how disheveled he looks, despite how ruffled his hair is even as he desperately tries to comb it down with his hands, Cassy is so incredibly turned on by how beautiful he is.

Braxton stands to the right of Ruin, beaming with delight. Ruin reluctantly allowed him to be their wedding officiant, but she knows he wouldn't have chosen anyone else for the job. Braxton himself is in a French blue suit, looking handsome and eloquent as he stands underneath the light cast by the large stained-glass window behind him. The image is made up of an array of colors, a random pattern that vaguely looks like some birds and a green hillside with a rising sun in the background. But that window casts the entire sanctuary with a magical aura, the multicolored lights like fairies dancing in joy at the prospect of their union.

Cerci walks Cassy slowly down the aisle, the song playing on the piano unfamiliar to her but chosen by Ruin. It is old and happy, joyous in a way only a bride can be. And as she reaches the end of the aisle, stepping up next to Ruin with an offer of his hand, she feels every bit the beautiful, blushing bride she is meant to be.

I can't believe I'm getting married. I never thought I would get married. I never thought I would be in a relationship, period. If I had never met Ruin, there isn't a single person I would have considered for this honor. I don't know how I got so lucky. I don't know why I am so blessed. I don't—I can't—Ruin is—

She watches as he takes her in, his Adam's apple bobbing as he swallows hard. She chose a Victorian-inspired dress, something she knew he would appreciate in his old age. It has long white sleeves that elongate into ruffles at the elbows, the matching white skirt large and voluminous. It has a layer of lace on its outermost skirt, a small opening left in the front where the lace doesn't connect. The lace is present around her chest, too, reaching up her neck and ending halfway up. She had ensured he could still see her cleavage with a sweetheart neckline, though. Her thin veil is long, starting from the headband placed atop her drooping silver curls and brushing against the red carpet they stand atop. It is beautiful, and magnificent, and everything she never knew she wanted.

Ruin licks his lips once, twice, then says, "You are everything I could have dreamed of and more."

"You're late," she says in return, smiling majestically.

Ruin lifts her veil off her face gently, slowly, giving her a cocky smirk. "I had a few last-minute errands, my beloved."

She shakes her head softly, turning to look at Braxton when he says, "Alright, lovebirds. Ruin has *ruined* the timing of this, so let's get down to business. The rest of us have to go back to work."

Cassy laughs while Ruin glowers, earning chuckles from the small crowd. Winter sits among the group of reapers in the two front pews, Cerci now beside her. Winter looks awkward and out of place, but she beams up at Cassy and Ruin with tears streaming down her cheeks despite it. Cassy and Ruin opted not to have bridesmaids and groomsmen, or Winter would be by her side through this. It is symbolic, having the two alone with only a reaper by their side. For the rest of eternity, it will be them and their reapers. Cassy and Ruin together will now make decisions for those loyal to their cause. It felt right at the time. It still does. Cassy's parents were not invited, for obvious reasons. They can't know about what Ruin is, or what he has turned Cassy into. She plans on spinning a wild tale about eloping in Vegas, as many young couples do. With her history of impulsiveness due to her ADHD, she knows her parents will believe it.

Cassy hadn't realized Braxton had gone through a whole speech, his voice tuned out, until Ruin squeezed her hand gently three times. "I'm sorry," she breathes, staring into the hazel eyes of the man she loves. "What did you say?"

"You're supposed to repeat after me," Braxton huffs, but she knows there is no real resentment there. "I, Cassiopeia Jaynes, take you, Ruin Morrigan, to have and to hold from this day forward, for better or for worse, for richer or for poorer, in sickness and in health, to love and to cherish, until the world rips me from your heart."

She almost laughs at the abrupt change at the end but repeats the phrase anyway. Her heart picks up its pace as Ruin does the same, following it up with his own additions as prompted by Braxton to do.

Ruin holds her steady gaze, words unwavering. "Do you know why we say until the world rips me from your heart? It's because it's an impossible feat, to have a heart full of love ripped away into the unknown. It's an impossible feat to forge a heart without you in it, to possess a single part of me that will not ache for you for eternity. I am not made as humans are. I am still composed of cells and tissues and organs, but my chemistry is different. And yet, despite those differences, I feel the same things. I feel love and loss, feel pain and worry. All those cells and tissues and organs...they have been infiltrated by you. Every inch of me now belongs to you, every pesky feeling now yours to control. When you look at me, I am merely a man in love with a woman. Not Death, the reaper of souls. Not an immortal, lonely monster desperate for companionship. With you, I am just Ruin. You granted me a precious gift when you came into my life, and I will owe you a debt for the rest of my life. The world can never rip you from my heart because you are already embedded there, a permanent change to the chemistry of my very being. I am yours, Cassiopeia Jaynes, just as surely as you are mine."

Why does he have to be so eloquent? Why does he have to be so romantic? How did I ever find him? What did I do to deserve this life, this love? I can't live without this man. I cannot exist without him next to me. I hardly remember myself before him. I cannot live unless he is by my side. I cannot—How did—Why does—

Cassy is weeping, an unexpected thing. She isn't one to cry at weddings and had never expected to cry at her own. But now her tears are so great she can barely get out her own vows. "I did not know I was alone until you came into my life. I did not know that I wanted love or companionship. I was a mess, Ruin, and you cleaned me up. You gave me a purpose, a reason for being. You chose me before either of us ever knew I was chosen, and I can't even imagine what I did to deserve the amazing twist in fate that led us to each other. I can't imagine a life without you in it anymore. I fought what I felt for you for so long. I was convinced I could *never* be with you. And once I let myself hope, it was all over. I was yours, and there wasn't anything that could change that. Not even the giant dog that had been sleeping in my bed for months who suddenly turned into a woman and waltzed into our bedroom unannounced." She laughs and so does everyone else, Cerci the most of them all. She mouths, "My bad," to Cassy, grinning and trying to contain the joyous laughter she so rarely expresses. Cassy's mouth wobbles, her voice cracking as she says, "My words aren't as eloquent as yours, but they come from my heart. I love you, Ruin Morrigan, and I can't wait to spend an eternity by your side."

Cheers erupt as Ruin pulls Cassy into his chest, his lips finding hers in a heated kiss that leaves her quaking in her heels. Her arms slip around his neck, pushing into him further as she briefly forgets they have an audience. That is, until Braxton clears his throat and announces, "The new Mr. and Mrs. Morrigan!"

It feels like a blur as Ruin drags her down the aisle, hand in his. Reapers disappear in flashes around them, taking off to go collect awaiting souls. He pulls her into his arms as they enter the foyer, lips on hers again in a passion-filled moment. She considers transporting them away, a new skill she has learned in recent months, but remembers Winter still needs a way home at the last second.

"I'll take her," Cerci says from behind them, Winter at her side. Winter leaps at Cassy, pulling her away from Ruin and into her best friend's arms. Winter weeps into Cassy's shoulder, congratulating her over and over.

"I never thought I'd see the day," Winter says through her tears, sniffling and wiping at her eyes. Black is smudged across them and runs down her cheeks, but Winter doesn't seem to mind.

"Me either." Cassy smiles as Cerci pulls Winter away, transporting her away and home. She turns to her husband, wrapping her arms around his neck and grinning. "Where to now, husband?"

Ruin grins, hands on her hips as his lips trail down her neck. "Our room."

Cassy and Ruin decided to stay in the Maldives for their honeymoon, renting out a small hut on the crystal clear waters with a private pool. She hadn't planned on leaving the small hut, hadn't planned on leaving the bed with Ruin for at least a full day. But when he jumps up in the middle of the night, panting and panicked, she knows something is seriously wrong.

She watches through blurry vision as he slides off the bed and begins gathering clothes, his scythe appearing at his side. "What's going on?"

"Cerci," he says simply, the pure rage in his tone making her blink in surprise.

"What happened to her?" She rises, the blankets falling in a pool in her lap. Ruin pauses to take in her bare breasts, a frustrated groan leaving his lips.

"I'm going to kill her for taking me away from you," he grinds out, blinking away the lust in his gaze as he pulls on a shirt.

"I'm probably going to kill her anyway. What she has done…it's unforgivable."

"What did she do? Is she okay?" She is truly concerned as Ruin grabs his scythe, spinning on her with wild eyes.

The words that leave his mouth are unexpected and leave her guts twisting in the same anger overcoming him. "Cerci has raised the dead."

Acknowledgements

I started this book with little more than a concept to go off of, and my little spark turned into a roaring flame. This series is an ode to the love I will always cherish and never feel deserving of. I want to say thank you to my beta readers, who helped push me to make great changes. I want to say thank you to Jessica, who is always honest and uplifting and beyond supportive of my work. I want to say thank you to my wonderful editor Sage, who made a huge impact on the quality of this work and who made me smile with her comments. I want to say thank you to my wonderful street team for helping me make my dreams come true, and to the arc readers who took a chance on my work. And last, but not least, I want to say thank you to my readers for choosing to embark on this journey with me.

See you in book two!

About the author

M.N. Lash, despite having a bachelors degree in biology and minors in chemistry/psychology, is a stay-at-home mom from Alabama. When she isn't reading or writing you can find her crocheting, sewing, or attending to her many pets. Kiss Me And Die is her fifth book, and she is readying to publish her sixth and seventh, an installment in the Draxmere Academy of Conjuring Series and in the Kiss Me Series. You can also find her on Instagram for updates on future works @m.n._lash

Also by